BBC DOCTOR WHO

Engines of War

DOCTOR WHO

Engines of War

George Mann

BBC BOOKS

1 3 5 7 9 10 8 6 4 2

Published in 2014 by BBC Books, an imprint of Ebury Publishing
A Random House Group Company

Doctor Who is a BBC Wales production for BBC One.
Executive producers: Steven Moffat and Brian Minchin

The Random House Group Limited Reg. No. 954009

Addresses for companies within the Random House Group
can be found at www.randomhouse.co.uk

A CIP catalogue record for this book is available from the British Library.

ISBN 978 1 849 90848 1

MIX
Paper from
responsible sources
FSC® C016897

The Random House Group Limited supports the Forest Stewardship Council®
(FSC®), the leading international forest-certification organisation. Our books
carrying the FSC label are printed on FSC®-certified paper. FSC is the only
forest-certification scheme supported by the leading environmental
organisations, including Greenpeace. Our paper procurement policy can be
found at www.randomhouse.co.uk/environment

Editorial director: Albert DePetrillo
Series consultant: Justin Richards
Project editor: Steve Tribe
Cover design: Lee Binding © Woodlands Books Ltd, 2014
Production: Alex Goddard

Printed and bound in Great Britain by Clays Ltd, St Ives PLC

To buy books by your favourite authors and register for offers,
visit www.randomhouse.co.uk

To my family,
who made time and space

Part One
Moldox

Chapter One

It had been three days since she'd last seen a Dalek. Three days since she'd notched another kill into the barrel of her gun. It was too long. She was starting to feel twitchy. What were they up to?

The Dalek patrols had been sporadic of late, as though they were no longer bothering with the outlying ruins. They were massing in the city, corralling any surviving humans they found and shepherding them there, too. Their plans had changed. Something new was happening.

Maybe she'd have to think about moving again. And just when she was starting to get comfortable, too.

Cinder lay on her belly in the dust and the dirt, perfectly still, surveying the road below the shallow escarpment. She'd heard that a Dalek patrol was coming this way, but that had been over an hour ago. Had one of the other resistance cells taken them out already? That seemed unlikely. If they had, she'd be aware of it by now. A message would have buzzed over the comm-link. No, the likelihood was that the Daleks had encountered another group of survivors and were processing them for enslavement, or else 'exterminating' them – or, as she preferred to call it, *murdering* them on the spot. Cinder clutched her weapon just a little harder, feeling a spark of anger at the thought. If they *did* come this way…

She brushed her fringe from her eyes. She had a bright shock of auburn hair, cut in a ragged mop around her shoulders. It was this that had originally earned her the name 'Cinder'. Well, that and the fact she'd been found in the still-burning ruins of her homestead, the only thing left alive after the Daleks had passed through.

It seemed so long ago now, when the planet had burned. When they had *all* burned. Cinder had watched as every one of the worlds in the Spiral had burst into candescence, lighting up the sky above Moldox; a twisting helix of flaming orbs, a whorl of newly christened stars.

She'd been a child, then, little more than a scrap of a thing. Yet even at that early age she had known what the fire in the skies heralded for her and her kind: the Daleks had come. All hope was lost.

Moldox had fallen soon after, and life – if you could even call it that – had never been the same again.

Her family died in the first days of the invasion, incinerated by a Dalek patrol as they tried to flee for cover. Cinder survived by hiding in an overturned metal dustbin, peering out through a tiny rust hole at the carnage going on all around her, scared to so much as breathe. It took almost a year before she felt safe enough to even make another sound.

Days later, confused and traumatised, she'd been found wandering amongst the wreckage of her former homestead and was taken in by a roaming band of resistance fighters. This was not, however, an act of kindness on the part of her fellow humans, but simply a means to an end: they needed a child amongst their ranks to help set traps for the Daleks, to sneak and scurry into the small places where the Daleks couldn't follow. She'd spent the next fourteen years learning how to fight, how to eke out an existence in the ruins, and growing angrier at every passing day.

Everything she'd done since – *everything* – had been fuelled by that burning fury; that desire for revenge.

She knew the years of living hand to mouth had not served her well – she was thin, despite being muscular; her skin was pale and perpetually streaked in dirt, and whenever she found the time to look in a broken mirror or shattered pane of glass, all she saw staring back at her was the pain and regret in her dark, olive eyes. This, however, was her life now: surviving day to day by scavenging food, and hunting Daleks whenever the opportunity arose.

All the while, out in the universe, the war between the Time Lords and the Daleks rolled on regardless, tearing up all of time and space in its wake.

Cinder had heard it said that in simple, linear terms, the war had been going on for over four hundred years. This, of course, was an untruth, or at least an irrelevance; the temporal war zones had permeated so far and so deep into the very structure of the universe that the conflict had – quite literally – been raging for eternity. There was no epoch that remained unscathed, uncontested, no history that had not been rewritten.

To many it had come to be known, perhaps ironically, as the Great Time War. To Cinder, it was simply Hell.

She shifted her weight from one elbow to the other, all the time keeping her eyes on the cracked asphalt road, watching for signs; waiting. They would come soon, she was sure of it. Earlier that day she'd destroyed another of their transponders, and the patrol that the others had spotted must have been despatched to investigate. The Daleks were nothing if not predictable.

She scanned the row of jagged, broken buildings lining the opposite side of the road, looking for Finch. It was his turn to draw the Dalek fire while she took them out from behind. She couldn't see him amongst the ruins. Good. That meant he was keeping his head down. She'd hate it if anything happened to him. He was one of the good ones. She might even go as far as calling him a friend.

The fronts of the shattered buildings all along the roadside were blackened and splintered; the result of both the Dalek energy rays and the incendiary bombs used by the human defence forces as they'd tried to hold the invaders at bay. Ultimately, they'd failed in the face of overwhelming odds and an unflinching, uncaring enemy. The Daleks were utterly relentless, and within days the entire planet had been reduced to a smouldering ruin.

Cinder could barely remember a time before the Daleks had come to Moldox. She had vague, impressionistic memories of gleaming spires and sprawling cities, of wild forests and skies overflowing with scudding transport ships. Here, in the Tantalus Spiral, humans had achieved their zenith, colonising a vast corkscrew of worlds surrounding an immense, ghostly structure in space – the Tantalus Eye. It glared down at her now, balefully studying the events unfolding below.

It must have borne witness to some horrors in the last decade and a half, she considered. Moldox had once been majestic, but now it was nothing but a dying world, miserably clinging on to the last vestiges of life.

There was a noise from the road below. Cinder pressed herself even deeper into the dirt and scrabbled forward a few inches, peering over the lip of the escarpment in order to see a little further along the road. The strap of her backpack was digging uncomfortably into her shoulder, but she ignored it.

The Daleks were finally coming, just as she'd anticipated. Her pulse quickened. She squinted, trying to discern their numbers. She could make out five distinct shapes, although her heart sank as they drew closer, and her view of them resolved.

Only one of them was a Dalek, hovering at the back of the small group as if herding the others on. Its bronze casing glinted in the waning afternoon sun, and its eyestalk swivelled from side to side, surveying the path ahead.

The rest of them were Kaled mutants, Daleks of a kind, but twisted into new, disturbing forms by Time Lord interference. These were Skaro Degradations, the result of Time Lord efforts to re-engineer Dalek history, to toy with the evolution of their origin species, probably in an attempt to sidestep the development of the Dalek race altogether. The results had been catastrophic, however, and in every permutation of reality, in *every single* possibility, the Daleks had asserted themselves. They were not to be stopped. Whichever way Cinder looked at it, it seemed the universe *wanted* the Daleks.

Many of these Degradations were unstable – unpredictable – which, to Cinder's mind, made them even more dangerous than the Daleks. And now they were being pressed into service here on Moldox.

Cinder readied her weapon – an energy gun ripped from the broken casing of a dying Dalek and lashed up to a power pack – and fought the urge to flee. It was too late now. They were committed. She only hoped none of the Degradations was carrying a weapon they hadn't faced before.

As the patrol drew closer, Cinder got a proper look at them. Two of the Degradations were near identical and of a kind she had seen many times before: a humanoid torso in a reinforced glass chamber, suspended beneath a normal Dalek head and eyestalk. Three elongated panels on black metal arms flanked this central column to the sides and rear. The panels were peppered with the same half-globe sensors as the standard Dalek casing, and from each side jutted energy weapons mounted on narrow sponsons.

The limbless torsos inside the glass chambers twitched nervously as the monstrous things glided along, propelling themselves through the air on plumes of blue light. Finch had dubbed these ones 'Gliders'.

The others, however, were like nothing she had seen before. One of them was egg-shaped and mounted on a set of three spider-like limbs, scuttling along the road like a massive, terrifying insect. Once again, its casing was dotted with the same, familiar half-globes, although in this instance they were coal black and embedded into panels of a deep, metallic red. The eyestalk was fatter, too, and from its body bristled four matching gun emplacements.

The final mutant appeared to be almost identical to a normal Dalek, except that its middle section – which typically housed the manipulator arm and gun – had been replaced by a revolving turret, upon which was mounted a single, massive energy cannon.

Cinder tried to swallow, but her mouth was dry. There was no way she could risk allowing that cannon to get off a shot. The results would be devastating, and Finch would have next to no chance of getting clear. That one had to be her first target.

She sensed movement in the ruins, and a quick glance told her that Finch was already on the move, dashing from cover to cover to draw the Dalek's attention. The Dalek sensed it, too, and its eyestalk swivelled in Finch's direction.

'Cease! Show yourself! Surrender and you will

not be ex-ter-min-ated.' The Dalek's harsh, metallic rasp sent a shiver down Cinder's spine as it echoed along the otherwise empty road. She watched for Finch, trying to discern him in the ruins, to anticipate his next move. There was no chance he'd obey the Dalek's order – even if it wasn't lying, extermination had to be a better alternative to being enslaved by these monsters.

There! She saw him move again, near to the remains of a burnt-out homestead, and the Dalek swivelled, letting off three short, successive blasts with its weapon. The high-pitched wail of the energy discharge was near deafening. There was a flash of intense white light, followed by the crump of an explosion, and the remains of a damaged wall toppled into a heap, close to where Finch had been hiding only seconds before. Smoke curled lazily from the ruins in the still air.

'Seek. Locate. Destroy!' ordered the Dalek. 'Find the human and ex-ter-min-ate.'

'We obey,' chorused the Degradations in their warbling, synthetic voices. The two Gliders rose up on spears of light, while the others fanned out, covering the ruins with their weapons.

The patrol had separated, and Cinder saw her chance. She pushed herself up onto her knees, hefting the Dalek weapon to her shoulder and sighting along the length of the notched barrel. She drew a bead on the head of the Degradation with the cannon, took a deep breath, and fired.

The weapon issued a short, powerful blast of energy, and the force of its discharge almost sent her reeling. She kept her shoulder locked in position, steadying herself. The air filled with the stench of burning ozone.

Her aim was true, and the energy beam lanced across the mutant's bronze carapace, scoring a deep, black furrow and detonating one of its radiation valves. It did not, however, have the desired effect of causing its head to explode in spectacular fashion, instead eliciting an altogether more unwelcome response.

'Under attack! Under attack!' bellowed the Degradation, rotating its head a full 180 degrees to scan the top of the escarpment. 'Human female armed with Dalek neutraliser. Exterminate! Exterminate!'

Panicked, Cinder glanced at the gun in her hands. What had gone wrong? She'd never known a Dalek to survive an energy blast from one of its own weapons. Did this new kind of mutant have specially reinforced armour? Whatever the case, all she'd succeeded in doing was broadcasting her own location.

She had to act quickly, take out the leader. She twisted, raising the gun and closing her left eye, drawing a line of sight on the Dalek as it shifted its own bulk around, preparing to return fire. She squeezed the makeshift trigger and the weapon spat another bolt of searing energy.

The shot found its mark, striking the Dalek just beneath the eyestalk. The casing detonated with a satisfying crack, rupturing the sensor grilles and spilling the biomass of the dead Kaled inside. Flames licked at the edges of the ragged wound as green flesh bubbled and popped, oozing out with a grotesque hiss.

Cinder didn't have time to celebrate, however, as the egg-shaped Degradation opened fire in response. Its four weapons barked in quick succession, like chattering artillery guns, churning up the impacted loam along the top of the escarpment. She threw herself backwards, rolling for cover, but it was too late – the impact had destabilised the ground, and the edge of the escarpment collapsed in a crashing landslide of mud and soil.

Cinder felt the world give way beneath her. She screamed, clutching on to her gun for all she was worth, as she tumbled head over heels towards the assembled Degradations below.

Chapter Two

High above Moldox, a blue box folded into reality, sliding effortlessly out of the Time Vortex. It seemed incongruous, here on the outer edges of the Tantalus Spiral, a relic from ancient Earth that had fallen through time and space, only to appear here, its domed light blinking wildly as it returned to corporeal form. If sound had carried in space, its appearance would have been accompanied by a laboured, grating wheeze, but instead, there was only silence.

The arrival of this anachronistic object did not, however, go unnoticed, and the appearance of the TARDIS flashed up warning sigils on a thousand Dalek control panels. Dalek saucers stirred into action, gliding through the void to adopt combat formations, lights stuttering as they powered up to full readiness.

Inside the TARDIS, the Doctor – or rather, the Time Lord who had, before now, lived many lives under that name – rotated a dial and stepped back from the console. He folded his hands behind his back, and waited.

Around him, the roundels on the walls glowed with a faint luminescence, causing the craggy lines of his face to be picked out in shadow: the map of a hundred years or more, worn thin through conflict and weariness.

The central column burred gently as it rose and fell, as if the machine was somehow breathing, in and out, in and out. The thought was comforting. It meant he was not alone. He sighed, and glanced up at the star field being projected through the de-opaqued ceiling of the console room.

Above him sat the ethereal form of the Tantalus Eye.

The Eye was an anomaly, a vast fold in space-time; an impossible structure that had no right to exist, and yet, nevertheless, did. How it had formed, whether it was natural or engineered – no one had ever been able to discern. All that the Doctor knew was that it predated the Time Lords, and that Omega, the great engineer, in those first, halcyon days of the Time Lord Diaspora, had written of the Eye and its many obtuse secrets – secrets that it still held to this day.

From this far out, on the edge of the Spiral, it had the appearance of an immense, gaseous body, a swirling human eye, encircled by a helix of inhabited worlds. It was pricked with the fading light of dying giants and the kernels of new, hungry stars, freshly reborn in an endless cycle of death of and resurrection; celestial bodies trapped within its event horizon and the influence of its temporal murmurations.

To the Doctor, it was utterly breathtaking. He had come here often in his other lives – particularly his fourth and his eighth, those of a more romantic persuasion – although now those days were like distant memories, dreams that had happened to somebody else. Now, there was nothing but the War. It had consumed him, remade him into something new. A warrior.

Just like the Doctor, the War had changed the Tantalus Spiral, too. Once a peaceful haven, it was now blighted by the Dalek occupation. It had become a war zone, like much of the universe – a staging post from which the Daleks could continue their crusade to populate eternity with their progenitors and wage their ceaseless campaign against the Time Lords.

That was why the Doctor had come to the Spiral – the Daleks were massing here, and he needed to get a measure of their strength.

There was one simple and effective way to do just that.

'Right then,' he growled. 'Come and get me.'

Above the TARDIS, the Dalek saucers began to converge. They were not yet in range for their energy weapons, but the Doctor knew that at any moment he could expect a barrage. He stepped forward and took the controls once again.

'Wait for it,' he mumbled to himself. 'Wait for just the right moment...'

He flicked a switch and opened the communication

channel. A hundred or more Dalek voices were chanting in a riotous cacophony. Their words were barely discernible, but he knew very well what they were saying: 'Exterminate! Exterminate!' Even now, the sound of it made his skin crawl.

They were getting closer. Still, the Doctor waited.

The lead saucer finally moved within range, scudding overhead.

'Now!' bellowed the Doctor at the top of his lungs, cranking a lever forward and gripping the edges of the console so that his knuckles turned white with the strain.

The TARDIS shot straight up like a rocket. It caught the saucer completely unaware, colliding with its dome-encrusted belly and ripping through at an immense velocity, erupting through the top of the ship and spinning off, twisting on its axis.

The electrics inside the saucer fizzed and popped, visible through the ragged hole. It listed, spinning out of control, its weapons blazing indiscriminately. One energy beam took out a neighbouring saucer, while the damaged ship itself went spinning into another, which proved too slow to take evasive action.

On his monitors, the Doctor watched the shells of damaged Daleks drifting away motionless into the void as the ships themselves burned up.

'That's done it, old girl,' he said, manipulating the controls once again to swing the TARDIS out of the path of another energy weapon. The Dalek saucers shifted like a flock of birds, swooping after him, their cannons spitting death all around him. 'That's right,' he said. 'Follow me…'

Like the pilot of a stunt aeroplane – which he'd made a point of watching with the Brigadier, back in his UNIT days on Earth – the Doctor ducked and weaved the TARDIS, left, right, up, down, looping across the void, leading the Daleks on a merry chase, but always staying one step ahead of their guns.

All the while, the baleful glare of the Eye regarded them impassively.

'Right, isn't it about time…' The Doctor broke off, grinning, as a hundred or more Battle TARDISes phased out of the Vortex behind the Dalek fleet. 'Now we've got you,' he crowed, rotating a handle and dipping the TARDIS, bringing it back around on itself so that he could zip underneath the oncoming wave of Dalek saucers to join his comrades.

Weapons transmuted from the outer skin of the Battle TARDISes – plain, white lozenges with an outer shell of living metal that could morph into shields, or any number of predetermined gun emplacements. The TARDISes scattered, shooting off in a hundred different directions as the Daleks attempted to reverse their course, coming about to face the enemy who had so easily outflanked them.

Time torpedoes launched in a wave, a score of them finding their mark and freezing their targets, trapping them in a temporal holding pattern, a locked second from which the saucers could not escape. The Dalek ships bloomed into silent balls of flame as the Time Lords followed up with a volley of explosive rounds.

The Daleks weren't backing down, however, and as the Doctor's TARDIS burst through the surface of another saucer, sending it spinning toward one of the planets below, they managed to set loose their own first volley, detonating TARDISes with every strike.

The Doctor watched as the dying time ships blossomed, their interior dimensions folding out into reality, unfurling like violent flowers to swell to their true size before burning up in the vacuum. His fingers danced across the controls and the TARDIS danced away, just as the Dalek ships spat a second volley.

'Phase!' he bellowed over the communications rig, and the Time Lords did as he commanded, their TARDISes blinking suddenly out of existence. They appeared again a moment later, having leapt two seconds into the future to avoid the crackling beams of the Dalek weapons, which faded away harmlessly into space.

Their return volley was far more effective, detonating countless Dalek saucers.

'Retreat! Retreat!' The chorus of Dalek voices, now diminished but still audible in the background, had changed. They were attempting to regroup, pulling back toward the Eye and using the wreckage of their fallen brethren as cover.

'We've got them on the run, Doctor!' called a satisfied female voice over the comm-link.

'Stay with them!' he replied. 'Press the advantage.'

The Time Lords, now outnumbering the Dalek vessels two-to-one, did precisely that, surging forward, some going high, others going low, trapping the retreating Daleks between them.

The time torpedoes did their work, stuttering the Dalek retreat, and within seconds, space above the Tantalus Eye was filled with the wreckage of the remaining Dalek fleet.

'Well done, Doctor,' said the woman on the comm-link. She sounded jubilant. This was Captain Preda, Commander of the Fifth Time Lord Battle Fleet. 'We led them on a merry dance indeed.'

'Don't count your victories too soon, Preda,' replied the Doctor, his tone grim. 'I'm not sure it's over yet. There could be more of them, lurking in the shadow of those planets.'

'Then let's take a look,' said Preda. The comm-link buzzed off, and the Battle TARDISes, assembling themselves into a spearhead formation, slid closer toward the Tantalus Eye.

Warily, the Doctor fell in behind them, keeping an eye on his monitors.

The ambush came without warning. There was no alarm, no indication that anything was awry, that they'd triggered some sort of trap. One second there was nothing, the next an armada of Dalek stealth ships had blinked out of the Vortex.

The Doctor had seen these ships only a handful of times before – sleek, ovoid vessels of the purest black, devoid of the usual winking lights that typically marked a Dalek saucer, and twice as dangerous. They were a recent and unwelcome development. They were said to sit in the Time Vortex like spiders at the heart of a web, detecting the vibrations of passing TARDISes. Only then would they make themselves known, shimmering into existence to catch the Time Lords unaware.

It was elegant and deadly and – the Doctor realised – Preda and her fleet had just been caught in their web.

The Time Lords had no time to react. Not a single one was able to dematerialise before the Dalek weapons cracked them open like tin cans, spilling their insides into the cold vacuum of space.

The Doctor roared, slamming his fists into the controls and sending the TARDIS spinning sideways in an evasive action that saved his life. Nevertheless, the TARDIS caught a glancing blow on her right flank and was sent into a wild spin. With the stabilisers unable to compensate, the Doctor slammed to the floor, rolling off the central dais as the ship juddered.

The TARDIS, out of control, hurtled headlong toward one of the planets below.

Chapter Three

The TARDIS plunged through the planet's upper atmosphere like a dropped stone, tumbling end over end, leaving a rippling trail of black smoke in its wake.

Inside, the Doctor clung to the metal rail that ran around the edges of the central dais. The engines were screeching and stuttering as the ship tried to right herself, but the trajectory was too sharp, and they were falling too fast.

The ceiling was still showing a projection of the view from outside, but now it was nothing but a disorientating jumble of images: snapshots of a bruised, purple sky; sweeping continents encrusted with bristling ruins; flames licking angrily at the edges of the ship's outer shell.

With a gargantuan effort, the Doctor released his grip on the railing and lurched over to the console, catching hold of a hooped cable in an effort to stop him from being sent sprawling to the floor. He tugged on it for support, but to his consternation it came away in his hand, one end decoupling from its housing and causing him to swing out wildly, windmilling his other arm until the ship tipped forward again and he could grab hold of a nearby lever.

He steadied himself as best he could, rocking with the motion of the tumbling ship. 'Right, let's see if this works…' he said, tossing away the loose end of the cable and jabbing at a series of buttons and switches on the control panel.

Its engines screaming in protest, the TARDIS made a juddering attempt to dematerialise. Outside, visible through the transparent ceiling, the world seemed to fade away to nonexistence, replaced by the swirling hues of the Time Vortex.

Just as the Doctor was about to issue a heartfelt sigh of relief, however, the view stuttered as if it were just out of reach, and returned to flickering images of the desolate, spoiled world beneath him, seen only in snatches as the ground seemed to rush up to meet the falling TARDIS.

He hammered at the controls furiously, to no avail. Even the central column had now ceased its ponderous rise and fall, as if the TARDIS herself had anticipated what would come next and was withdrawing into herself, shutting down her vital systems.

'I'm sorry, old girl,' said the Doctor, hanging on to the console for all he was worth. 'I think we're in for a bit of a bumpy landing…'

*

Her mouth was full of soil, her left cheek was smarting and she was pretty sure she'd broken at least one of her ribs. She couldn't remember where she was, what she'd been doing. Comforting blackness offered to consume her. She welcomed it. *Sleep*. Sleep was what she needed. Sleep would –

'Locate the other hu-man.' The rasping, metallic sound of a Degradation stirred her to wakefulness. Of course! The escarpment. The landslide. The *Degradations*. Only a few seconds could have passed. She remained rigid and still. Did they think she was dead?

She was partially covered by the loose soil. She could feel it weighing down on her legs. That was good – at least she could still *feel* her legs. The mud must have cushioned her fall. She shifted her foot, ever so slightly, and felt the heaped earth give way. She'd be able to break free, then. She wasn't buried too deep.

She was still clutching the stolen Dalek weapon. It felt smooth and cold against her palm, and hummed with power. Not only that, but she had the element of surprise. They weren't expecting her to suddenly start shooting again. And by the sound of it, they hadn't found Finch. They hadn't –

'Cinder!' Finch's worried cry echoed from the ruins. Cinder wanted to scream in frustration. What was he doing! He'd give away his position, make himself an easy target.

Well, she supposed he'd forced her hand…

With a gasp, Cinder heaved herself up out of the heaped earth, twisting as she rose, spitting soil. She didn't have time to take stock of what the Degradations were doing. She saw one of the Gliders, hovering a few metres off the ground with its back to her, and took aim, releasing two shots. Still turning, she got the other Glider in her sights and squeezed off another two shots.

They detonated into bright balls of flame, one after the other, showering the ground with burning debris, and Cinder dived for cover, rolling behind the shell of the Dalek she had taken out from above. There would still two Degradations to contend with, and she didn't much fancy her chances against the cannon.

'Cinder!'

She scrambled to her feet to see the tall, broad silhouette of Finch up ahead, bursting from behind a broken wall and rushing out into the road. He was wearing dirty black coveralls and carrying an old-fashioned machine gun, with which he rained down shells on the remaining Dalek creatures as he ran. The bullets pinged ineffectually off their armour, but his plan – if indeed it was a plan – had worked, and he'd distracted them long enough for Cinder to take cover.

'Cinder – get to safety, now!' he bellowed. He sprayed the Degradations with another burst of useless ammunition, then turned and ran.

'Eradicate!' burred the Dalek with the cannon, rotating its mid-section to track him as he ran.

'Finch!' cried Cinder. 'No!'

The cannon fired, emitting a pulse of eerie, ruby-coloured light. It struck Finch in the back and seemed to engulf him entirely, encircling his body, whispering around him as if looking for a way in. He stopped running, twisting around in obvious agony and thrashing as if trying to free himself of the beam's deadly embrace. There was no escape.

He opened his mouth to scream, and the stream of light rushed in through the orifice, pouring into his body, choking him. He clutched at his throat with both hands, scrabbling for breath.

As she watched, tears pricking her eyes, Finch's flesh began to glow, taking on the same odd, pinkish hue as the light. He seemed to disintegrate before her, fading out of existence, as if the light inside of him was pushing out and expanding, dissolving him from within.

In less than a few seconds, there was nothing left of him whatsoever, aside from a faint wisp of slowly fading light.

Crouching behind the burned-out Dalek, Cinder felt an odd sensation. She knew she'd just witnessed something horrific, but, for some reason, she couldn't quite understand what. Her memory seemed suddenly fuzzy, confused.

She had the unsettling notion there was something she couldn't remember, scratching away at the back of her mind. She could have sworn the Degradations had just exterminated someone, maybe even someone she knew, but she couldn't imagine who it could have been. After all, she'd planned this ambush alone, with no help. Hadn't she?

Nevertheless, she couldn't deny the overwhelming feeling of hollowness, as if she was experiencing the absence of an emotion akin to grief. She didn't have time to dwell on it, however, as even now the two remaining Degradations were moving, turning towards her…

She glanced behind her, looking for somewhere to run. There was nowhere but the ruins on the other side of the road, and she didn't much fancy her chances in the open. Then again, the wrecked shell of a Dalek wasn't going to provide much in the way of a shield for very long, either.

Cinder glanced up at a high-pitched whistling sound from overhead, her mouth falling open in slack-jawed awe. Something was falling from the sky – a large, blue box, with illuminated window panels and a flashing lamp on top. It was coming in at quite a speed, glowing white hot around the edges, and leaving a long, dark smear in the sky to mark its passing. Whatever it was, it was clearly out of control, and it was going to make landfall any second…

'Evade! Evade!' The egg-shaped Degradation turned and skittered toward the ruins, its spider-like limbs clawing at the broken ground for purchase.

Cinder cringed, dropping to her knees and burying her face in the crooks of her arms. There was little else to do. The roar of the falling box had grown to such intensity that it was all she could hear. There was no time to run, to seek cover. It was coming down, and it was coming down *now*.

It impacted with a tremendous *crunch*, sending up a spew of displaced earth that bowled Cinder, and the shell of the dead Dalek she'd been cowering behind, at least two metres into the air. She landed on her back, knocking the wind out of her lungs, just as the box – which had rebounded from the edge of the escarpment and was sent careening into the road – crashed for a second time, this time causing a colossal *bang*. For the second time that day, she was doused in a spray of loose soil and debris.

The blue box screeched across the asphalt, rending what appeared to be *wood*, until it struck the remains of a brick wall and came to a sudden, jarring halt.

Cinder took a deep breath and opened her eyes. The first thing that struck her was the fact that she was still alive. The second was the eerie silence that had settled over proceedings. The only sound was the hiss of the scorched box melting the asphalt on the road surface where it had come to rest. She had no idea how a box made of wood could have survived the violence of re-entry into the planet's atmosphere.

Cinder picked herself up, dusting shards of Dalek casing and dirt from her clothes. She gasped for breath, forcing air back down into her lungs. Her ears were ringing. She staggered forward a few steps, but then thought better of it, deciding she'd have to wait until her head stopped spinning.

She tried to get her bearings.

The entire scene was a mess. The initial impact had blown a crater in the side of the escarpment, the force from which had rippled out, crumpling the surface of the road and churning up an area the size of a house.

The shell of the Dalek was lying on its side about three metres away, still rocking gently with the motion of the impact.

Smoke curled from where the blue box had finally come to rest, lying on its side. A hatch was open in the top, but she couldn't quite see inside. The lights were still glowing softly in the windows, although the lamp on top had gone out. She wondered if that was the distress beacon or homing device.

It appeared the box had inadvertently saved her life, too – half of a Dalek casing – presumably belonging to the cannon-bearing Degradation – still stood upright beside the overturned box, but the top half was nowhere to be seen. It seemed the box had decapitated the ponderous thing before it had had chance to move out of the way.

Of the squat, spider-like mutant, there was no sign.

Cinder crept forward, peering into the box. All she could see was a pall of thick smoke and the impression of some bright, internal lighting. She thought about calling out, to see if there was anyone still alive inside, but was worried about attracting attention. And besides, she had no idea who – or what – might be in there. No, she'd just get a little bit closer and take a look inside...

She froze at the sound of a man spluttering. It had come from inside the box. So – the occupant *was* still alive.

Quickly, she cast around for her gun. It was jutting out of the damp earth close by, and she hastily dug it out with her hands, getting thick, grimy clay wedged beneath her broken fingernails. She yanked it free, trailing cables, then dusted it off and checked it over.

The light on the power pack had dimmed and turned red, indicating that all of the stored energy had been discharged. Clearly, it had been damaged in the explosion. She cursed beneath her breath. Still, whoever it was who'd come down in that blue box didn't have to know that. The weapon would still make an effective deterrent.

Brandishing it like a shield, she advanced slowly on the box, wary of any sudden signs of movement that might indicate hostilities. Was it an escape capsule? It certainly didn't look very big, and the way it had fallen from the sky suggested it had been ejected from an orbital craft. The edges of the box were still glowing from its abrasive entry into the atmosphere, and a dark, sooty streak across its outer casing indicated that it had taken a glancing strike from an energy weapon. Had a Dalek saucer shot down the ship? She wondered if the occupant of the escape pod might even be human. But why were the words 'POLICE BOX' written on the side in big, bold letters? Nothing that was happening seemed to make any sense.

The man gave another cough, louder this time. Cinder sensed movement. She stopped walking and thrust the barrel of her gun in the direction of the box, just in time to see a head emerge from the open hatch.

With a loud huff, the man threw his arms over the sides of the box and hauled himself up, so that his head and shoulders were poking over the rim.

Cinder glared at him, unsure what to say or do. He was an older man, with a craggy, careworn face and startling green-brown eyes. His hair was silvery grey and brushed up into a tuft at the front, and he wore a bushy white beard and moustache. He frowned at her, looking perplexed. He appeared to be wearing a battered leather coat and a herringbone patterned scarf.

'Well?' he said, as if waiting for the answer to an unasked question.

'Well, what?' she replied, jiggling her gun to ensure that he'd seen it.

He raised both eyebrows as if taken aback by her insolence. 'Oh, so waving a gun at me is the best thing to do in the circumstances, is it?'

'Well…' Cinder thought for a moment, confused. 'Look, you're the one who's just fallen out of the sky!'

'And just as well that I did,' he said. 'I'd argue that my timing is impeccable.'

'What are you *talking* about?' said Cinder, failing to quell her exasperation.

'Look at you,' he said. 'Clearly in need of my help.'

Cinder felt a surge of indignation. 'Oh, *really*?' She shook her head at the sheer arrogance of the man. '*I* need *your* help?'

'I should say so,' replied the man.

'And what makes you say that?' asked Cinder. She was growing tired of this irritating newcomer and his ridiculous posturing.

The man made a gesture that might have been a shrug, if it hadn't been for the fact he was hanging on to the edge of his box with both arms. Come to think of it, the position did appear a little odd, given how shallow the box actually was. He sighed. 'If you don't want to end up getting yourself exterminated, then I suggest you get a move on and hop inside.

'What?' she said. 'You want me to get in that box with you?' She pulled her best 'not in your lifetime, mister' expression.

'I don't *want* you to do anything,' said the man, 'but

unless you're as stupid as you look, you'll do as I say.'

Cinder had to fight the urge to pull the trigger on her gun in the hope that there was enough residual charge in the power pack to blast him into tomorrow. 'Right,' she said. 'You're on your own.' She turned to walk away.

'NOW!' bellowed the man. There was a sense of urgency in his voice that hadn't been there before, an edge to it that made her suddenly decide to pay attention.

'Ex-ter-min-ate!'

Cinder twisted on the spot to see the spider-thing emerging from the ruins on her right. She cursed, loudly. She'd been so intent on her argument with the man in the box that she hadn't been paying attention. She should have known better. She pointed her gun at the Degradation and squeezed the trigger, but as she'd expected, nothing happened. The power had completely drained.

Cinder was quickly running out of options. She could stay out here and attempt to fight off a Degradation with a gun that would prove about as useful as a wooden club, try to make a run for it and expose herself to being shot in the back, or dive into a small blue box with an old man who had just fallen out of the sky.

'Out of the frying pan, into the fire,' she muttered. As the Degradation came clambering over the remains of a wall, dislodging a flurry of loose bricks, she backed up, took a run-up and leapt into the open hatch of the escape pod. She brought her knees up to her chest as she jumped, preparing to fall into a crouch as she landed inside the shallow box.

'Incoming!' she screamed, to give the man chance to take cover before she landed on him.

She crashed down on her backside, slamming painfully into what felt like metal floor plates, and rolled to her left, putting a hand out to stop herself. With her other she still gripped the Dalek weapon close to her chest.

The momentum carried her over onto her side, and she ended up with her face pressed against cool metal, which seemed to thrum gently with the vibration of an idling engine.

Something didn't feel right.

She'd screwed her eyes shut during her fall. She opened them, expecting to see the old man pressed up against her in the confined space, taking cover from the Degradation outside. Instead, the sight of a large, circular room greeted her.

She sat up, clutching the gun to her chest.

The room was utterly incongruous with what she'd expected. The walls were aglow with a series of odd, round impressions – sunken lights, perhaps – and rough stone pillars arched overhead to support the roof.

A raised dais housed what looked like a control panel, of sorts – although the controls in question appeared to be patched up and cobbled together from scavenged components that had been made to fit. Nests of cables drooped from the ceiling.

The whole place had a higgledy-piggledy sort of feel to it, like it was constantly being made over by an inveterate tinkerer, or mended by someone who was never able to get the right parts. It was the control room of a ship. She supposed she could have knocked herself out during her leap into the escape pod and had only just come round, hours later, in a different place. But try as she might to convince herself, she didn't believe that for a moment.

The man whose head and shoulders she had seen sticking up out of the box was now standing by the control panel, attempting to adjust the picture on a small computer screen. He had his back to her, but it was definitely the same man – he was wearing the same brown jacket and his hair was the same silvery grey.

She glanced behind her. Bizarrely, she was sitting with her back to the hatch. She studied it for a moment, assessing the size and shape of the opening. She supposed, on reflection, it was technically more of a door, but it looked about right. It was definitely the hatch she had jumped through.

'It's… it's…' she stammered.

The man stopped what he was doing and looked over at her. 'Bigger on the inside. Yes, I know. Let's get that bit over and done with quickly, shall we?' he said.

'It's the right way up,' finished Cinder. 'The box was on its side, and now I'm the right way up.'

'Oh. Right. Hmmm. I wasn't expecting that one,' he said. 'Yes, I suppose it is. That'll be the relative dimensional stabilisers. Stops you from, well… falling over.' He looked down at her and raised an ironic eyebrow. 'The inside can be orientated differently to the outside.' He waved his hand, as if explaining away a miracle as nothing but sleight of hand.

'And it's bigger,' said Cinder.

The man laughed. 'And there we are. *That's* the one I was expecting.'

'Which means…' Cinder's expression darkened. 'Is this a TARDIS?'

'It is,' said the man. He returned his attention to the console and began examining the readouts on the computer screen. It looked antiquated and a little decrepit. He tapped at the keypad, as if trying to get something to work.

Cinder peered over his shoulder to see what he was looking at, but all she could see on the screen was a mass of unfamiliar pictograms, scrolling and shifting about in an apparently random dance.

'Blast it!' he barked suddenly in response to something he'd read, and Cinder started, her finger brushing the trigger of her gun.

'If this is a TARDIS,' she said, 'then that means you're a—'

'Time Lord,' he said, interrupting. 'Yes, that's right. Well done.' His tone was patronising.

Cinder took a deep breath. She edged back, shuffling on her behind. She brought the barrel of her weapon up so that it was pointing at the Time Lord. She was beginning to think she'd have better luck out there with the mutant Daleks. She could hear one of the Degradations now, hammering at the door, trying to force its way in behind her. Thankfully, the doors of the TARDIS seemed to be holding.

'What are you going to do with me?' she said, her voice wavering.

The Time Lord sighed. 'Drop you somewhere safe

as soon as I possibly can,' he said. 'That way I might be able to get a little peace and quiet.' He glanced at her, as if to weigh up her response.

'Tell me why I shouldn't just kill you now?' she said, brandishing the Dalek weapon. There was no way he could know it was damaged, that the charge had all bled away.

'Because I saved your life?' he said, reasonably. 'Because you don't look like a murderer, and because the power pack for your salvaged gun is completely dead.' He reached around the control panel and began flicking switches.

'Saved my life!' she snapped, indignant. 'You almost crushed me to death, hurtling out of the sky in your... your... *box*!' She cursed under her breath in frustration. He must have seen her try to fire at the Degradation, and worked out she had no power left. That meant she was exposed. Nevertheless, she might still be able to take him in a fight if he tried anything. She was a lot younger than he was, after all.

'Oh, I see. So it would have been simplicity itself to extricate yourself from that Dalek patrol?'

She didn't think much of his condescending tone, given that he'd basically crashed his ship. He withdrew something from just inside the fold of his jacket, but she couldn't quite see what it was.

'They weren't Daleks,' she countered. 'I'd already dealt with the Dalek. Those were mutants. Degradations.'

The Time Lord shrugged. 'A Dalek is a Dalek,' he said, 'whatever their form and from whichever epoch or permutation of reality they originate.'

'Is that true of Time Lords, too?' asked Cinder, the sarcasm dripping from her voice.

'Sadly, I believe it is,' he replied.

'But, you *are* a Time Lord?' she said, waving the gun to ensure he hadn't forgotten about it. He wasn't looking. He'd returned to tinkering with the object in his hand – a thin, metal cylinder with a glowing end, which made an infuriating buzzing sound every time he pressed a button on it.

'Yes,' he said, drawing out the word, as if indicating his impatience. He held the device up to his ear and pressed the button, listening intently to the sound. Then, frowning as if frustrated with the thing, he banged it repeatedly against his palm.

'Then where are your skull cap and robes?' said Cinder. 'You don't *look* much like a Time Lord.'

'I'm told there are exceptions to every rule,' he replied. He raised his device to his ear again, listened to the sound, and then, apparently satisfied, slipped the device into a leather hoop on the empty ammo belt he was wearing and dusted his hands.

'What is that thing? A weapon?' she said.

He offered her an impatient look. 'No. It's a screwdriver. Now, why don't you put down that gun? You're upsetting the old girl.' He patted the TARDIS console fondly. 'And to be perfectly frank, you're upsetting me.'

Cinder ignored the last part of his jibe. 'You mean, more than you've just upset her by crashing her into a planet?' she retorted. She lowered the barrel of the gun all the same, although she refused to relinquish her grip on it entirely.

'There, now,' said the Time Lord. 'Doesn't that feel better?'

Cinder gave an exasperated sigh. 'Look, what are you doing here, on Moldox?'

'Ah, so that's what this dreadful-looking planet is called, is it? Moldox.' He said the word like he was trying it on for size, then shook his head, as if deciding it wasn't for him. 'More to the point, what were you doing out there, facing off against those Daleks?'

'An ambush,' she said.

The Time Lord gave her an approving look. 'An ambush?' he echoed. 'Just you, your friend and a single, salvaged Dalek energy weapon. I'm impressed.' He looked momentarily forlorn. 'I'm sorry I couldn't save him.'

Cinder looked at him, confused. 'My friend? I was alone.'

The Time Lord frowned. 'The TARDIS picked up two human life signs in the crash zone. One of them disappeared just after a massive energy discharge from one of the Daleks. I'd assumed you were together.'

Again, that strange itch at the back of her mind, as if there was something she should be able to remember, but couldn't. 'I...' She hesitated. 'I don't think so,' she said.

The Time Lord nodded, but it was clear he was troubled by her answer. 'Well, you might as well make yourself at home for a minute or two,' he said, doing a lap of the console, making adjustments to the controls. 'I'm just going to get her started up again.' He grabbed a lever with a worn wooden handle and pulled it towards him. The tall glass chamber at the centre of the console flickered briefly with bright, white light, and the nest of tubes at its heart began to rise up inside the column. But then the light dimmed, and there was a deep, unsettling groaning sound from beneath the floor.

'Damn it!' said the Time Lord, striking his fist angrily against the control panel. 'She's out of action. She's going to need some time to heal before I can take her off-world again.'

'Off-world?' said Cinder. A sudden, unbidden thought had entered her head. Was this it? Was this the chance of escape she'd been looking for? Could she hitch a ride off the planet with this eccentric old Time Lord? The thought was appealing. She'd toyed with the notion of leaving Moldox hundreds of times over the years, but the opportunity had never presented itself. Could this be it? Her chance for a fresh start, some place where the war was nothing but a distant memory, a fairy story told to the young to encourage their good behaviour. Places like that had to exist somewhere out in the cosmos.

'Well, it's not as if we're in a particular rush,' she said, finally getting to her feet. She propped the gun against the metal railing, but made sure to remain within grabbing distance of it. It wouldn't really do her much good in a tight spot – at least until she found another power pack – but if things got ugly, it was all she had.

'We?' said the Time Lord.

'You said you were going to take me somewhere safe,' said Cinder. 'And I can assure you, Moldox is *not* safe. It's difficult enough avoiding the Dalek patrols. I'd rather die than let them take me prisoner.'

'Prisoner?' said the Time Lord. 'That's not like the Daleks. Not unless they've got plans for this planet. What happens to the people they've taken?'

Cinder shrugged. 'All I know is that they're taken to the cities. That's what the patrols are for – to round people up. They only exterminate you if you try to run or fight back.'

'Are they sinking shafts into the ground? Digging out mines?'

Cinder shrugged. She had no idea.

'I think you'd better show me,' said the Time Lord.

Cinder's heart sank. 'What about the Daleks?' She realised the hammering at the door had ceased. Perhaps the Degradation had given up and scuttled off to report. Nevertheless, she rather avoid going back out there to find out.

'We can cross that bridge when we come to it,' he said. 'What's the nearest city?'

'Andor,' she said. 'About ten miles from here.'

'You know the way?'

Cinder nodded. 'It's dangerous,' she said. 'There're thousands of them there. There's stories… about the mutants, and the new weapons they're developing.'

'That's what I'm afraid of,' said the Time Lord. He took one last look at the monitor, and then started toward the door. 'Come on. There's no time like the present.'

'If I do this,' she said, still standing by the console, 'if I take you to Andor and show you the Daleks, then you'll take me away from here in your TARDIS, to somewhere safe?' Her voice cracked as she said the words. She jammed her hands into her pockets so he wouldn't see she was trembling.

'Yes,' he said. 'I will. I promise.'

'How do I know I can trust you?'

His eyes met hers, before he turned and walked through the door. 'You don't,' he called behind him.

Thinking that she didn't have anything else left to lose, Cinder grabbed her gun and ran after him.

Chapter Four

Before the Daleks had come, Jocelyn Harris had been the governor of the planet Moldox, along with the four outlying human settlements on the planet's moons. She'd been good at her job, too: the colony had flourished under her dutiful eye. Birth rates were up, the construction programme continued at a steady pace and the terraforming process had proved relatively smooth, with only one memorable malfunction causing a single, harsh winter.

Jocelyn had taken pride in her work. The people of Moldox, who had re-elected her three times in succession, had celebrated her as the herald of a new age. And to repay them for their unwavering faith, she had betrayed them all to the Daleks.

She hadn't done it out of a desire for power, or because of any sort of devotion to a higher cause.

They were the sorts of thing that drove most defectors, in her limited experience. No, what she'd done had been motivated by cowardice, and in Jocelyn's own opinion, that made her the very worst sort of defector. She had done it to save her own skin. When the Daleks had swarmed over Moldox, stripping the planet bare and culling the population, she had agreed to become their human mouthpiece, their puppet, their plaything. All to make sure that she lived.

Over the years, she'd tried to tell herself that she'd had no choice, that surely it was better if she worked against the Daleks from the inside, inveigling herself into their plans, warning her people on the ground. Only she'd always been just that little bit too afraid to act, to pass any of the information on to the resistance, worried that the Daleks would find out what she was up to. Their retribution would be swift and effective, and that would be an end to it all. She knew that, whatever happened, one thing was certain: she was eminently replaceable.

She wondered what the Daleks had in mind for her today. Two of the dreadful, brass-coloured tin cans had come to her room – a cell by any other name – and demanded she leave with them immediately. As usual, there was no attempt at niceties, no explanation – just the simple command that she was required in the audience chamber.

She rose from behind her desk, setting down her data tablet, and did as she was told. The artificial gravity on the Dalek command station was weak, despite its size. The Daleks, she'd learned, had no real need of it – they could magnetise themselves to the metal floors to avoid floating away, and even if they did, they had propulsors that would enable them to fly. The gravity, then, was a simple concession to the prisoners they held onboard the station, and as such, they weren't particularly given to expending power to ensure it was set at a comfortable level.

As such, Jocelyn found herself bouncing along behind the Daleks, taking exaggerated strides as she tried to keep up.

The audience chamber was less than five hundred metres from her cell, and during the many years she'd been held on the station, she'd visited it innumerable times.

Today, it seemed, the Eternity Circle was in full session. All five of them were here, resting upon their raised pedestals, glaring down at her as she loped into the large, hexagonal chamber.

She'd never quite been able to establish the function of these particular Daleks, or what set them apart from their more lowly kin. Save for their colouring, of course. They were identical in size and shape to the two guards that had brought her from her cell, but where the standard Dalek casings were decorated with burnished bronze and gold, the five members of the Eternity Circle were a deep, metallic blue, with domed heads of polished silver and matching silver sense globes spotting their lower halves.

All Jocelyn knew was that they'd been charged by the Dalek Emperor with fashioning new weapons to deploy against the Time Lords, some of which they had been testing on the people of Moldox and the other worlds of the Tantalus Spiral. She knew this because she'd had to file the reports.

To Jocelyn, they were nightmare creatures; demons encased in blue shells. These were the monsters responsible for what had happened to her beloved planet, her home – and her children.

'Wait,' barked one of the Dalek guards. Its voice was like nails being driven into her skull. She stopped walking. She was standing in the centre of the chamber, looking up at the five blue Daleks. They seemed to regard her with menace, but none of them spoke.

The guards retreated, sliding back soundlessly into two recesses by the door. She decided to remain silent until she was prompted to speak.

High above her, a holographic screen flickered to life, tinting a patch of the air a bright, hazy blue. Its appearance was accompanied by a smell that reminded her of fresh ozone.

'Report,' boomed the low, grating voice of the Dalek Emperor. Jocelyn glanced up in surprise. The ominous image of its massive, unblinking eye was projected on the screen, but the voice seemed to emanate from all around her, filling the chamber. She sensed the bass rumble of it in her gut, and felt her hackles rise.

'The weapon approaches completion,' said the Dalek on the far-left pedestal, drawing out the words in its rasping monotone. 'Soon the Eradicator will be ready.'

'Excellent,' replied the Emperor. 'We stand on the eve of Gallifrey's destruction.' A pause. 'What of the progenitors?'

'Twelve of the seventeen epochs identified have now been seeded with Dalek progenitors,' replied another of the Eternity Circle. 'The Time Lord forces are spread thin. The War is fought on multiple fronts.'

'As it was proscribed,' said the Emperor. 'What progress has been made on development of the new paradigm?'

'Testing on the planet Moldox is almost complete,' replied the Dalek on the central pedestal, its radiation valves flashing as it spoke. 'Data suggests the new Temporal Weapon paradigm is almost ready for distribution through the time-space continuum.'

'Show me,' purred the Emperor.

'I obey,' replied the Dalek. Its head swivelled in Jocelyn's direction. 'Jocelyn Harris. You have served the Daleks well,' it said.

'I've tried,' she stammered, unsure precisely where this was going.

'Your betrayal of your own kind shows only that you cannot be trusted,' continued the Dalek. 'You will be ex-ter-min-ated.'

'No!' she screamed. 'No! I'll do anything. Tell me what I have to do to prove myself to you.' She started backing away towards the door, but she knew there was nowhere to run. She was on a Dalek command station, orbiting a vast space-time anomaly. Any reprieve would be temporary. It wouldn't stop her from trying, though.

She turned around, intending to bolt for the door, but cried out in frustration at the sight of a Dalek silhouette in the doorway, blocking her path. As she watched, trying frantically to figure out what to do, the new Dalek glided slowly into view.

It was different from the others. The same bronze and gold patterning, the same height and general appearance, but the midsection had been replaced, so that instead of the usual arm and gun stick, there was an enormous black cannon mounted on a ball socket.

She backed away, lurching in the low gravity.

The Dalek edged towards her, levelling its cannon. 'Eradicate! Eradicate!' Wisps of ruby-coloured energy began to gather around the nozzle of its weapon.

'No! Please!' screamed Jocelyn, raising her hands to cover her face as the cannon spat a stream of light at her.

The last thing she saw was the eye of the Dalek Emperor glaring down at her from the screen above with maleficent intent.

Chapter Five

'Careful. It might still be out here,' said Cinder, crouching by the TARDIS and scanning the ruins for any sign of the Degradation. 'That one was armed with four energy weapons.'

'I'm sure it's scuttled off to warn its friends by now,' said the Time Lord. 'They won't like the fact I'm here very much at all.'

Cinder stared at him. She'd heard that Time Lords were famously arrogant, but this was different. He didn't seem as if he were being boastful. In fact, if anything, he'd delivered that last comment with a weary inevitability that suggested he didn't really *want* to be here. She was warming to him, although, for now, she'd have to remain cautious. He was difficult to decipher, and she had no idea whether she could trust him or not. She just hoped he wasn't going to make any trouble if she did manage to get him into Andor. A quick look, and then back here to the ship. That was her plan. If they were swift, they could return by morning.

He had his screwdriver in his hand again. She watched as he raised it up over his head and pressed the button. He moved his arm back and forth in a sweeping motion, listening to the sound it made, before shrugging, and then tucking it away into his ammo belt again.

Cinder walked over to stand beside him. She glanced around her, still feeling a little too exposed in the gully. 'I'm Cinder, by the way,' she said. She didn't offer him her hand.

The Time Lord nodded.

Cinder sighed. 'Usually when someone tells you their name, the polite thing to do is respond by telling them yours.'

'Is it?' said the Time Lord, a little bluntly. They lapsed into silence for a moment.

'Well?' prompted Cinder.

'What sort of name is "Cinder"?' he said, deftly changing the subject.

'It's the only name I have, these days,' she said. 'I used to have another, a long time ago, before the Daleks came. But after they killed my family and left me to die inside a rusty old dustbin, I left that life behind. The people who found me named me "Cinder", on account of my hair.' She reached up and tousled her mess of orange locks.

The Time Lord regarded her thoughtfully. 'I understand,' he said. 'I used to have a name, too, but I can barely recall the last time I used it.'

'Why?' she said. 'Was it *terribly* embarrassing?'

The Time Lord cast her a sidelong glance. 'It was a name that stood for something. I'm no longer worthy of it.'

'Isn't that for others to judge?' said Cinder.

'Perhaps,' he replied.

'Tell me,' she said. 'Tell me what it was.'

He seemed to think about it for a moment. 'The Doctor,' he said. 'I used to be called the Doctor.' He turned and trudged off down the road, his head bowed.

'Well, Time Lord who used to be called the Doctor,' she called after him. 'You're going the wrong way.'

The temperature had dropped with the fading light as the afternoon slowly turned to dusk. Thankfully, Cinder's compact backpack had not been damaged during her fall from the escarpment, and she was able to wrap herself in the warm, hand-knitted jumper she carried with her for the purpose.

Night never fell entirely on Moldox. The light from the Tantalus Eye kept the planet enshrouded in an eerie twilight. Cinder had never known any different, of course, and the thought of utter darkness, impenetrable black, filled her with dread. In her experience, the darkness harboured the monsters. At least on Moldox, you could see them coming.

They had taken a path through the ruins rather than keep to the roads. It meant scrabbling over broken lintels and walls and taking a more circuitous route, but it was harder for the Daleks to move about in the ruins, and if they took to the air they were easier to spot.

They'd seen only one further patrol as they'd trudged the first five miles through a landscape of broken habitation domes and civic buildings: two Daleks and two Gliders, skimming over the rooftops, looking for signs of life below. The Doctor had pulled Cinder into a temporary shelter in the archway of a shattered doorway as they'd passed overhead. They'd waited there for a further ten minutes, just to ensure the patrol was not doubling back.

She'd told the Doctor they had a quick stop-off to make en route, and they were approaching it now – the last known location of the rebel camp. It was a motley assortment of tents, lash-ups and temporary structures built from the debris of fallen buildings. From above, it was designed to look like any other waste-strewn field, but from down here it resembled the encampment of a marching army, nestled amongst the splintered structures that had once formed a square or recreational park.

Around thirty men, women and children, all dressed in scavenged rags, milled around cleaning weapons, cooking food and tending to each other's wounds. This was the only family that Cinder had known since the age of 7. This was the sum total of the human resistance movement, and, as far as she knew, the last of the free people of Moldox – the ones who had chosen to fight back against the Daleks and had been strong enough and light enough on their feet to survive.

'What is this place?' said the Doctor. 'I thought you

were taking me to Andoc.'

'An*dor*,' corrected Cinder. 'And I *am*. This is the stop I told you about. I need to collect some things.'

'This is where you live?' said the Doctor.

Cinder shook her head. 'Not for more than a couple of days. We have to keep moving if we want to stay ahead of the Daleks. But yes, this is it. This is my life. These are my people.'

The Doctor said nothing, but simply stood, regarding the place with his old, watery eyes.

'Come on,' said Cinder. 'I don't want to be here any longer than necessary. I just need to throw a couple of things into my backpack.'

She led him through the makeshift hamlet, drawing open stares from the people they passed.

'Don't mind them,' said Cinder, her voice low. 'It's rare enough we find another living human to join our little gang. Imagine what they'd think if they knew you were a Time Lord?' She grinned, deciding not to add that they would probably lynch him, given the opportunity.

'Cinder!'

Damn it! She recognised the voice. She kept her head down. Coyne was the last person she needed to run into now. She'd hoped to slip away without having to see him, without facing the guilt of leaving him here – of leaving them *all* here – while she ran away with a stranger in a blue box. What she was doing wasn't brave. She knew that deep down, but she'd grown so tired of the ceaseless running, of scratching out an existence amongst the ruins and constantly watching over her shoulder for Daleks. She'd never wanted to be a warrior, but the role had been thrust upon her by circumstance, and now, finally, this was her opportunity to escape, to do something different with her life. She knew if she saw Finch that the debt she owed him risked pulling her back in.

'Cinder! Who's your friend?'

With a sigh, she turned to see Coyne making a beeline for them from around the other side of his tent. 'Hello, Coyne,' she said.

He was lean and muscular, around 40 years of age and was one of the leaders of their small troupe. He was also the veteran of numerous encounters with the Daleks, as testified by the deep purple scar across the left side of his face, where a glancing energy beam had incinerated his ear and chewed up the flesh of his cheek.

It had been Coyne who had plucked her from the dustbin in the burning ruins of her homestead, and Coyne who had taught her how to survive, how to fight.

'Aren't you going to introduce us?' he said, with a wary look at the Doctor.

'This is…' She hesitated. 'This is—'

'John Smith,' said the Doctor, extending his hand.

'Well, John Smith,' said Coyne, looking the Doctor up and down. 'Where have you been hiding?'

'Anywhere the Daleks can't find me,' said the Doctor, with a thin smile. 'Moving about from place to place, never staying still for very long.' He glanced at Cinder, and she could tell this wasn't a lie. 'I found Cinder here trying to singlehandedly take down a Dalek patrol,' he continued, 'and decided to drop in and help.'

Coyne laughed amiably. 'Yes, that sounds like Cinder.' He put a protective arm around her shoulder. 'But why didn't you take anyone with you? You know the rules. It's not safe to go out there alone.'

'I wasn't alone,' she replied. 'I had John Smith here, didn't I?'

Coyne rolled his eyes. 'You know precisely what I mean, Cinder,' he said. 'Look, I bet you could both do with something to eat. Come on, the stew's almost ready.'

Cinder glanced apologetically at the Doctor. 'Well, we…'

'That sounds like a marvellous idea,' said the Doctor.

The stew was a thick broth made from vegetables and herbs, but it was hot and welcome, and Cinder gulped it down, enjoying the rare sensation of a full belly.

It was now what passed for night on Moldox, and the strange, ethereal light of the Eye rippled across the sky, an aurora of yellow, pink and blue striations. It bubbled like the surface of some unfathomable lake, like a colourful oil painting being smeared across the sky.

The Doctor, who'd been deep in conversation with Coyne for the last half an hour gleaning details about the Dalek occupation force, came to sit down beside her on an overturned drum. He followed her gaze, looking up at the sky.

'Beautiful, isn't it?' she said.

'Do you know what they are?' he replied. She

shook her head. 'Time winds.' He took a long swig from a metal mug of tea. 'Temporal radiation from the Eye. What you're seeing up there is a billion years of history, a glimpse into the night sky of the ancient past and the furthest reaches of the future. The radiation causes anomalies, glitches in space-time. It's a window right through to another time, only the world on the other side is shifting in constant flux. And yes, you're right – it is rather beautiful.'

Cinder glanced up at it again, this time with new eyes. 'All that time, all those years of peace. Now there's only the War.'

'The universe is full of wonders, Cinder. The things I've seen… the glass moons of Socho, the Red Veil of the Eastern Parabola, the sky beaches of Altros. There are things out there that would make you weep with joy.' He was watching her intently.

'Moldox was like that once,' she said. 'Before your war. Before the Daleks came. The skies used to be filled with transport ships, bringing in new and exotic people every day. The cities heaved with life. People were happy. Out on the plains they erected pleasure palaces that overlooked the Barian Sea, with its golden water and beaches formed from grains of ice. They built towers that seemed to reach almost all the way up to the Eye itself, and machines that looked and thought like men. It was an empire to behold. Now it lies in ruins.'

She shuffled the dirt around with the edge of her shoe. 'All those other places you mentioned, those wondrous worlds – you're going to destroy them all, aren't you? Every last corner of the universe. By the time you've finished there's going to be nothing left.'

'Not if I can help it,' said the Doctor. 'That's why I'm here, Cinder. That's what I'm trying to stop, why I need to see what the Daleks are doing here on Moldox.'

She nodded. Could she really trust this man – this *Time Lord*? There was something about him, something different. Spending time in his company, she felt herself starting to believe, for the first time in years, that there might be a way out of this mess they'd found themselves in; that there might be hope. It was an unfamiliar emotion, and she wasn't yet ready to embrace it.

'Did you get what you came for?' he said, after a moment. The question pulled her right back to the here and now.

'Yes,' she said, indicating her backpack, which she'd dumped on her bunk a few metres away beneath a canvas awning. 'Just a few mementoes. Things I didn't want to leave behind.' She held up her arm, showing him the bracelet encircling her wrist. It was nothing, really, just a hoop of twisted copper wires, burnished with age. It had been made for her by her brother, all those many years ago, and she'd held on to it ever since. She wouldn't leave Moldox without it. It was all she had left of him, save for her memories.

'I understand,' said the Doctor. He frowned, catching sight of something. 'Tell me, whose is that bunk over there, beside yours?'

Cinder glanced at the other makeshift cot, only a metre or two from her own. It seemed oddly familiar. 'I don't…' She hesitated. 'I feel as if I should know, but I don't,' she said. 'It's the strangest feeling. Like something's missing.'

The Doctor nodded, his expression grave. 'Well, it's nothing to worry about now. It's time to drink up and go and find out what the Daleks are up to at Andor.'

Cinder placed her beaker down and swept up her backpack, slinging it over one shoulder. All she really wanted to do now was sleep, but she'd made a promise to the Doctor, and he in turn had made a promise to her. She was going to see this through, one way or another.

Chapter Six

'Shhh!'

'I didn't say anything!' said the Doctor.

'No, your feet,' hissed Cinder. 'On the gravel. Walk on the mud instead.'

The Doctor looked at her as if she were mad. 'But then my boots would get filthy,' he said. 'It'll get all over the TARDIS. Who's going to clear it up? You?'

Cinder rolled her eyes. 'Yes, if I must. Just do it. It's better to have muddy boots than to be lying in a ditch with a hole in your chest. We're nearly there. The place will be swarming with Daleks.'

The Doctor tutted dramatically, but did as she said and stepped up onto the verge, abandoning the gravel path.

They were standing on the outskirts of Andor, just beyond the boundary of the city walls. The walls themselves had been largely torn down during the years of Dalek occupation, and now formed heaps of rubble and broken slabs. It looked disturbingly like a painting she'd seen as a child in one of her picture books, of a citadel from old Earth, sitting on a craggy outcrop above the ocean.

The net result was that any approach to the city would prove hazardous and, more troubling, exposed.

It was clear to see that Andor had once been spectacular, a jewel at the heart of the colony. What had begun in the early days of the human occupation as a rag-tag collection of functional architecture – hab-blocs, basic schools and boxy civic halls – had, over the years, evolved into a picturesque metropolis.

Buildings from a myriad of original Earth cultures stood shoulder-to-shoulder, here – churches, skyscrapers, theatres and mosques – and the thin bands of aerial walkways crisscrossed the sky. Many of them were now broken, splintered during the shelling. The buildings were largely abandoned, too, with any survivors like Cinder, left to fend for themselves in the outlying ruins whilst the Daleks had taken up residence in the city.

Cinder beckoned the Doctor over to where she was crouching inside the shell of a homestead, peering over a tumbledown wall. Creeping ivy clung to the brickwork, running rampant, the only thing left alive in this forsaken place.

Ducking down so to stay out of sight, the Doctor crept over to crouch beside her. 'Over there,' she said, pointing to a large breach in the city walls. 'Can you see those domes?' The Doctor nodded. 'Those are the Dalek buildings. They've co-opted an old school, adapting it and adding to it. We think it's their base of operations.'

'What about the people?' said the Doctor. 'The ones they're bringing here to the city. Where are they?'

Cinder shrugged. 'No one knows. They're taken into those domes for "processing" and never seen again. In the early days we used to speculate about what was happening to them in there, but after a while everyone stopped talking about it. I think we all just assumed they were dead. I've never heard of anyone making it out alive.'

'Then that's where we need to go,' said the Doctor.

Cinder shook her head. 'Oh no, that's not what we agreed. You said you needed to take a *look*. You've seen it now. It's time to head back to your TARDIS and get as far away from here as possible.'

'Cinder, I need to see what they're doing to those people. If the Daleks are simply killing them, why are they going to the effort of rounding them up and leading them here? Why not just exterminate them on sight? That's the Daleks' modus operandi, isn't it? They're not exactly known for their mercy.' He stroked his beard thoughtfully. 'They're up to something, and I want to get to the bottom of what it is.'

Cinder kicked out at a rock in frustration. It bounced away across the gravel path, striking the opposing wall. Deep down, though, she'd always assumed that this was going to happen.

'You can wait here, if you like,' said the Doctor. 'I won't be long.'

'I can't let you go in there alone,' she said. 'Especially unarmed.' What she was thinking, however, was: *if the Daleks find you sneaking about, I have no chance of figuring out how to operate your ship.* And besides – despite all of that, she was starting to like him.

She heard a dull, mechanical whirr from around ten metres away, and hurriedly ducked back behind the wall. The Doctor had clearly heard it too, as he did the same. He peered over the top of the wall, his eyes gleaming.

'What was that?' she whispered. 'Can you see anything?'

'Over there,' said the Doctor, inclining his head. 'They're coming this way.'

Cinder twisted, peeking through a hole in the wall. Through the bushy ivy, she could see a long line of humans, around fifteen or twenty of them, being marched toward the city gates. They looked exhausted, pale and close to death. They were flanked by at least five Daleks, two of which were hovering, one on either side of the line, scanning the surrounding ruins for any signs of resistance.

She dipped her head as an eyestalk swivelled in her direction. She held her breath, waiting for the bark of a Dalek voice, or the blast of an energy weapon. Thankfully, none came. It seemed the Daleks were preoccupied with transporting their prisoners.

Four, five minutes passed, with neither Cinder nor the Doctor daring to move or speak. Then came the sounds of the city gates creaking open, the distant squawk of two Daleks exchanging orders and the wail of a human finally succumbing to fear or fatigue.

Cinder wanted to stick her fingers in her ears and drown it all out.

The Daleks rasped more orders at their prisoners, and a minute or two later the gates closed again behind them. Cinder slowly exhaled, for what felt like the first time in hours.

'They've gone,' said the Doctor, taking a quick look. 'We should move quickly, see if we can find a way to sneak in behind them.'

He stood, offering her his hand, and as she took it she froze in horror at the sight of the glowing tip of a Dalek eyestalk, peering over the wall at them.

'Intru-der! Alert! Alert!'

Only its head and eyestalk were visible, its manipulator arm and weapon hidden behind the ruined wall.

'Elevate! Elevate!'

'Come on!' The Doctor wrenched her up from where she was crouched. 'Run!'

'No!' she yelled, twisting out of his grip. Her weapon was slung over her shoulder and a makeshift leather strap, and she swung it around, sliding it into her hands and searching for the trigger.

The Dalek was rising steadily into the air. 'Extermina—'

There was a tremendous explosion as a lance of energy burst from the end of Cinder's gun, taking off the Dalek's head and sending the remaining shell spinning to the floor. It crashed into the side of a nearby building and bounced across the ground, finally coming to rest a few metres from them. Steam curled from the crater where its head had been.

The Doctor stared at her. 'I thought that thing had run out of power,' he said, surprised but clearly relieved.

'I picked up a new power pack at the camp,' she said, with a grin. 'Thought it might come in handy.'

The Doctor smiled. 'Well, you've certainly given them something to talk about. They'll be on us in moments. Come on, while we've got a distraction. Now's our chance to get inside.'

'*Really?*' said Cinder. 'You really want to go in there?'

'I thought we'd been through this,' said the Doctor.

'Just checking,' said Cinder. 'Because it is about the worst plan I've ever heard.'

A chorus of Dalek voices rose in the distance, coming from behind the city walls.

'I don't see that we have much choice,' replied the Doctor. He started off, his boots crunching in the gravel. 'Come on. This way.'

As the Daleks converged on the spot where they'd been standing just a few moments before, the Doctor and Cinder made a mad, panicked dash for the city walls.

The Doctor led the way, keeping to the muddy verge – somewhat ironically, Cinder noted – and sticking close to the walls of the abandoned homesteads, hiding in the shadows.

Behind them, she heard a Dalek issuing a tirade of instructions to its vile kin. 'Seek. Locate. Exterminate!'

This was utter, unadulterated madness. She'd never done anything quite so reckless in her entire life. She was certain there was only one way this way going to end… and yet, it was exhilarating, too. For the first time in as long as she could remember she had a purpose other than simply destroying as many Daleks as she could before she died. She had something to live for. Which, she supposed, was *also* ironic, given that she was charging headlong into enemy territory, where the most likely outcome was the bolt of an energy weapon between her shoulder blades.

The Doctor had reached the foot of the wall and was scrabbling up onto a heap of rubble, aiming for a narrow crevice through which he could gain entrance to the city proper. He was unexpectedly athletic for an old, curmudgeonly man – spritely, even – as he hauled himself up, not even bothering to glance back to see if the Daleks had spotted him.

'Wait for me!' she hissed as she followed suit, scrabbling up behind him. It was a daunting climb, but she had little choice. It was this or the Daleks.

The Daleks had now found their dead comrade and were fanning out, combing the ruins in search of the perpetrator. Cinder realised they didn't have much time before they were spotted.

She reached up, catching hold of a ledge, but her fingers slipped on the smooth granite and she swung out, dangling by one hand. She stifled a cry of alarm, which came out as an unseemly grunt.

The cold, sharp lip bit into her remaining hand, and she felt her grip loosening. She reached up, trying again, but without the momentum she couldn't quite get a hold. She was going to slide back down, back to the rocks below where, no doubt, the Daleks would find her, if she wasn't dashed upon the rocks first. She looked down, trying to assess the distance. Her vision swam.

A hand suddenly grasped her own. She looked up to see the Doctor peering down at her, holding her by the wrist. 'Hurry up,' he whispered. 'Places to go, people to see.'

He dragged her up onto the ledge. 'You're *enjoying* this, aren't you?' she said, a touch of accusation in her voice.

The Doctor grinned. 'Aren't you?'

Cinder shrugged, but gave an impish smile. 'Maybe,' she replied, noncommittally.

The crevice in the wall seemed far bigger from up here than it had from below. She'd anticipated having to wriggle through sideways, but in fact it was big enough that they could easily walk through side by side. As they did, Cinder realised the Doctor still had hold of her hand. She didn't know if it was more for his comfort than her own, but she didn't mind either way.

There was a drop of around twenty feet on the other side of the wall, into what looked like soft, sticky mud. Beyond that was a small patch of wasteland, which terminated in a line of abandoned human structures. As far as she could tell there were no Daleks to observe them. Evidently, her quick reactions out there in the ruins had proved a rather successful distraction.

'You first,' said Cinder, glancing at the Doctor. 'It was your idea.'

'Oh, together, surely?' he said.

Cinder sighed resignedly. 'Very well.' She peered over the edge again, considering the wisdom of this next move, but decided she wasn't about to start being sensible now. It was far too late for that. 'On the count of one, two—'

The Doctor jumped, still holding her hand, and she was forced to leap after him. They both landed on their feet, and, with a synchronous movement that would have been funny if it hadn't been for the circumstances, fell to their knees in the wet, cloying mud.

'Urgh,' said Cinder, letting go of the Doctor's hand and getting to her feet. 'My leggings are soaked through.' She helped the Doctor up.

'Don't worry,' he said. 'I'm sure there'll be something similar in one of the TARDIS's wardrobes.'

She raised an eyebrow. 'Fond of women's clothes, are we?'

'Yes,' he said, indicating his muddy trousers. 'Clearly, I have a penchant.'

She laughed, covering her mouth with her hands.

'Right,' he said, pointing at the sombre-looking buildings up ahead. They were very much abandoned, shrouded in darkness, with broken windows and plants poking inquisitively through holes in the roofs. 'I think it was this way.'

'No,' said Cinder. 'I've studied maps of this place. If you want to get closer to the Dalek domes we should follow the wall round this way for a while. Then we can cut across, keeping to the shadows. They shouldn't be expecting anyone to approach from that direction.'

The Doctor grinned. 'Aren't you glad you came along? I know I am.'

They were untroubled by Daleks as they crept through the empty streets of the city, passing long abandoned homesteads and shop fronts in which, years later, goods still stood on display in the windows, now slowly turning to mulch and mould.

The threat of the Daleks was an ever-brooding presence, however, depressing Cinder's earlier good humour. She could hear their rasping, tinny voices, barking indiscriminate commands at one another as they combed the ruins, searching for whomever had destroyed one of their patrols.

Cinder had no idea how they were going to get out of this. Scrabbling back up the wall was no option – it was far too high. They would need to find an alternative route out of the city – preferably one that wasn't being guarded by Daleks.

That, however, was for later. Right now, she needed to concentrate on getting them to the Dalek base without triggering any warning systems or bringing down the wrath of a patrol.

She stopped at the corner of an intersection, putting a hand on the Doctor's chest to hold him back, and peered around. At the end of a long, narrow street she could see the curve of one of the Dalek domes, its outer surface stippled with familiar globes. Before that, however, was a single Dalek, standing with its back to them, its eyestalk swivelling from side to side, as if keeping watch.

She pulled back. 'Dalek,' she whispered.

'Now I wasn't expecting to find one of those here,' whispered the Doctor.

Cinder punched him gently on the shoulder. 'Seriously, what are we going to do? If I fire my weapon this close to the dome, they'll hear it. There'll be swarms of them on us in moments.'

The Doctor stuck his head around the corner, assessing the situation for himself. 'We could just ask it nicely?' he said. 'Tell it we're lost and that we want to go back to our cells in the camp. It's as good a way as any of getting inside.'

Cinder looked at him as if he were mad. 'My liberty is more important to me than getting inside that dome,' she said. 'And my life. I have my limits.'

The Doctor grinned. 'In that case, let's go round.'

They backtracked until they found a gap between two rows of houses, forming a narrow alleyway. Quietly, they traversed the length of it, their feet sloshing in the unwholesome effluvia that ran in a constant stream from the overflowing drains.

'Come on, in here,' said the Doctor, pulling her into the doorway of an empty house. It looked relatively intact – a standard-issue, prefabricated habitation bloc, built for a family. He tried the door, but it was locked.

Cinder watched as he removed his screwdriver from its hoop in the ammo belt he wore slung across his chest, and tinkered for a minute with the settings. He held the tip of it to the lock and pressed the button. The end of it lit up, and it emitted an electronic warble. Seconds later, she heard the lock mechanism slide open.

'What did you do?' she asked.

'Agitated a few molecules,' he whispered, tapping the end of his nose. 'Let's go inside.' He led her into the building.

It was dark inside, without the flickering glow of the Tantalus Eye and the radiation storms still raging overhead. What light there was seeped in through the gaps between the lichen that was growing over the downstairs windowpanes, just about allowing her to see once her eyes had adjusted to the gloom.

She swallowed. She felt as if her heart were in her mouth. The room they'd entered was laid out as if the family who had once occupied it had simply upped and left; had got up and walked out, with every intention of returning later to pick up where they'd left off. Children's toys were strewn across the carpet. An empty glass rested on a side table. A picture frame on the wall still projected the holographic resemblance of a man and a woman, clutched in a happy embrace.

Cinder felt the weight of guilt upon her shoulders, of immense sadness. How had she survived all this time, while the Daleks had taken these people and their families? What right did she have to still be alive? How had she been allowed to live on while her mother, father and brother had been exterminated?

Her entire life up until this point had been about eradicating those memories, those insidious, guilt-ridden thoughts; about burying them in violence and revenge, turning them into the burning hatred of the Daleks that now festered at the very core of her being.

She'd never once thought of trying to rescue anyone, of trying to change things. It had always seemed so futile, so far beyond her means. And so she had settled for taking pot shots at passing Dalek patrols, or hunting them in the ruins of her former home, counting each death as a victory.

Then the Doctor had come along, tumbling out of the sky in his magical box, and in a few short hours had forced her to face up to this, to recognise that perhaps there *were* things that could be done, that nothing was quite as impossible as it might seem. There were different ways of fighting back. She wasn't quite sure what he intended to do with the information he gleaned here on Moldox, but she knew it wasn't simply for his own gratification. He was getting involved, because he wanted to help, wanted to make it all stop.

She could see now that all she'd been doing was screaming into the wind. Those victories she'd notched up on the barrel of her gun had been hollow, every one of them. She hadn't *changed* anything, hadn't really made a difference. She'd wasted so much time.

Yet something in her had known there was still time to make a difference. She'd followed the Doctor here, a Time Lord she barely knew, and now, standing in the remnants of Andor, she realised he might prove to be her salvation. This wasn't simply about helping her to run away from her old life. It was about showing her how to change it for herself. What was more, she thought he knew that, too.

She looked round for him and realised he'd already moved on, deeper into the house. She heard his footsteps on the stairs and followed after him.

Cinder found him in one of the children's

bedrooms on the second floor, standing by the window, the brightly coloured curtains pulled aside so that he might look out upon the Dalek base. She joined him there.

From this distance the Dalek structures didn't appear quite as sophisticated as she'd imagined. In fact, they looked rather lashed together, with narrow metal causeways erupting from the flank of each dome to puncture its neighbour. There were five domes in total, forming a loose circle around a central courtyard. They were large and seemingly identical, disc-shaped with a raised central turret, and decorated with the same bronze and gold patterning as the Daleks themselves.

The base had an economical, practical layout that had little or nothing to do with aesthetics and everything to do with function. The whole place had a temporary, transitory feel to it, despite the fact it had been in situ for well over a decade.

'What are they?' said Cinder.

'Spacecraft,' said the Doctor. 'Dalek vessels. They haven't co-opted the old school, so much as levelled it and landed their saucers on top of it. They've erected walkways between the ships, but they're only temporary structures. The whole base could be disbanded at any moment. They're clearly not intending to stay on Moldox.'

'Then what are they doing here?' asked Cinder. She'd always supposed the occupation was about the Daleks wanting control of the planet. She'd never even considered that there might be another, less permanent purpose.

'That's a question I'm very keen to know the answer to,' said the Doctor.

Cinder thought she saw a sign of movement in the courtyard and leaned forward, until her nose was almost touching the dirty glass of the window. She narrowed her eyes, trying to see what was going on. There was definitely movement – people, in fact – a group of humans being shepherded out into the paved area that had once been a children's playground.

Floodlights blared suddenly, causing her to wince as everything was brought into sudden, sharp relief. Three Daleks were jostling the human prisoners – around ten of them, both male and female – making them form into a long line, standing shoulder to shoulder. Cinder could hear nothing from this distance, but she could imagine the threats being issued by the metal monsters in order to force the humans to comply.

The Doctor put his hand on the sill, peering out, watching with interest.

Why were they forming a line?

'Oh, no!' said Cinder, with sudden realisation. 'They're going to execute them!'

'Perhaps,' said the Doctor, his voice a low growl. 'But again, why do it like this? Why go to all the trouble of taking them prisoner, leading them here half-starved, only to line them up in the courtyard to shoot them down. There has to be more to it.'

Cinder didn't really want to watch, fearful of what she might see, but nevertheless she was transfixed, unable to tear her gaze away. As she watched, the three Daleks backed away, two of them disappearing from view, while another moved forward into focus.

This one had a slightly different, yet familiar outline. 'That's like the one I saw during the ambush,' said Cinder. 'The one you decapitated when you crashed. It's one of the mutants, a Degradation.'

It was precisely like the monstrous thing she had encountered earlier that day, the size and shape of a standard Dalek, save for the fact its midsection had been replaced by a fat, black cannon.

'That's no Degradation,' said the Doctor. 'That's different. That's something new.'

The Dalek swivelled to face the sorry-looking line of human prisoners. One of the other Daleks hove into view, and Cinder could tell it was speaking by virtue of the flashing lights on its domed head.

In response, the cannon-wielding Dalek powered up its weapon. An aura of intense, ruby-coloured light flickered to life at the end of the barrel. There was a sudden, massive discharge as the weapon spat a stream of pink light, which engulfed four of the people, warping around them as they screamed and tried to back away.

The remaining prisoners staggered out of the way, clearly terrified as they looked on upon their own likely fate.

The four victims writhed in obvious agony, as the pink light appeared to seep into their bodies, pouring into their open mouths, their eyes, permeating through their skin. Then, as if their flesh were simply unable to contain so much raw energy, they blossomed, their forms dissolving, the pink light flickering brightly before dispersing and fading away, like wisps of trailing smoke.

Cinder staggered back from the window feeling nauseous. She put her hand to her brow. She could tell that something was badly wrong, put she couldn't put her finger on what it was. She stared at the Doctor, put her hand on his arm as if to steady herself. 'What just happened?' she said. 'I know something awful has just happened, but what was it?'

She glanced back at the courtyard, where the Daleks were surveying the six prisoners they had brought out into the courtyard a few minutes earlier.

The Doctor stepped away from the window and, taking hold of Cinder's forearm, led her away too. 'It's a temporal weapon,' he said. 'A dematerialisation gun. The Daleks have developed a new template, a new paradigm, which has the power to eradicate a person from history.'

'How can you tell?' said Cinder. 'How do you know just by looking at it?'

The Doctor narrowed his eyes. 'Didn't you see it? Didn't you see what it just did to those four people?'

Cinder shook herself free from his grip. She went back to the window. No, there were six people there, just as there had been before. 'Four people?' she said. 'There are six of them down there.' Even as she said it, though, she knew something was awry. She could feel it, nagging away at her. She was missing something. Couldn't she even trust her own mind any more?

'It's the weapon, Cinder. That's what's doing it,' said the Doctor. 'That cannon – it can erase a person's timeline from history, removing every trace of them, as if they never even existed. It's what happened to your friend, out there in the ruins, the person whose bunk was next to your own at the camp, the one you can't quite remember. Your mind is struggling to comprehend it. You know there's something wrong, something missing. The memories are still there, buried inside your head, but they no longer add up, they no longer relate to a person you've known or seen, because reality has warped around you.'

Cinder shook her head, as if trying to clear it. She didn't understand. A weapon that not only killed someone, but rewrote history as if they'd never even been born? It was the most awful thing she'd ever heard. The sheer violence of it – to not only take a life, but to undo every action, every thought, every emotion ever enacted or experienced by that person… it had to be the most evil device ever conceived. She wiped tears from her eyes, remembering the grief, if not the people.

'I'm sorry,' said the Doctor. 'I truly am. But that trip in the TARDIS is going to have to wait a little longer. If the Daleks are able to disseminate this weapon, then the War is all but lost.' He stepped towards her, put his arms around her and pulled her close, hugging her to his chest. 'I'm going to stop them doing this to anyone else.'

Sniffing back her tears, Cinder pushed the Doctor away. She fixed him with a defiant stare. Her resolve hardened. 'I'm in,' she said. 'Whatever it takes, I'll help you stop them.'

The Doctor gave a grim smile. 'That's my girl,' he said.

Chapter Seven

'How are we going to get in?' said Cinder.

They'd left the house, emerging onto the still, empty street outside. The Dalek domes loomed large and foreboding at the next intersection. Cinder was trying to work out the best plan for getting inside.

'I always find at times like these,' said the Doctor, 'that the best recourse is to use the front door.'

'The front door? You can't seriously mean that you're just going to walk on up there and try the handle?' said Cinder. She couldn't tell if he was naive, confident, or just dangerously reckless. Nor did she know if the doors on Dalek space vessels even *had* handles.

'Precisely,' replied the Doctor. 'It usually does the trick.' He strode off in the direction of the dome.

Exasperated, Cinder rushed after him. 'You find

yourself in these sorts of situations often, do you?' she asked.

'More than you'd care to know,' said the Doctor, with a heavy sigh. His eyes looked rheumy and tired.

She wondered how old he really was. He certainly *looked* old, but she had no idea how long a Time Lord could actually survive. She'd heard tell that they were immortal, that they couldn't be killed, but also that they could change their faces at will, become someone different and new. She didn't know if any of that were true. For all she knew, the Doctor was as mortal as she was, and just as susceptible to the blast of a Dalek energy weapon.

'But what about the Daleks?' she said. 'You've seen what they can do. That new weapon, the dematerialisation gun – what if they come at you with one of those?'

'The Daleks are as arrogant as the Time Lords,' said the Doctor. 'Perhaps worse. That's the beauty of a plan like this. They won't be expecting anyone to simply roll up and invite themselves in.'

'I'd hardly call it a plan,' muttered Cinder. She clutched her gun a little tighter. When she'd said she was in on this escapade, she'd expected him have a bit more of an idea about exactly how they were going to go about it.

At the end of the street she glanced left, ready to make a run for it, but the Dalek they'd seen earlier had moved on. She checked in the other direction, looking along the street.

The city was arranged in a basic grid pattern, designed to a plan the colonists had brought with them from Earth. They'd arrived with a certain amount of prefabricated materials in their hold, and these had formed the basis of the very first buildings – those, and the skin of the ship that had brought them here. As the colony had developed and they'd learned to manufacture, to harvest the local wood and mine for minerals and metals, the buildings had grown more sophisticated, but still they had followed the plan from Earth. Month after month, year after year, the colony had grown, soon forgetting it was a colony at all and becoming a home.

People had flourished here, and in time they had spread across the other planets of the Spiral. Moldox, however, had been the first, the origin of human life in this sector. Now, billions of those people were dead, possibly erased entirely from history, whilst billions more were enslaved to the Daleks.

The Doctor was right. They would stop this happening to anyone else. They had to. It was time to stop doubting him. If brazenly walking up to the saucer and strolling in through the nearest entry point was going to be the best way into the Dalek base, then she would follow him. There was something about the Doctor – something that inspired her to trust him.

They crossed the intersection and continued down the filthy street, until they were standing in the shadow of the nearest saucer. It was immense, towering over her, and she could see here, from ground level, that it sat upon three domes that sprouted from its base. Beneath it was the rubble of one of the old school buildings. The ablative armour that formed the outer skin of the ship was pitted and covered in verdigris.

None of the lights appeared to be functional. Creeping vines had begun to make inroads, curling up from below like willowy green fingers, clutching at the alien interloper. It looked as abandoned as the human buildings that surrounded it.

They edged forward, glancing from side to side. High above, on one of the gantries, a Dalek and two Degradations – the squat, egg-shaped variety with the spider legs – were crossing from one saucer to another. The Doctor didn't appear to have spotted them. Cinder grabbed his arm and dragged him into the shadows beneath the belly of the ship. She jabbed her gun silently in the direction of the Daleks and he nodded his understanding. They waited for a moment until the Daleks had passed.

'There should be a ramp on this side, if I'm not mistaken,' said the Doctor, fiddling with the knot of his scarf. He moved on, following the rim of the saucer around until they were close to the edge of the central courtyard, but still largely hidden by the shadows.

The Daleks appeared to have finished their weapon testing, and the remaining humans – six of them, she counted, relieved – were being herded back into the saucer on the other side.

It seemed incomprehensible to Cinder that this site, this old children's playground, could have become such a place of death. The faded markings of hopscotch squares and painted circles on the ground seemed incongruous, wrong. She was filled with a sharp feeling of disquiet. It was almost as if the Daleks had chosen this location in order to mock their human captives, to remind them of happier times, now lost to them for ever.

'Move, or you will be ex-ter-min-ated,' said one of the Daleks, shoving a prisoner in the back with its manipulator arm. The man staggered forward, but didn't acknowledge the Dalek, didn't even cry out. The fight had clearly gone out of him, and he shuffled onto the boarding ramp, his head bowed.

This was a man waiting to die, Cinder realised. They all were. Every one of those prisoners, men and women – they knew it was only a matter of time, and in some ways, they'd probably begun to look forward to it. To crave it, even. At least death would be a release from the torment inflicted upon them by their captors. Anything else was just an extension of their agony.

She watched the final stragglers of the small party mount the ramp and disappear into the other ship.

'Right,' whispered the Doctor, touching the top of her arm to get her attention. 'This is our chance. There's a ramp just around here.' He indicated by waving his thumb. 'Slowly and quietly, and stay by my side.'

Cautiously, they crossed the courtyard and ascended the ramp. Cinder kept her weapon slung at her hip, her finger close to the trigger. She could hardly believe what she was doing. If Coyne could see her now…

Side by side, the two of them stepped into the yawning maw of the Dalek ship.

Inside, the walls were comprised of a series of crystalline archways patterned with small roundels, and through which lurid colours – yellows, greens, ochres and purples – pulsed like blood pounding through a network of arteries and veins.

A wide passageway appeared to run around the circumference of the ship, offering them the choice of going left or right. Cinder's heart was hammering in her chest, expecting a Dalek to round one of the bends at any moment. For now, though, they seemed to be alone.

'Well, that was easier than I thought,' she whispered.

'Getting in is the easy bit,' replied the Doctor. 'It's getting out that's usually the problem.'

'Oh, thanks for that,' she muttered. She realised her hands were trembling as she tried to hold her gun level. 'So, what now?'

The Doctor shrugged. 'We take a look around. Each of these domes will be given over to a specific purpose. Let's find out which of them we're in.'

Staying close to the wall, they followed the passage as it snaked around to the left, peering ahead for any sign of oncoming Daleks. Sheer luck had got this far, Cinder was sure, and she was convinced they would find themselves surrounded at any moment. Surely the Daleks must have monitoring systems aboard their ships?

After a while the passage branched to the right, splitting into a number of narrow tunnels that appeared to lead deeper into the ship. The Doctor – who seemed to be arbitrarily deciding which way to go – led her down one of these smaller, tributary corridors with a wave of his hand.

Here, there was a row of panels in the wall resembling doors; large metal sheets inset into archways. They didn't appear to have any controls. Or, Cinder considered, any handles. Well, that answered *that* question, at least.

'Are these cells?' asked Cinder. 'Might there be prisoners inside?'

'Possibly,' said the Doctor. 'It's hard to tell from out here, although I imagine they're keeping them all together on the other saucer, or in some of the buildings nearby.'

'We should check,' she said. 'How do I open the door?'

'Walk towards it. They're motion activated,' he replied.

Cinder crept towards the door, but nothing happened.

'No, not like that,' said the Doctor. 'Walk at it with purpose, like a Dalek.' He strode forward confidently, puffing out his chest. There was a click and a mechanical whirr, and a second later the door *whooshed* open, sliding up into the roof.

The room revealed beyond was a relatively large chamber, filled with all manner of bizarre equipment and technological ephemera. The stench that wafted out, however, was almost enough to cause her to keel over and vomit. Immediately, she wished she'd kept on walking.

The Doctor stepped inside, and she followed, wrinkling her nose at the smell. It was foul, like rancid, rotting meat. Something inside the room was very wrong indeed.

Five glass structures stood against the rear wall. They were transparent, but shaped in the archetypal form of a Dalek, complete with a glass manipulator arm and weapon.

Cinder hefted her gun, expecting them to swing into action at any moment. She backed up, glancing from side to side.

The Doctor held out his hand, reassuring her. 'They're not living Daleks,' he said. 'At least not yet. Take another look.'

Still a little unsure, she crept closer. Through the glass walls of the casing she could see the organic matter inside, a heaving, glutinous mass of flesh and tubing, steadily inflating and deflating like a sticky, diseased lung.

The room was some sort of incubation chamber.

This in itself was enough to cause another involuntary gag, but it was when she looked at the second of the incubation chambers that she realised the true extent of the horror. In this one, the organic component still had a human face.

It had once been a woman, but now, if there was anything left behind the darting, yellow eyes, it was only madness. The head had mutated, becoming hairless, misshapen. The flesh had blistered and bubbled, caked in gnarled tumours. The woman's limbs had been removed, and cables extruded from her chest, wiring her into the incubation housing.

Cinder staggered back, looking away, unable to process exactly what she was seeing. It was simultaneously the most disgusting and most pitiful thing she'd ever seen.

'This is what they're doing here?' she said. 'Experimenting on the prisoners?'

'Turning them into Daleks,' said the Doctor, his voice grim.

'Turning humans into Daleks?' echoed Cinder, unable to adequately display her disgust.

'Yes, it rather seems they're not quite as concerned with racial purity as they used to be,' said the Doctor. 'Funny how ideals go out the window when your back's against the wall.'

'But why? What could they possibly have to gain?'

'They're making foot soldiers,' he said. 'Cannon fodder. They're dousing people in radiation so that their cells mutate into forms resembling the mutant Kaleds. Once they've altered them physiologically, they'll remove all of the emotion, effectively lobotomising them, and re-house them in normal Dalek casings. They'll take orders as well as any other Dalek, and if they're destroyed, well – at least they weren't a *real* Dalek.'

'It's obscene,' said Cinder.

The Doctor nodded. 'It's just the tip of the iceberg,' he said.

Cinder looked around the room. Besides the five incubators there was little else worthy of note: a bubbling vat containing something that looked disgustingly like melting flesh, and a web work of trailing cables hooked up to the incubators, that disappeared into the ceiling and walls. Clearly, it was these that carried the power and nutrients needed to keep the human mutants alive during their transition.

She glanced at the Doctor, a question in her eyes.

He nodded his understanding, and crossed to the door to keep watch.

Cinder dropped her gun, allowing it to swing loose on its shoulder strap, and grabbed a bundle of wires in both hands. She yanked down on them hard, using all of her weight to try to tear them free of their ceiling mounts. On the third attempt at least half of them sheared, ripping loose, horrible black fluid spraying in gouts from the frayed ends like blood spurting from a fresh wound. Cinder dropped the frayed ends to the floor. She continued like this for a few moments, ripping all of the cables out of their sockets, allowing her anger to burn brightly and violently in her chest.

When she was finished, she crouched down before the incubator housing the once-woman, and stared into the thing's eyes. Its pupils fixed on her, but the look was vacant, disturbing. 'Find peace,' said Cinder. She got to her feet and walked over to the Doctor. He was still waiting just inside the doorway, keeping watch for Daleks.

'Let's see what else they've got here,' he said. He stepped from the room and immediately leapt back, catching Cinder in the chest with his arm and almost bowling her over. 'Daleks,' he whispered.

They fell back, one on each side of the open doorway, pressing flat against the wall as three Daleks slid past. They moved almost silently, their eyestalks swivelling, their manipulator arms twitching as if feeling the air for disturbance.

Cinder held her breath, waiting for them to pass, assuming at any minute one of them would note that something was wrong in the incubation chamber and turn to investigate.

Thankfully, they didn't appear to be paying attention, and trundled on, heading deeper into the ship.

She waited for the Doctor to indicate the all-clear before she allowed herself to exhale. 'Do they live aboard these things?' she said, when she was sure they would not be overheard. 'The saucers, I mean. Is this their home?'

'In as much as a Dalek does live,' said the Doctor. 'They don't sleep, eat, or drink. They don't have a concept of friendship, companionship. They're single-minded, relentless in their pursuit of their end goal – to eradicate all life in the cosmos save for their own.'

'Yeah, I pretty much got that,' said Cinder, with a crooked smile.

They moved on, continuing their circuit of the ship.

'The flight deck is at the heart of the ship,' said the Doctor. 'That's where most of the Daleks will be. I'm far more interested in what's going on elsewhere.'

He walked towards another door, which slid open as he approached.

The contents of this room were just as disturbing – and, Cinder noted, just as foul smelling – as those of the last. Here, experiments were clearly being carried out on the Degradations.

The casing of a Glider lay in pieces on the floor, while the torso had been removed from inside the glass chamber and was splayed open on a metal slab. It looked as if the Daleks had been carrying out an autopsy investigation, and had simply abandoned it part way through. Excised organs sat in metal bowls, slowly turning putrid, and the uncovered carcass was drying out and beginning to rot.

Components from other unusual-looking Daleks were strewn about the room: an elongated eyestalk, the bottom half of a travel unit in which all of the sensor globes were transparent and flickered with an exotic blue light, a golden head dome with four radiation valves.

'Is it true,' said Cinder, covering her mouth and refusing to look at the corpse, 'that these are the result of Time Lord experiments, attempts to re-engineer Dalek history and evolution?'

The Doctor shrugged. 'There's some truth in that,' he said, 'of course there is, but only inasmuch as it gave the Daleks an idea, a means of experimenting on and adapting themselves. They've taken it to far greater extremes than the Time Lords ever did.'

'You mean they're doing this to *themselves*?' said Cinder. The very idea of it appalled her.

The Doctor nodded. 'A Dalek eugenics programme,' he said. 'Dipping into as many alternative realities as they can find and tampering with their own DNA, trying to nurture the perfect killing machine to deploy against the Time Lords.'

'You must be quite the fearsome enemy,' said Cinder, 'to inspire that.'

The Doctor looked away, unable to meet her gaze. 'We're not going to find what we're looking for here,' he said. 'I think it's time we checked one of the other saucers. These are just experimental laboratories.'

Cinder wanted to ask him exactly what he *was* looking for, but before she had the chance he'd set off again, disappearing out into the passage. Her questions would have to wait – trying to engage in conversation as they crept around the ship only risked bringing the Daleks down on top of them. She hurried to catch up.

They continued with their reconnaissance around the outer passages of the ship, until they happened upon an access ramp leading to the upper level. They hurried up it, spurred on by the sound of muffled Dalek voices, echoing through a doorway behind them.

The upper tier of the vessel appeared very much the same as the one below, although they found themselves facing a large, open hatchway as they emerged from the top of the ramp. Here, the metal walkway jutted from the hole, neatly spanning the open space to the opposing saucer.

It was makeshift; it looked as if it had been lashed up in nearly as much of a hurry as the temporary buildings that had served as her home for so long. It didn't look particularly safe – there were no handrails or lips, just a smooth band of metal, about four metres wide, stretched between the two vessels for the Daleks to glide over. Unlike a Dalek, however, if Cinder fell, she wouldn't be able to fire a quick burst from her thrusters to stabilise herself or fly away.

She inched to the opening and peered down, while the Doctor checked there were no Daleks coming from the other directions. It was quite a drop. Below them, the courtyard now appeared to be empty, the prisoners and the Daleks having returned to one of the other saucers.

'It doesn't look particularly safe,' hissed Cinder, as the Doctor joined her at the foot of the metal bridge.

'You'll be *fine*,' said the Doctor, in what sounded like an attempt to reassure her. He didn't, however, sound particularly sure himself. He tapped the metal gantry with the edge of his boot, and then lurched out, trying it with his weight. 'See, fine,' he said. He set off in the direction of the other ship.

Feeling rather too exposed, and decidedly unsafe, Cinder followed him across the bridge, trying not to look down. If she focused on the Doctor's back, and hurried, then it wasn't quite so bad…

Too late, they realised that in the eerie stillness of the base their footfalls sounded like gunshots, ringing out against the metal plating with every step.

Halfway across, the Doctor stopped for a moment, looking back. 'Better hurry,' he whispered. 'Any minute now, one of them is bound to come investigating. We're not being terribly inconspicuous.'

Cinder gave him her best 'you don't say' look and carried on, simultaneously trying to walk faster while making sure she remained upright on the polished metal surface. She almost went over on her backside as she reached the point where the bridge bowed, leading down into the other Dalek ship, and wheeled her arms frantically, trying to keep her balance. Her gun swung loose on its shoulder strap and caught in the crook of her elbow, threatening to slip free and over the edge.

'Hang on!' said the Doctor. He reached for her,

fumbled for a moment, and then finally managed to get hold of her arm. He waited for a moment, still clinging onto her, as she regained her footing and hitched her gun strap back up onto her shoulder, and then guided her to safety, bundling her through the hatchway. She was glad to have her feet back on solid ground, even if it was onboard a Dalek ship.

'Where are they all?' she said a moment later, once she had her breath back.

'There'll be fewer here than you think,' said the Doctor. 'They'll have other bases elsewhere on the planet, similar to this one, and patrols out in the ruins like the ones you've encountered before. Most of them will have moved on, though, deploying to the other battlefronts, or joining their attack fleets up there near the Eye.'

'I just assumed there'd be a whole army of them,' said Cinder. 'Thousands and thousands of them. I mean, look what they've done to this place. Look at the devastation they've wrought. And yet here we are, sneaking around their base, and we've hardly seen sign of them.'

'This is what they do,' said the Doctor, 'Move in, destroy, and move out. They've no interest in the planet itself. I think I'm starting to realise that it's more to do with Moldox's proximity to the Eye. I think that's why they're here.'

'What do you mean?' said Cinder.

'That temporal radiation I talked about,' said the Doctor, 'the thing that causes the aurora in the sky?'

Cinder nodded.

'It leaks from the Eye, a constant discharge.

The Eye is an anomaly, a structure that shouldn't exist. It's a wrinkle in space-time: a hole, if you will, between universes. Those temporal weapons, the dematerialisation guns, I think they're being powered by it. The Daleks have found a way to harness the radiation and bend it to their will.'

Cinder looked up involuntarily, as if searching for the Eye. All she saw, however, was the inside of the Dalek saucer. 'What about the prisoners, then?' she said. 'Why keep them here?'

The Doctor shrugged. 'Biological matter they can use to construct new, mutant Daleks, or fodder to test their experimental weapons. That's all, I'm afraid.'

The sheer callousness of it was staggering to Cinder. To have such blatant disregard for life – it seemed anathema to her. 'And this is what they'll be doing on all those other planets in the Spiral?'

'Probably,' said the Doctor, 'or they'll have sunk mines and enslaved people to dig, harvesting minerals and precious metals for their war effort. They don't have a great deal of imagination, unless it's to do with killing people.' He smoothed down the front of his waistcoat. 'Come on, there'll be plenty of time to talk later.'

The interior of the second saucer looked much the same as the first: identical almost, except for the fact there was a series of doors facing them almost immediately as they went in.

'I want to find one of their computer terminals,' said the Doctor. 'Let's try in…' he waggled his finger back and forth as if counting out 'eenie, meenie, miney, mo', '…here.' He strolled purposely towards one of the doors and, just as before, it slid open to accommodate him.

This one opened into a large chamber from which a series of other doors stemmed off into adjoining rooms. It appeared to be a laboratory, with a bank of nine monitors set into the far wall, all of which were displaying complex sequences of numbers, animated to form twisting double helixes against a faint green background.

Two tables were laid out with an array of vicious-looking surgical tools and equipment, although thankfully, thought Cinder, this time none of them bore the remains of a Dalek experiment.

'Watch the door,' said the Doctor. He crossed to the bank of screens and began tapping on the glass, calling up strange-looking sigils and dragging them around to create unusual patterns. It looked like utter gobbledegook to Cinder, but she supposed it must have meant something to the Doctor.

'Can you read that?' she said.

'A little,' replied the Doctor, but he was distracted, paying attention to the data scrolling before his eyes. Now schematics were blinking across the screens, wireframes that appeared to describe a building or other massive construction. She wondered if they were maps of the saucer or the base.

Cinder waited just inside the doorway, holding the gun across her chest so that she was able to cover the passageway outside, as well as the entrance to the ship. Her heart was still juddering, and her palms were slick with sweat. Despite the bravado, she was feeling somewhat terrified, and the initial surge of adrenalin was beginning to wear off.

'It's worse than I thought,' said the Doctor, suddenly. She glanced over her shoulder to see what was wrong, but he still had his back to her, reading from the screens. 'They're cloning Dalek mutants here, and through there,' he looked over his shoulder to see if she were paying attention, pointing to one of the doors, 'that's a hatchery. They're breeding Daleks so that they can put their new paradigm into full production.'

'The ones with the cannons?' she asked.

'Yes,' confirmed the Doctor. 'But it gets worse. They're building something else, too.'

'What?' hissed Cinder.

'A planet killer,' said the Doctor. 'A mega-weapon. They're planning to turn the Tantalus Eye itself into one, massive energy cannon, and fire it at Gallifrey.'

'What does that mean?' said Cinder.

'The end of everything,' growled the Doctor. 'They'll erase Gallifrey entirely, remove it from existence, rewrite history as if the Time Lords never existed. They'll condemn the universe, overrun everything.' For the first time since arriving at the Dalek base, the Doctor actually looked worried.

'What can we do?'

'We can start by giving them something else to worry about,' said the Doctor. He returned to playing with the icons on the monitor screens, and one of the door panels on her right slid open to reveal a small antechamber.

She swung around, half expecting to see a Dalek emerge from the doorway, but there was nothing there. She backed up, keeping her gun pointed at the main door, until she could take a glance inside the newly revealed room.

Clear vats filled with pale blue fluid lined benches on both sides the room. Inside, ugly green creatures about the size of a human head, with a single, pale eye, fat worm-like tentacles and sharp hooked claws, were suspended in the bubbling fluid. There were hundreds of them. Just the sight of them made Cinder want to gag, let alone the acidic stench that assaulted her nostrils with every intake of breath.

'What are they?' she said, the disgust evident in her voice.

'Kaled mutants,' replied the Doctor, coming to stand beside her. 'Clones, at a fairly late stage of development. These will soon be ready to be placed inside Dalek casings.'

'*That's* what's inside a Dalek,' said Cinder, peering a little closer. 'No wonder they have image problems.'

The Doctor stepped into the room and began fumbling with a metal grille on the floor.

'What are you doing?' she said.

'Something I should have done a long time ago,' he replied. He thumbed a lever and removed a small access panel by his feet, revealing a nest of coloured cables beneath. He grabbed a fistful and yanked them loose, sorting through until he found the one he was after.

'Ah, that's the one,' he said.

'What is it?'

'Coolant pipe,' he replied, tugging at it violently until it tore, shearing apart in his hands. Pale grey vapour began to seep from the ragged ends, condensing in the warm air and spattering across the floor. He cast the ruined piping away. Somewhere else in the saucer an alarm began to blare; an insistent warble, echoing around the empty corridors.

'You're killing them,' she said. There was no accusation in her voice. It was a statement of fact. She could already see the mutants beginning to squirm in their tanks, growing uncomfortable as the temperature of the water began to increase. 'They're going to overheat, boil alive in those vats.'

The Doctor fixed her with a hard stare. 'I've been here before,' he said. For the first time, his voice sounded *old*, weary with the weight of centuries. 'I've faced this in the past, and I didn't act in time. If I'd only had the guts to do what was necessary back then, things might be very different now. But I'm a different man now. I don't live by the same ideals. I have a job to do, and this time, I have no such qualms.'

Despite the coldness of his words, she could tell he didn't really believe this. He was trying to convince himself as much as convince her.

'Are you sure?' she said.

He nodded. 'Leave them.' He left the room, marching directly toward one of the other doors. It slid open, revealing another small antechamber. This one appeared to be a store cupboard, holding a variety of Dalek components: manipulator arms, sensor globes, energy weapons. The Doctor approached a rack housing a row of broad, black cannons, just like the ones fitted to the new Daleks.

He grabbed one, hefting it, testing its weight. He

turned it over in his hands, checking the power pack, and then nodded at Cinder, clearly satisfied. 'Time to go,' he said.

The alarm was still blaring, and as they stepped out into the corridor, Cinder fell back in terror at the sight of a Dalek no more than a couple of metres away, heading directly for them.

'Stop! Intruder! You will be exterminated!'

'Not if I can help it,' said the Doctor from behind her. She threw herself against the wall of the ship as the Doctor depressed the trigger on the cannon, blasting the Dalek with a dose of temporal radiation. The Dalek screeched in fury, backing away, but the crackling pink light from the gun seemed to form a cocoon around it, warping and weaving as it tried to find a way in.

'Expunge! Expunge!' shrieked the Dalek.

Something was wrong. The weapon wasn't behaving in the way he'd expected, having observed it being used against the human prisoners. Instead of seeping inside of the Dalek, eating it away from within, the light began to disperse in shimmering wisps, dissolving into the air, until a moment later, it had faded entirely, and the Dalek remained before them.

The Doctor lowered the cannon. 'They've made themselves immune to it,' he said.

The Dalek fired its energy weapon and the Doctor dived to the floor, cracking his shoulder off the wall and rebounding, landing on his knees. The energy beam missed him by a whisper, scorching a long, black line into the wall.

'They're not immune to this,' Cinder said, raising her gun and squeezing the trigger. A bolt of white energy lanced through the Dalek's sensor mesh, cracking its armour plating and bursting out through the back of its head, showering the corridor in fragments of Dalekanium and biological matter. Its eyestalk dimmed and stilled.

'Now we've done it,' said the Doctor. 'Now we've really got their attention.' Cinder could hear the chant of Dalek voices coming from deep within the ship. They were stirring, summoned by the alarm and the blast of the energy weapons.

'A simple "thank you" would have sufficed,' she said, helping him up. 'But let's just say I was returning the favour.'

The Doctor grinned. The sound of the Dalek voices was growing closer. 'Let's go,' he said. 'Now!'

They charged out of the ship onto the gantry by which they'd boarded. They were ten metres up, at least, and below them Daleks were swarming out of the other saucers. There was no way they could jump without doing themselves an injury, and if they did, they'd never be able to get away in time.

'Back to the other ship,' cried the Doctor, grabbing her by the upper arm and charging up the slope.

'Exterminate!' An energy bolt zipped past them, close enough to scorch the back of the Doctor's jacket. They charged across the walkway towards the other ship.

Ahead of them a Dalek emerged from the open hatchway, but Cinder didn't hesitate. She squeezed off another shot and watched the Dalek explode, the momentum carrying its casing back into the mouth of the ship.

Daleks were taking to the air now, screeching a chorus of threats as they unleashed shot after shot, but the Doctor and Cinder ran on regardless, sliding haphazardly into the other saucer. Somehow, they'd managed to make it across the bridge without getting shot. It didn't seem like much of a consolation.

With a shove, the Doctor sent the remains of the dead Dalek trundling into the path of another two that were coming down the corridor toward them, and led the charge in the opposite direction, circling around the ship to head back the way they had come, down to the lower level and past the human hatchery.

They burst out into the courtyard to see a least ten Daleks heading straight for them. Cinder knew she couldn't take them all before they brought her down, and the cannon still being clutched by the Doctor would prove utterly ineffective.

They were all here, all the various types of Dalek and Degradation she had seen before: standard ones in bronze and gold, Gliders, Spiders, Temporal Weapons. There were new ones, too, versions she'd never encountered on patrol: black ones; silver ones with blue domes; another of the purest white, like a pale ghost – each of them as deadly as the others.

She levelled her gun at the oncoming tide, resolved that she would take at least half of them down with her.

'The walkway!' bellowed the Doctor. Cinder glanced up. There were three Daleks coming over the gantry above.

She swung the barrel of her gun round and fired three consecutive shots – not at the Daleks themselves, but at the metal gantry on which they stood. The metal twisted and buckled, causing the Daleks to wobble uncontrollably, and a fourth shot split the walkway in two, sending them crashing down on top of the Daleks beneath. At least five of them were sent spinning off across the courtyard, their weapons blasting indiscriminately, whilst two more were incapacitated, sent sprawling, their domed heads caved in by the impact from above.

It wouldn't stop them for long, but it was enough of a distraction for the Doctor and Cinder to get out of the line of fire.

'Head for the city wall,' said the Doctor. 'I'll lead them off.' He started off in the opposite direction.

'What about the prisoners?' called Cinder. Surely they couldn't abandon them now?

The Doctor hesitated, stopping in his tracks. He looked pained, as if trying to decide whether to risk it. 'Damn it!' he barked. 'Hold them off.'

He turned around, charging diagonally across the courtyard towards the ship, where earlier they'd seen the Daleks shepherding the human prisoners.

Cinder ran after him, as he charged up the ramp, but stopped short, turning to face the three remaining Daleks who were rounding on her. 'Come on, then!' she screamed. 'Come and get me, you stupid metal cans!'

Just as she was about to empty the remains of energy pack into the Daleks, there was a terrific explosion from inside one of the saucers. She felt the vibration of it as a rumble beneath her feet, rattling her bones.

A plume of flame and dark, oily smoke erupted from the top of its dome, and the Daleks swivelled in the opposite direction, barking commands. She realised it must have been the hatchery which the Doctor had rigged to overload, finally reaching critical mass.

She took her chance and brought her weapon up, loosing off three shots, blowing the domes off the remaining Daleks while they tried to decide what to do.

Yet more Daleks were arriving on the scene, however, and she knew she only had seconds before she'd be overwhelmed.

'Doctor!' she bellowed, just as a swarm of people came hurtling down the ramp behind her, spilling out into the old playground. There were scores of them, and she realised they must have been crammed into cells on board the ship.

She heard the Doctor calling to them from the top of the ramp. 'Go on! Run for your lives! Fight back! Now's your chance.' The freed prisoners responded with gusto, rounding on the Daleks. Even with no weapons they were finding ways to disable them, tipping them over by sheer weight of numbers.

Daleks swarmed in from above, firing indiscriminately into the crowd, but the prisoners were now in full rebellion and not about to be dissuaded.

'It's really quite impressive, what a handful of humans can achieve when they put their minds to it.'

Cinder turned to find the Doctor was at her side. In one hand he still held the cannon, while in the other he clutched his sonic screwdriver, which he'd clearly used to open the locks on the cells.

'Now, Cinder. It's time to run,' he said. 'Make for the main gates. We'll find a way through.'

Exhilarated to see her people overwhelming the Daleks, Cinder did as the Doctor said and fell back. They ran, side by side, ducking into one of the side streets and braving a dash for the main gates.

With the insurgency raging at the main base, the gates themselves – as clearly the Doctor had anticipated – were unattended. Cinder didn't bother to find a way to unlock them, however, and blasted at the old wooden doors with the Dalek gun, punching a hole big enough for them to scramble through.

Within moments, the Doctor and Cinder had disappeared once more into the ruins. Behind them, the orange glow of the burning Dalek base lit up the sky above Andor.

They didn't stop until they reached the TARDIS. Exhausted, out of breath, they stumbled to the lip of the crater caused by the Doctor's earlier unorthodox landing. The remains of the dead Daleks still lay in the road, cold and unmoving.

The TARDIS was perhaps the most welcome sight Cinder could have imagined, this funny blue box, lying on its side in the mud. To her, it represented safety, a chance to get away, to leave the War behind. But now it also represented something else – liberation. The day the Doctor fell out of the sky and made her look differently at the world, at what was possible. And now, although she knew it was only a mote in the eye of the War, the tiniest of victories, she'd helped to liberate some of her people.

Gratefully, Cinder hopped inside of the TARDIS, this time preparing herself for the odd shift in alignment between the outer and inner dimensions. Nevertheless, disorientated, she still staggered to one side like a drunk, forced to catch hold of the metal rail to steady herself.

The Doctor closed the door behind them, and she sank to her knees, flinging her gun on the floor and wrapping her arms around herself. She felt tears welling up, tears of relief, but she fought them down, sniffing and wiping her eyes.

She noticed the Doctor still had the Dalek cannon in his hands. 'Why did you bring that?' she said. 'You know it won't work against the Daleks.'

The Doctor glanced down at the gun, and then tossed it on the floor, where it clattered loudly before coming to rest. 'I need to take it to Gallifrey,' he said. 'I need to show the Time Lords what we're up against.'

Cinder gaped at him. 'But we had a deal,' she said. 'I thought you were going to take me away from all this, from the War?'

The Doctor nodded. 'I will. I promise. I'll take you somewhere safe. But first I have to visit Gallifrey. What the Daleks are doing here – it could mean the end of the War. Worse, the end of the universe. If they're able to deploy that weapon there won't *be* anywhere safe, in any corner of reality.'

'Then I'm coming with you,' said Cinder defiantly.

'You're not leaving me here.'

The Doctor shook his head. 'I travel alone. I haven't got time for waifs and strays. You'll only get in the way.' He started to turn away, but Cinder got to her feet, catching him by the arm. There was more to it than that. She could see it in his eyes. He was afraid of her in a way he hadn't been afraid of even the Daleks.

'Oh no,' she said. 'You don't get off the hook that easily. I said I was in, and that means you don't get to leave me behind.'

Their eyes met. They stared at each other in silence for a moment, neither of them willing to give ground.

Finally, the Doctor relented. 'All right,' he said, throwing his hands up in a gesture of resignation. 'All right. You can come. But this is a temporary arrangement. I haven't got time to be worrying about anyone else.'

Cinder grinned. 'I think more to the point, Doctor, is whether I've got any time to worry about you.'

'I've told you – I don't go by that name any more,' he said, with a frown.

'Oh, I think you've earned it today,' said Cinder. She ambled over to stand beside him at the console, examining the odd assortment of levers, dials and flashing buttons. 'Right then,' she said. 'Are you going to show me how this thing works?'

'Don't push your luck,' said the Doctor, as he hit the dematerialisation switch.

Chapter Eight

'Report!'

The Dalek slid effortlessly into the hexagonal chamber of the Eternity Circle, its head rotating as its eyestalk peered at each of its five masters in turn. 'Dalek operations on Moldox have been compromised,' it said. 'The temporary base in the city of Andor has been destroyed.'

'Explain,' barked the blue and silver Dalek on the central plinth.

'A human rebellion,' said the Dalek. 'The prisoners escaped and destroyed the hatcheries.'

'What of the progenitor?'

'Rendered inoperable. The clones are unviable,' said the Dalek.

'Unimportant,' purred another of the blue and gold Daleks on the plinths. 'Testing is complete. The template for the new paradigm can be disseminated. Transmit instructions to the other progenitors in the Tantalus Spiral. Order them to begin production immediately.'

'I obey.'

'Did the humans have Time Lord assistance?' asked the Dalek on the central plinth.

'Yes,' replied the bronze and gold Dalek. 'Transmissions from the base indicate the presence of the Predator on Moldox. We have confirmed the energy signature of his TARDIS.'

'Excellent. The plan nears completion.' The blue and silver Dalek made a sound that might almost have been a chuckle. 'Soon, the Predator will lead the Daleks to their ultimate victory. Soon, he will be ours.'

Part Two

Gallifrey

Chapter Nine

Karlax hunched over his desk, wearily stabbing at a data screen with his index finger. Scrolling glyphs indicated countless reports coming in from the front – or rather, from the numerous fronts on which the Time Lords were currently engaged against the Daleks.

He selected one at random and pulled it up on the screen, then scanned the opening lines, not even bothering to check which epoch it referred to. They were all blurring into one, anyway – every period of Gallifrey's history was now under assault from the vile Kaled mutants.

The story was the same. In each and every report, it was always the same. No matter how well they fought, how many Dalek saucers or stealth ships the Time Lords managed to destroy, more took their place. The things were relentless, and worse, somehow capable of replicating themselves at a rate of knots. They were wily, too – they'd taken to seeding their progenitors into uncontested eras, cloning themselves and manufacturing entire legions, which would then lay dormant, sometimes waiting for years for the right moment to strike. Inevitably, they would deploy to strengthen an existing Dalek attack force or else lay siege to an unsuspecting Time Lord stronghold during some chaotic period in Gallifrey's history. They'd even attempted to purge prehistoric Gallifrey of its primitive life forms in an effort to stop the Time Lords from evolving.

To the Daleks, life was cheap and easily replaced. That gave them an edge. A Time Lord might have thirteen lives, but, reflected Karlax, regeneration was no good whatsoever if you'd been atomised in a detonating Battle TARDIS or eradicated before you'd ever been conceived.

Karlax sighed. His collar and robe felt heavy, today. He had the foreboding sense that they were only moments away from the apocalypse, that all of their efforts, all of their so-called victories against the Daleks would, ultimately, be for nothing. They were locked in a stalemate, and it would only be a matter of time before the Daleks found a way to break it and the countdown continued. They were trying to hold the inevitable at bay.

His data screen bleeped. More reports were coming in by the second, and they all needed to be read and summarised for the Lord President. The trouble was, Karlax simply couldn't keep up, not whilst he had other duties to consider. Still, he supposed, they weren't going to read themselves. He pressed the icon for another report, but as he leaned back in his chair the shrill cry of an alarm sounded overhead. His shoulders sagged. What was it now?

Karlax looked up at the sound of the door sliding open, only just audible over the din of the alarm. A soldier of the Chancellery Guard came running into his chambers. He stopped before Karlax's desk, catching his breath.

'Well? What is it?' Karlax snapped at the guard. 'What's this infernal racket about?'

'It's a level nine emergency, sir,' said the guard, still a little breathless. He sounded worried.

'Level nine?' queried Karlax. He could never quite remember what they all meant.

'An unauthorised time capsule is attempting to materialise in the Panopticon,' said the guard.

'What?' said Karlax. The timbre of his voice altered dramatically as the man's words registered. The Panopticon. 'How have they managed to bypass the sky trenches and the transduction barriers?'

The guard looked at him, blank faced. 'I've no idea, sir. It's… it should be… well, it's impossible.'

'Clearly not,' said Karlax, sarcastically. He stood, tossing aside his data screen. 'Send for the Castellan. Tell him to gather his troops immediately. If this intruder manages to gain entry, only Omega himself knows what might happen.'

'He's already attending to it, sir,' said the guard. 'It was the Castellan who sent me to inform you.'

'Good,' muttered Karlax.

The guard looked at him expectantly.

'Yes?' said Karlax, 'is there more?'

'The Castellan requested your presence, sir,' said the guard, clearly uncomfortable to be the one delivering the message.

Karlax sighed. 'Very well.'

He followed the guard from the room and along the passageway. The man seemed to want to walk at a hurried pace, even a jog, but Karlax was having none of that. He wasn't very much interested in being summoned by the Castellan.

They passed along a wide corridor, which terminated in a massive door. It opened automatically as they approached, sliding up into the roof. The view beyond was immense, breathtaking – the eye of the Capitol, the citadel that was the beating heart of Time Lord civilisation. Its flared base rose high above their heads, narrowing as it reached up to scrape the clouds, clustered with the spines of towers and communication arrays. The shimmering energy of the dome was just visible from below, curving across the sky and tinting the light a faint orange.

Karlax and the guard marched across the large, rail-less gantry, which led from the Cardinals' habitation complex, across a moat-like chasm, to the entrance of the citadel. Ahead of them, he could see other uniformed soldiers gathering. It seemed the Castellan was taking no chances.

So, could this be it. Had war finally come to the Capitol? Had the Daleks at last managed to discover a way in, a means of breaching their security? It seemed unlikely, and yet – who else would make such a brazen attempt to barge their way in? Who would be insane enough to even try?

He decided that perhaps the guard was right, after all, and picked up the pace, hurrying past the milling guardsmen while barking at them to get out of his way.

Everyone was converging on the Panopticon – the vast chamber that served as the Time Lords' parliament and seat of State. It was pandemonium.

'Move!' bellowed the guard who'd been escorting him. 'Allow the Cardinal through.' Karlax regarded the man with a little more respect. The crowd of onlookers – some guards, others simple underlings who were eager to discover what was going on – parted to allow him to pass.

Smoothing his robes, he strode on down the central aisle and into the Panopticon proper. The Castellan was in the process of clearing a space in the centre of the room, surrounded by a score of guards all armed with energy weapons. He caught sight of Karlax walking toward him.

'Have you sent word to the Lord President?' he said, by way of greeting.

'And a good morning to you, too,' said Karlax.

'Damn it, Karlax. This is serious. Has the Lord President been informed?' The Castellan's face was reddening.

'Not yet,' said Karlax. 'Not until I actually have something to tell him. What's going on here? The guard said something about a level nine emergency, about an unauthorised time capsule attempting to materialise here, in the Panopticon. I know that can't be right. I know you're too good at your job to allow something like that to happen.'

Karlax smiled inwardly. Good to establish now whose fault it would be if the enemy did manage to breach the Citadel's security. Karlax always found it useful to apportion blame early on in the process, particularly if doing so meant that he could prove that none of it rested upon his own shoulders.

The Castellan looked exasperated. 'We've tried to jam it, but it's passed through all of our defences, one by one. Whoever, or whatever it is seems to know all of our protocols. The Lord President needs to know because he needs to evacuate. He needs to leave the Capitol now in case the enemy are deploying a weapon.'

Karlax regarded the Castellan. This wasn't just hyperbole. The man was seriously worried. 'Very well,' he said. He beckoned to one of the guards. 'You. Do you know where the Lord President's chambers are?'

'Yes, sir,' said the guard, wide-eyed. Evidently the idea of visiting them terrified him more than the possibility of an unknown enemy appearing in the immediate vicinity.

'Good. Then I need you to go th—' Karlax stopped mid-sentence as a deep, grating whine filled the air around them. The hubbub of the chattering crowd immediately died to a whisper.

'Too late,' said the Castellan, redundantly. 'They're here.'

Karlax turned to watch as the outline of the incoming vessel began to solidify in the air just to the left of where he was standing. The guards encircling the space raised their weapons, readying themselves to fire. A dreadful suspicion stirred in the back of Karlax's mind. He recognised that sound…

The noise grew to a bass, elephantine roar, and then, with a final wheeze, the vessel slid into existence, bypassing all the Time Lords' security measures to shift out of the Time Vortex and into the Panopticon.

For a moment, everyone in the room stood in silence, as if scared to so much as exhale. The ship was a tall, battered blue box with the words 'POLICE BOX' written on it in bold white letters.

'Oh,' said Karlax, with a disgusted shake of his head. 'It's him.'

'We're here,' said the Doctor.

'Here being Gallifrey?' asked Cinder.

The idea of visiting the Time Lords' home world filled her with both inquisitive excitement and abject fear. She couldn't imagine they were going to prove particularly welcoming to a human refugee. She wasn't even sure they were going to welcome the Doctor with open arms, judging by the way he talked about them.

Still, at least it wasn't Moldox. In for a penny and all that…

The Doctor grinned. 'Yes, Gallifrey,' he said. 'Although I think I might have given them something of a shock.' He stooped and picked up the Dalek cannon he'd left propped against a chair during their short flight. If, indeed, it could be called a flight. Cinder wasn't entirely sure.

'Come along,' he said. 'You'd better stick with me.' He strode purposefully toward the door.

Cinder glanced at her discarded Dalek weapon, propped against the metal railing, and considered for a moment whether she should take it or not. She decided against it. She didn't know how trigger-happy the Time Lords might be, and she didn't want to give them any opportunity to show her.

With a shrug, she followed the Doctor as he hurried out of the TARDIS.

She stepped out into the light of the Panopticon, and immediately raised her hands. A sea of guards surrounded them, all dressed in matching red and white uniforms and brandishing weapons that didn't look as if they were designed to incapacitate or stun.

'Quite the welcoming committee,' she said, edging closer to the Doctor. 'I can see you're very popular with your friends.'

The Doctor didn't seem to be paying any attention – to her, or to the guards. 'Karlax,' he growled, eyeing one of the crowd, a figure dressed in the flamboyant traditional garb of the Time Lords – a skull cap, robes and exuberant pink-purple collar. He looked utterly outlandish. 'Where's Rassilon?'

'Doctor, you cannot keep on just turning up like this. There are protocols,' replied the man, whom Cinder took to be Karlax.

'Even now you worry about protocols,' said the Doctor, with a dismissive tone. 'No wonder we're losing the damn war.'

Karlax scowled, ignoring the barbed comment. 'You could use the front door like everybody else,' he said.

'I was trying to get your attention,' said the Doctor. 'Even you have to admit, Karlax,' he glanced around at the assembled mass of guards, who were still brandishing their weapons, 'it worked.'

Karlax smiled, a thin, calculating smile. 'I'll give you that, Doctor. You've certainly got our attention.'

The man standing beside Karlax, dressed in similar robes and skull cap, only orange and red and without a collar, gestured to the guards to lower their guns. There was a palpable sense of relief in the room. Cinder dropped her arms, feeling a little ridiculous.

'Now, tell me,' said the Doctor, 'where's Rassilon?'

'The Lord President is currently engaged in important matters of State,' said Karlax, pompously.

'He'll want to hear about this, Karlax,' said the Doctor. He hefted the Dalek cannon and Cinder saw the man beside Karlax lower his hand to his belt, as if preparing to draw a pistol.

'Doctor,' she interrupted, stepping forward and putting her hand on the barrel of the Dalek weapon. 'With so many guns in the room, I think it might be a good idea to keep that one out of the mix.'

Karlax laughed. 'I see you've found yourself a new… companion,' he said. He spoke the word as if it left a particularly bad taste in his mouth. 'Another stray?'

Cinder bristled. This was exactly what she'd imagined the Time Lords to be like – snide, presumptuous and dripping with self-importance.

'You'll have to leave her here,' continued Karlax. 'You can't bring her into the council chamber.'

'I can do what I like,' said the Doctor. 'She's with me. She's under my protection. And she's seen what the Daleks are up to on Moldox. Her perspective will be useful.'

'She's also here, in the room,' said Cinder pointedly. Both of them looked at her for a moment before resuming their argument.

'Lord Rassilon won't like it,' warned Karlax.

'No,' said the Doctor. 'But then I don't much like you, and I have to put up with it,' he added.

Karlax's cheeks flushed scarlet, and Cinder had to stifle a laugh. 'Be it on your own head, then, Doctor,' he said. 'You'd better come with me.'

The Doctor glanced at Cinder, and there was a glimmer of something she hadn't seen there before, a twinkle in his eye. He was having fun. 'Lead on, Macduff,' he said, with a smile.

Chapter Ten

The War Room wasn't at all what Cinder had expected when she'd overhead Karlax telling the Doctor where they were headed. If this was the nerve centre of the Time Lord's entire operation against the Daleks, then perhaps they really were in more trouble than she'd thought. It was rather... well, she supposed the word for it was *understated*.

The room didn't even look that impressive, and nor was it particularly well equipped, at least as far as she could tell – most of the Gallifreyan technology was beyond her understanding, more akin to magic than anything wrought by a person.

Nevertheless, the War Room amounted to little more than a large, oval chamber, flanked by crumbling stone pillars and dominated by an enormous ebony table. The table's surface gleamed with the hazy blue light of holographic pictograms and runes. They seemed to glide just below the lacquer, like fish in a pond, blooming into new, elaborate shapes every time they touched or interacted with one another. It was a strange and hypnotic dance, and she could not decipher any meaning from it.

This, she supposed, was the language of the Time Lords. It certainly looked complex and logical enough to be a language, and precise enough to belong to the only race in the universe who seemed to make pedantry into an art.

There was little else in the room worthy of note, besides a number of screens hung like picture frames upon the walls, streaming relayed footage from what she assumed to be Time Lord warships or TARDISes. The silent images slid by in a confusion of explosions and flashing lights; windows onto the Time Lords' encounters with the Daleks. As she watched, she saw ships on both sides of the engagement blossom into flame and then extinguish almost instantly, their dead hulks left to drift in the cold, airless void.

She couldn't tell whether it was a live feed, or whether the man sitting in the chair was reviewing the footage of battles that had already passed. She supposed in a war of time, the point was probably moot.

The strangest thing about the whole setup, however, was the fact the War Room was hidden in a quiet corner of the citadel, well away from the staterooms and Panopticon. It felt to Cinder as if the Time Lords were attempting to hide it away, to sweep all evidence of the war into a dusty, disused corner of the building so that they might simply ignore it. Did they think that if they chose not to acknowledge it, it somehow wouldn't be real, and life could go on in the Capitol as it always had? She got the distinct impression that for many of the Time Lords the War was someone else's business, a perturbation that would all be resolved in due course. Nothing to get their feathers ruffled about.

She wondered about the other people of Gallifrey, the men drafted in to be soldiers, and whether they felt the same about protecting a way of life that had probably become stale and archaic before the surface of Moldox had even cooled from its fiery creation.

Cinder knew the Doctor felt differently, of course, judging by his reaction to what he'd seen on Moldox. That was the reason for their visit. He'd come to warn them. These were his people, and he planned to protect them.

The man in the chair didn't rise or turn to look at them as they filed into the room. A show of power, perhaps – a reminder of who was in charge.

This, then, was the Lord President of Gallifrey, the man the Doctor had referred to as Rassilon. Despite herself, Cinder felt her stomach knot. Only yesterday she'd been fighting for her life against a Dalek patrol on Moldox. Now she was here, in the presence of one of the most powerful beings in the universe.

She could only see him in profile. He was an older man, lean and rugged. His hair was close cropped and dark, turning to grey. The light from the monitors cast his features in stark relief: the sharp, shallow brow, the aquiline nose, the square, set jaw. Here was a man who didn't see much humour in the universe, who'd been blunted by the burden of duty. The weight of that burden was almost palpable in the room.

'Ah, Doctor,' said Rassilon, still refusing to drag his eyes from the monitor above him. 'I understand your arrival caused quite a stir. You're to be applauded for your inventiveness.' He was well spoken, and his voice was deep and smooth. He laughed. 'I'm only glad you're working for us, rather than against us.' He turned his head and offered the Doctor a crooked smile. His eyes, however, were hard and cold. 'Don't you agree, Karlax?'

'Indeed, sir,' said Karlax, with a sickening obsequiousness.

'News travels fast,' said the Doctor, glancing at Karlax. 'I've only just arrived.'

Rassilon laughed. 'Come, join me,' he said, beckoning the Doctor forward. His fingers gleamed in the reflected light, and Cinder realised he was wearing a metal gauntlet on his left hand.

The Doctor did as he was bid. Cinder remained just inside the doorway, attempting to remain invisible, while Karlax took a seat at the table, from where he could observe proceedings.

'Gallifrey's wayward son. See here,' he indicated the monitors with a sweep of his hand. 'Our bowships burn, our TARDISes bloom, our children die at the hands of the Daleks. We fight for our very existence.' He sighed. 'But you know this, of course. You've been out there, in the thick of it. Tell me, Doctor – what brings you home from the front?'

'I bring a warning,' said the Doctor drily.

'A *warning*,' said Rassilon, evidently amused. 'We are privileged indeed, Doctor.' He laughed. 'First, though, I would hear news of your search. Have you found him yet? Have you located the Master?'

The Doctor shook his head. Cinder had no idea who or what they were talking about. 'He's abandoned you, Rassilon. He's abandoned all of us. He's run for cover, and I doubt we'll see him again. Not until the War is over, at least.'

'He looked into the eye of the storm, and what he saw there was too much for him to bear,' said Rassilon. 'He is weak, and thinks only of his own survival. Still, I cannot blame him. We are all of us standing on a precipice, looking down.' He studied the Doctor for a moment. 'And now you, Doctor, bring news of further unpleasantness.'

'I'm afraid so,' said the Doctor. 'I've come directly from the Tantalus Spiral, where I saw Preda's fleet destroyed by an ambush of Dalek stealth ships.'

Rassilon indicated the screens with an expansive wave. 'I watched the dying moments of her TARDIS with a heavy heart.' Cinder thought that he didn't sound in the least bit bothered.

The Doctor nodded. 'My TARDIS was damaged in the attack. I survived a crash-landing on the planet Moldox, where I discovered a Dalek testing facility. They've developed a new weapon, housed in a new paradigm. It harnesses the temporal radiation leaking from the Tantalus Eye.'

'The anomaly?' said Rassilon.

'Precisely,' replied the Doctor. 'They've created a demat weapon. I saw them testing it on their human prisoners. It's ready to be disseminated to their frontline forces.'

'This is... troubling,' said Rassilon.

'It gets worse,' continued the Doctor. 'I managed to get inside one of their saucers and interrogate their databanks. They're using the technology to build a planet killer. They intend to fire it at Gallifrey.'

'To dematerialise an entire world,' said Rassilon. 'I admit it, Doctor – I'm impressed by their ingenuity.'

'We need to act,' urged the Doctor, 'and soon. That precipice you mentioned – we've just moved uncomfortably close to the edge.'

Rassilon seemed amused. 'Karlax?'

'Yes, my Lord?'

'Arrange for an emergency session of the High Council. We shall meet in one hour. The Doctor and his assistant will present their findings.' Rassilon glanced at the Doctor, and smiled.

'Very good, sir,' replied Karlax.

Cinder couldn't shake the feeling that the Doctor had just made himself the subject of a different sort of ambush.

Karlax ushered them into the council chamber. The Doctor went first, hauling the Dalek cannon he'd retrieved from his TARDIS, and as Cinder followed after him, she stopped at the touch of a hand on her shoulder, pressing just a little too hard to be comfortable. She turned to see Karlax looming over her.

'You wait with me, over here,' he said, as he pushed her forcibly towards the corner of the room, just on the left inside the door. Reluctantly she relented, allowing him to guide her out of the way.

'Oh, I *see*,' she said, smartly, crossing her arms over her chest and putting as much distance between herself and the odious little man as possible. 'Only *important* Time Lords are allowed a seat at the table.'

Karlax scowled at her, but otherwise didn't respond. She watched as proceedings began to unfold, mindful of what Karlax was up to beside her.

Given that this was the meeting hall of the High Council of Gallifrey, it was far less ostentatious than she'd come to expect from her brief time in the Capitol: the walls were plain white, the floor laid in a smooth, cream marble, and the furnishings sparse.

A large oval table filled most of the space. It was similar in size and shape to the one in the War Room, but with a gleaming surface of lacquered wood, inlaid with fine traceries of gold. It didn't appear to have any embedded technology, but it was difficult to tell.

Aside from this, the only other objects in the room were a large golden harp, a painting of a decrepit-looking Time Lord playing the harp, and a platform containing two spurs and a computer interface.

Around the table, a number of Time Lords had already taken to their seats. Rassilon sat at the head, dressed in the full regalia of his office, and clutching a golden staff in his left hand. It was a thin metal pole, crested with an elaborately wrought finial. Cinder had no idea of its purpose, but she assumed it was ceremonial in origin.

One of the chairs was empty, and Cinder noted the Time Lord sigil that had been carved into its high back in exceptional detail. She wondered if this denoted the rank of the person who should have been seated there.

To Rassilon's left sat a female Time Lord. She looked young, with a bob of dark hair framing a pretty, delicate face. She too was dressed in elaborate robes, this time in deep purple with platinum trim, with a wide, golden collar resting upon her shoulders.

Opposite the woman was the Castellan – the head of the security service, whom Cinder had encountered briefly upon arrival in the Panopticon – and two other men, one of them older, with dark, puckered skin and close-cropped hair, the other younger but still turning to grey, with a neatly trimmed beard and darting blue-eyes. Both were wearing elbow-length gloves, their knuckles dusted with rings.

It was all pomp and ceremony, Cinder realised. They seemed more concerned with their rituals than with hearing what the Doctor had to say. If the fate of the universe truly rested in the hands of these people, then she had grave doubts over whether there'd be anything left worth fighting over once the Daleks had made their move.

It seemed that everyone who was supposed to be in attendance was there. Karlax pulled the door to and then returned to his place in the corner beside her. She watched him for a moment. His eyes were fixed on the President, taking in the man's every move.

Karlax must have sensed her looking, because he turned and offered her a sneer. 'You are privileged,' he whispered. 'I know of no human who has ever been permitted to attend a session of the High Council.'

Cinder shrugged. 'Desperate circumstances call for desperate measures,' she said.

'Quite,' said Karlax bitterly.

Rassilon rose from his seat, striking his staff firmly upon the ground.

Metal rang out against marble, and all eyes turned toward the President. 'This session is hereby convened,' he said. 'The Doctor will address us now.'

The Castellan smiled and leaned back in his chair. He watched the Doctor with an amused look in his eye. 'I understand there's a small matter you wish to bring to our attention, Doctor?' he said. His tone was patronising, and Cinder felt indignant on behalf of the Doctor.

The Doctor, of course, could look after himself. 'Small, you say? *Small?*' He glared at the Castellan. 'The only small thing this room, Castellan, is your mind.'

The Doctor slung the Dalek cannon upon the table, where it clattered loudly, causing the Time Lords to flinch as if it the Doctor had been uncouth enough to toss a dead animal onto the dinner table.

The Doctor began pacing on the spot, his hands folded behind his back. Cinder could see that he was brimming with simmering rage. 'It's time to wake up!' he said. 'We're at war, and by all accounts we're losing on every front. We're outnumbered and outclassed, and we're burying our heads in the sand, refusing to acknowledge what's clearly evident to the rest of the universe. While we're gazing at our navels, the Daleks have established a presence in the Tantalus Spiral and are building their forces there.'

The Cardinal with the beard gave an exasperated

shrug. 'We should send out a flotilla to deal with it, then.'

The Doctor slammed his fists upon the table, leaning forward to tower over the man. He stuck out his chin, pushing his face close to that of the other man. 'We've tried that already, Grayvas,' he said. 'We've left it too late. There are too many of them and we're spread thinly enough as it is. I watched as Preda's entire fleet burned up, the Battle TARDISes blooming under the fire of a hundred or more Dalek stealth ships. And that's just the tip of the iceberg. They've been incumbent on a dozen planets for years now, shaping their plans, building their fleets.'

'We've seen this before,' said the Castellan, his tone dismissive. 'The Daleks are building armies everywhere we look. It's just the same. They seed their infernal progenitors throughout history and harvest biological matter from the local populace to create new mutants. This is nothing new, Doctor. The War grinds on.'

'Oh, but it is, *Castellan*.' The Doctor used the honorific like a curse. 'They are mining the temporal radiation that seeps from the Tantalus Eye, using it to create dematerialisation guns such as this.' He pointed to the weapon on the table. 'This is taken from one of their new paradigms. I've seen what it does, watched as it rewrote time and totally eradicated four human beings from history.'

Rassilon leaned forward, peering at the weapon. The Castellan reached out his gloved hand as if to touch it, and then withdrew, changing his mind. His expression was gaunt.

'That's right,' said the Doctor. 'You remember what a demat gun can do to a Time Lord. No chance of regeneration – just simple oblivion. We locked ours away, burying them in a vault because of the horrors they were capable of inflicting upon others.' He ran a hand through his hair. 'Now the Daleks have them, and they're putting their new paradigms into production as we speak.'

Grayvas cleared his throat. 'This Temporal Weapon Dalek, Doctor – you've seen it more than once?' he said.

The Doctor nodded. 'It's viable. I destroyed one of their hatcheries on Moldox, but there'll be hundreds more, thousands even. The Tantalus Spiral has become a breeding ground. If we don't stop them soon they'll begin seeding them through time, to all of the different epochs in which we're fighting, and others in which we are not. The genie will be out of the bottle, and we'll never be able to put it back in.'

Rassilon sat back, looking thoughtful. He rapped his gauntleted fingers upon the table, *rat-ta-tat-tat*, *rat-ta-tat-tat*. 'Tell them the rest of it, Doctor. Tell them of the real threat.'

'This is only the beginning,' said the Doctor. 'I gained access to their computer systems while I was onboard one of their saucers. They're building a planet killer. They're using the same technology to turn the Tantalus Eye into a massive energy weapon. A temporal weapon.' He paused for breath. 'They're planning to erase Gallifrey from history, from every single permutation of reality. The Time Lords will cease to exist, history will be rewritten as if they *never* existed, and the universe will fall to the Daleks.' The Doctor stood back from the table, glowering at Rassilon. 'We have to act *now*.'

Rassilon frowned. 'If you're wrong, Doctor, and we show our hand, we might leave ourselves utterly exposed to the Daleks. As you so ably put it, our forces are already spread too thin. If we commit to an offensive in the Tantalus Spiral we risk allowing the Daleks an opportunity to establish a beachhead elsewhere.'

'I'm not wrong,' said the Doctor. His tone was forceful. 'Here's the evidence, right before your eyes.' He gave the Dalek cannon a shove, so that it slid across the table toward Rassilon. 'Have the technicians examine it if you doubt me.'

Rassilon smirked. 'Then what is to be done? Tell us, Doctor. What do you suggest?'

The Doctor sighed, his shoulders slumping. 'I don't know,' he said. 'They appear to have a command station at the heart of the Spiral, just above the Eye. I'd guess that would also be the location of the weapon. The problem is getting to it. There's an armada of saucers stationed there, let alone countless stealth ships, hiding in the void. It would take everything we've got.'

'Impossible,' said the female Time Lord. 'We simply don't have the resources.'

'There is a way,' said the Castellan, his tone grave. 'There's a weapon in the Omega Arsenal.'

The other cardinal, who until this point had remained silent, turned to the Castellan. 'You can't seriously be referring to the Moment? Surely it's not yet come to that?'

'No,' said the Castellan, firmly. 'Not that. The Tear of Isha.'

The Doctor frowned. 'But the Tear's designed to collapse black holes,' he said. 'It's a tool for stellar engineering. How would you… Oh.' He stopped, his mind catching up with his mouth. 'Yes, I see…'

'I see you understand, Doctor,' said the Castellan. 'If we were to deploy the Tear into the heart of the anomaly, we could close the Eye. It would allow us to re-engineer the fold in space-time and neutralise the source of the Daleks' temporal power for ever.'

'You can't do it,' said the Doctor. 'Billions of lives would be forfeit. There're a dozen inhabited worlds in the Spiral, colonies that have been established there for centuries. The Tear would cause the Eye to implode, and the ensuing storm would ravage the planets, ageing them to dust. I can't allow it.'

'*You* can't *allow* it?' said Rassilon. 'Really, Doctor, I think you have an inflated sense of your importance. Who are you to say what we can and cannot do?'

'Rassilon, you'd be condoning genocide on a massive scale,' countered the Doctor. 'The stakes are far too high. There must be another way.'

'Then tell us, Doctor. Enlighten us. What other way do you see?' Rassilon rose to his feet, closing his gauntleted fist. 'You come to us with word of impending doom, and yet you expect us to sit back and refuse to act because of your petty fondness for a handful of human beings?'

Cinder couldn't stand it any longer. 'A handful?' she said, strutting forward. She'd had enough of listening to all this casual talk of genocide. 'That's my home you're talking about. *Billions* of lives. There are more people on those worlds than the sum total on Gallifrey. They are not pawns in your game, to be sacrificed at will.'

Rassilon glared at the Doctor. 'Kindly silence your assistant, Doctor. She has no voice in this room.'

Cinder felt Karlax's grip on her shoulder once again, and this time he squeezed until it was painful.

The Doctor glanced at her, and she could see the frustration in the set of his jaw. Clearly he wanted to grab Rassilon by the shoulders and shake him until he listened.

'Please, Lord President,' he said, with an effort that must have been clear to everyone in the room. He was holding back a tirade. 'If you give it time, give it proper consideration, there will be other ways. We just cannot see them yet.'

Rassilon waved his arm at the assembled Time Lords. 'Go,' he said. 'All of you. This session is at an end. I will make my decision and you shall be informed.' He looked up, fixing the Doctor with a menacing stare. 'Doctor, you may wait in the observation lounge. I will speak with you shortly.'

'Very well,' said the Doctor. The other councillors stood and filed out of the room, each of them refusing to meet Cinder's gaze. Whether this was down to their sheer arrogance, or their inability to face a human being after their complicity in what would amount to the genocide of her people, she did not know. Neither did she particularly care. She wanted them to squirm.

Karlax left her side to go and speak with the

President, and she rushed over to the Doctor, who was leaning heavily on the table, his brow creased. 'Come on,' she said. 'Come and show me this observation lounge.'

The Doctor looked round and she smiled at him hopefully. She knew she needed to get him out of the room. There was still time. He would find a way. The look on his face now, however, suggested that if she left him here with Rassilon and Karlax, things were not going to end well. Besides, she didn't think she could bear to look at them any longer, either.

The Doctor straightened up, collecting the Dalek cannon from the table. 'This way,' he said, storming abruptly from the room.

Chapter Eleven

From the observation panel in the antechamber they had a view right across the Capitol. Cinder stood before it, shoulder-to-shoulder with the Doctor, both of them lapsing into awed silence. She couldn't help but marvel at the sea of bristling spires, the orb-like crystal domes, the oddly angular complexes of buildings and transport platforms. This was the urban sprawl of an ancient, god-like race; this was the pinnacle of Time Lord civilisation. It was beautiful and terrifying in equal measure, a far cry from the blighted wilderness of Moldox.

'I haven't looked out upon Gallifrey like this for too long,' said the Doctor, after a while. 'It reminds me what I love about the place, and what I hate about it, too.'

'It reminds you what you're fighting for?' said

Cinder.

The Doctor laughed. 'Yes, I rather suppose it does.'

With the Time Lords, Cinder shared a common enemy in the Daleks, and peering out across the expanse of this, their premier city, she felt a sort of bitter empathy with them. This was what they were trying to protect: their home. It was only natural that, backed into a corner, they would lash out and do anything in their power to defend it.

Many of her people claimed the Time Lords were nothing but self-deluding fools, an ancient people who had taken it upon themselves to attempt to police the universe, to meddle in the evolution and development of other races. They argued that the Time Lords' power had gone to their heads and corrupted them, and that they had started the war with the Daleks in the first instance, all those many centuries ago. Perhaps worse was the thought that it was their interference, or even the sheer fact of their very *existence*, that had driven the Daleks to evolve into the heartless killing machines they were today.

Cinder didn't know if any of this was true. It didn't alter the fact, however, that when faced with the same problem as the Time Lords – a marauding army of Daleks threatening to obliterate her people from history – she had behaved in exactly the same way. She had fought with every ounce of her being, deploying every available weapon in her arsenal. That, she could understand.

Nevertheless, she couldn't forget the things she had seen during this long and dreadful conflict: the sheer arrogance of the Time Lords, their disregard for human life, and the horrifying inventiveness of their weapons. Empathy was one thing; trust was quite another.

Nor could she simply ignore the fact that, if the Time Lords had their way, her people might still face extinction, only this time at the hands on an entirely different enemy.

It was approaching dusk and, as Cinder watched, tiny lights began to wink in the sky around the habitation domes. At first there were only a handful, but as she watched they seemed to multiply, until there were scores of them, hundreds even, drifting slowly into the sky from the city below. They looked like fireflies, buzzing about chaotically on the breeze.

'What are they?' said Cinder. 'Paper lanterns?'

The Doctor shook his head. 'No, although the principle is the same. Those are memory lanterns.'

'Memory lanterns?' echoed Cinder.

The Doctor glanced at her. 'They all think they're going to die,' he said. 'All of those people down there think the Daleks are coming for them, and that they're going to be exterminated.' He sighed, and the weariness in his expression spoke volumes. Perhaps he thought they were right. 'So they're recording all of their thoughts and memories into those lanterns, and scattering them through time and space. It's the last act of a desperate people. They're terrified that they're going to be forgotten, so they're seeding themselves into all the distant corners of the universe to be remembered.'

'It's beautiful,' said Cinder, softly. She stepped closer to the observation screen, watching as more of the tiny pinpricks of light drifted up into the sky, before winking out of existence, transmitted somewhere deep into the Vortex. She wondered where they'd all emerge, into the distant, long-forgotten past, or perhaps the battle-scarred future, long after the end of the War.

'It's vain,' replied the Doctor, 'and unseemly. A waste of time. Most of those lanterns won't survive the journey through the Vortex. They'll break up on the time winds, and all of those cherished memories will be dashed to the breeze.'

'That's not the point,' said Cinder. 'To those people, the lanterns represent *hope*. Hope that some small part of who they are might survive all of this. Don't take that from them.' She suddenly felt cold, and folded her arms across her chest, hugging herself.

The Doctor smiled, for the most fleeting of moments. 'You're marvellously human, Cinder,' he said, quietly. Their eyes met for the briefest of moments, before he looked away and the tired, haggard expression returned.

'What do we do now?' said Cinder.

The Doctor shrugged. 'We await their answer,' he said.

Half an hour passed, maybe more. Cinder paced the room impatiently, while the Doctor remained standing at the window, looking out upon the city that had once been his home.

She wondered how long he had been running. Rassilon had called him 'Gallifrey's wayward son'. That suggested a deeper, more interesting history than she had so far managed to glean. What had he done to earn a reputation such as that? It was clear he was non-conformist, of course – the simple matter of his appearance, the tarnished leather jacket, the red and white scarf, not to mention the strange external aspect of his TARDIS – all of these marked him out as different from the other Time Lords. Yet Cinder got the sense there was more to it than that.

She supposed it might simply be down to his antagonistic approach to authority and his blatant disregard for the Time Lords' obsession with ceremony and ritual. He certainly hadn't done himself any favours in the way he'd spoken to Rassilon. Although, seeing how Karlax fawned over the Lord President, it was probably a healthy attitude to adopt. Someone had to speak up. Cinder herself, of course, probably hadn't helped matters with her outburst. Still, at least she'd been able to make her point.

She turned at the sound of the door sliding open. A guard stepped into the room. His eyes seemed to pass over her, despite the fact she was looking right at him. He waited for the Doctor to turn and acknowledge him before speaking. 'Lord Rassilon will speak with you now, Doctor,' he said. 'You may bring your... *companion*.'

Cinder stiffened. The man had delivered the word in such a way that the implication was clear: he did not consider her in any way to be the Doctor's 'companion', but rather his 'pet'. The Doctor knew it too, as he crossed the room and pointedly put a hand on her arm to reassure her. 'Come on,' he said, beneath his breath. 'Let's go and see what the musty old fools have come up with.'

They followed the guard along the passageway to the council chamber. He ushered them in, but did not enter.

Rassilon sat alone at the head of the table, still clutching his staff. He looked up as they entered the room. Cinder noted that, thankfully, Karlax was nowhere to be seen.

'Have you reached your decision?' said the Doctor.

Rassilon narrowed his eyes. 'You forget your place, Doctor. You assume a standing here, in the chamber of the High Council, where you have none. You are a renegade, a runaway. A deserter.'

'I am a former President of Gallifrey,' said the Doctor angrily.

Rassilon scoffed. 'In name, perhaps, but never more. You could never appreciate the importance of such an office.'

'On the contrary, Rassilon. I was the only one who did.' The Doctor pulled out a chair, scraping it across the floor, and dropped into it heavily, facing Rassilon. 'The Tear of Isha. What is your decision?'

'That it will be deployed into the Eye,' replied Rassilon.

Cinder felt her heart lurch in her chest. She felt suddenly nauseous. They were going to do it. They were really going to murder every single living thing on a dozen worlds.

'Rassilon,' said the Doctor, clearly exasperated. 'You're condemning a billion souls to a terrible death. More. How can you even consider it?'

'What are a billion human lives to us, Doctor?' said

Rassilon. 'They are but motes of sand on the breeze. They breed like a virus, infesting every corner of the universe. Where some die, others will take their place.'

He paused, his sharp, green eyes fixed on the Doctor, as if boring into him. 'We're talking about Time Lord lives, now, Doctor. What you've described to us is a doomsday device, a weapon with the power to annihilate us, to bring an end to the War in the Daleks' favour. Worse, if you're right, if the Daleks manage to deploy this weapon, then Gallifrey and all her many children will be utterly eradicated from history. It shall be as if we never even existed. And where will your precious humans be then? At the mercy of the Daleks, with no one to watch over them, to keep the monsters at bay. The fate of time itself is in the balance. The death of billions is as nothing to us, Doctor, if it helps defeat the Daleks.'

'Rassilon, you can't honestly believe that. We're talking about a dozen inhabited worlds,' said the Doctor, getting to his feet. The exasperation – and disbelief – was evident in his voice. 'You're talking about genocide.'

'Worlds now inhabited by Daleks, Doctor, lest you forget,' said Rassilon.

'Nevertheless, we don't have the right to decide who lives and dies. Not on that sort of scale. We're not gods, no matter how much posturing you like to do in your fancy capes and funny hats.' The Doctor allowed his words to hang for a moment. 'You don't get to decide this,' he continued, quietly, reasonably. 'If you deploy that weapon, we're as bad as the Daleks, the very thing we're fighting against. Don't you remember why we're even at war in the first place?'

'Enough!' bellowed Rassilon, striking his gauntleted fist upon the table. Spittle flecked the table surface before him. He stood, glowering at the Doctor. 'We're fighting, Doctor, because we must. Because we're under attack, and we have no other option. We're fighting to save ourselves from extinction.'

'That's not good enough,' said the Doctor. 'That's not a good enough justification for what you're suggesting. Sealing the fate of twelve planets to save one. That's the choice you're making. You're putting your own lives above those of everyone else.'

'What if I am, Doctor? Is that not the burden of the Time Lords? If we survive this war, as well we must, we shall go on to ensure the sanctity of the timelines. We will restore history; unwind the damage wrought by the Daleks. Only the Time Lords have the capability, the ingenuity, to achieve this. It is our *duty* to survive.'

The Doctor laughed. 'Oh, how grand the view must be from up there on your pedestal, Rassilon. Your *duty*. You're starting to sound more like a Dalek every day.'

Cinder could see that Rassilon was grinding his teeth, flexing his fingers inside his gauntlet. 'This conversation is at an end,' he said, getting to his feet. 'Once again, Doctor, you have outstayed your welcome. I have made my decision. The Tear shall be deployed. But rest assured – despite your allegations to the contrary, we are not monsters. If there is a way to neutralise the Eye and deploy the Tear of Isha without any... collateral damage, then I shall find it. I shall consult the possibility engine.'

'The what?' said the Doctor.

'The means of our salvation,' said Rassilon cryptically, 'and none of your concern. The time has come for you to leave. Go, and return to flitting about the universe, meddling in the affairs of the lower species.'

'I have seen some "low species" in my time, Rassilon, but none so low as the Time Lords have sunk.'

Rassilon raised his gauntleted hand, poking the Doctor hard in the chest with an extended index finger. The Doctor's shoulder rocked back, but he retained his footing. 'Get out. Now!'

'Come on, Cinder,' said the Doctor, not taking his eyes off Rassilon. 'It's clear there's nothing more to be done here.' He took a step back, and then turned and grabbed her by the arm, leading her hastily toward the exit.

She glanced back over her shoulder to see Rassilon still standing, his arm raised, his finger pointing to the door.

Once in the corridor outside, the Doctor pulled Cinder to one side, stopping her in her tracks. He glanced down the passageway, checking for guards. There was no one there.

'Wha—' she began.

He put his finger to her lips to silence her. She furrowed her brow, giving him a quizzical look.

'I want to see what he does next,' he whispered. 'I've got a feeling that I should know what this "possibility engine" is all about.'

Cinder nodded. She watched as the Doctor crept back toward the open doorway that led to the council chamber. He stopped just short, peering in around the frame.

With a shrug, Cinder decided to join him. She sneaked up behind him and, placing a hand on his back for leverage, peeked over his shoulder.

Rassilon was still inside the room, standing with his back to them. As she watched, he turned and mounted the small platform she had noted earlier, standing between the two black spurs. He made an adjustment to something on the control panel, pressed a button, and then, in a glimmer of coruscating light, he winked out of existence.

She felt the Doctor heave a sigh of relief. He stepped out into the doorway.

'What happened to him?' she whispered, confused. 'Where did he go?'

'Two very different questions, with two very different answers,' said the Doctor. 'That device is a transmat, designed for matter transference.'

'Teleportation?' asked Cinder.

'In a sense,' said the Doctor. 'That's what happened to him. As for where he went…' He glanced over his shoulder, and then strode into the room, crossing to the transmat device. He hopped up onto the platform and punched at the controls, frowning at the display. 'Ah, yes. Just as I thought.'

'Well?' said Cinder, 'don't leave me in the dark.'

'He's gone to the Tower,' said the Doctor. He was clearly distracted, trying to fathom his next move.

'Right,' said Cinder. 'Now I'm clear.' She folded her arms across her chest.

The Doctor looked up from the transmat controls. 'Listen, Cinder. Go back to the observation room. Wait for me there. I won't be long. Try to stay out of trouble.'

'Wait! Hold on. Where are *you* going?' she said.

'I'm going after Rassilon,' he replied, before flickering into nothingness.

Cinder was left staring at an empty platform, in an empty room. 'Great,' she said.

Chapter Twelve

The Doctor shimmered into existence in the blustery wasteland that had once been the Death Zone.

It took him a moment to get his bearings. It wasn't often that he travelled by teleport any more, and he felt momentarily disorientated.

The landscape here was wild, overgrown, and dangerous. Rocky outcrops were exposed to the elements, and the woodland had been left to grow unchecked, harbouring all manner of feral beast, left over from the days of the games. Heather had run rampant over the fields, but the Doctor knew that, hidden beneath the long grass, there were deadly bogs and swamps. Worse, there were cave systems that were prone to collapse, some of them the only means of passing from one part of the zone to another.

Here, the Time Lords of old had carried out brutal

games of life and death, during which they would scoop unwitting alien species from their natural habitats and pit them against each other in this untamed corner of Gallifrey. It was a spectator sport, similar to those of the ancient Romans of Earth, a violent, bloodthirsty pastime from a less enlightened era that many Time Lords now wished to forget.

The Doctor had played those games once, a long time ago, when a madman had torn five of the Doctor's incarnations from their own time streams and tried to deposit them here, in the hope that he might lead them to the tomb and the secret of Rassilon's longevity. The man responsible had transpired to be an old friend and mentor, Borusa, who'd become obsessed with his desire to achieve immortality and his need to retain a grip on his waning power.

He'd been granted his wish, too, upon following the Doctor to the tomb, where the ancient Time Lord President had tricked him, entombing his living consciousness in a stone relief for the rest of eternity.

Rassilon himself had been resurrected in the early days of the War, encouraged to take corporeal form once again to lead the Time Lords in their crusade against the Daleks.

The Doctor had once imagined him to be a benign leader, an innovator and a great statesman, just as the ancient legends had claimed, but now he knew that Rassilon was just as flawed as any other Time Lord. Worse, his ideals were outdated, and his bloated sense of his own importance was the driving force behind his policies. In his own mind, Rassilon had become a god, able to do whatever he saw fit.

The Time Lords had always preferred an autocratic society – they were overly fond of being told what to do – but what he had seen during the meeting of the High Council had convinced the Doctor more than ever that things were going badly awry. The only question was how he was going to successfully intercede.

He turned up the collar of his coat and tugged thoughtfully at his beard. He'd emerged from the teleport at the foot of the Tower – a tall, imposing structure that sat at the heart of the Death Zone. It was carved from slabs of dark, imposing granite, and crested with a finial in the form of a golden globe, intersected by a half moon. It had to be one of the most unwelcoming places the Doctor had ever seen, its brutal architecture dating from those primitive days of Gallifrey's first forays into the stellar engineering that had granted them the power to step through time. Inside the Tower was the former tomb of Rassilon.

This had to be where the President had gone. But what was he up to? Why return to this place, where he had slept in peace for so many millennia, but was now, surely, disused? Had Rassilon found another use for the place, something he didn't wish to share with the rest of the High Council?

The Doctor supposed there was only one way to find out. He risked incurring Rassilon's wrath but, he reflected, it was already a little late for that, and he was curious now to discover exactly what this 'possibility engine' was all about.

He strode up to the tower, approaching the main

gates. Here, two immense pillars flanked the entrance, and iron braziers were mounted on ornately wrought spikes, their bowls guttering with bright orange flame.

He hoped that Cinder was staying out of trouble back at the Capitol, although he doubted it. She was probably giving Karlax hell. It was no more than he deserved. It would be good, however, if at least one of them didn't end up in a cell.

With a deep breath, the Doctor crept inside.

The interior of the Tower was cavernous, and lit by further braziers that cast long, flickering shadows, lending the place a sombre tone. Which, the Doctor considered, was only natural for a tomb.

It was dominated by the tomb itself, which sat on a large plinth in the centre of the chamber, with impressive marble pillars at each corner, and a short flight of steps leading up to the raise dais. Tattered banners in greys and blues hung from the ceiling. Once, they might have been splendid, but now they were dusty and rotten, representative, that Doctor decided, of the faded glory of the Time Lords themselves.

The Doctor watched as Rassilon swept into the great hall, his billowing robes trailing across the marble floor and swirling eddies of dust in his wake. His staff *tap-tapped* with every step, echoing out in the desolate, abandoned place.

He crossed to a small hexagonal console and ran his hands over it, waking the system so that a series of runes lit up across its surface. He then turned and approached the empty tomb, upon which his body – or rather, the body of his previous incarnation – had once lain.

'Borusa!' he called, his voice booming, as if trying to wake the dead. 'Borusa! I have need of you.'

Was Borusa still here, his essence trapped inside the carved relief on the side of Rassilon's granite coffin? During that fateful episode when the Doctor had been forced to endure the Death Zone, this was where Rassilon had incarcerated Borusa.

There was a whirring sound from atop the tomb, and as the Doctor watched, a platform began to raise itself up, pivoting so that the figure lying on top of the tomb would be presented upright to anyone standing below.

Rassilon stood at the bottom of the steps, looking up as the machine completed its cycle. The Doctor, still standing in the doorway, crept forward in order to get a better look, edging round to stand in the shadow of a buttress. He cringed as his boots scuffed against the polished marble, but thankfully the grating sound of the mechanism muffled his steps, and Rassilon didn't look behind him.

The sight of the thing on the tomb was something the Doctor would never forget, not in all his lives. It was utterly monstrous. Borusa had been lashed to the steel frame, his wrists and ankles bound with rope, so that his body formed the shape of a cross. He was still wearing his ceremonial robes, but where they fell open over his chest, it was clear they were hiding a multitude of sins.

His body was a mess, resting at the heart of a

nest of wires and cables. His pale flesh was puckered where incisions had been made in his chest and tubes had been inserted, pushed deep into the cavity, presumably to inflate his lungs and keep at least one of his hearts beating.

His head was crowned with a metal skullcap, and a knot of cables erupted from the back of his skull, trailing away to the blinking box of a neural relay.

Most terrifying of all was his face, which appeared to be trapped in a cycle of endless transition, accompanied by the soft glow of regenerative energy. It twisted and reformed as the Doctor watched, passing through the likenesses of all Borusa's previous incarnations – or at least the ones the Doctor recognised – as well as many others he did not. His eyes flickered with bright, electrical energy, as he stared, unseeing, down at Rassilon.

This, then, was Rassilon's 'possibility engine'.

'Tell me, Borusa, what do you see?' said Rassilon, almost reverentially.

'I see Gallifrey burning,' croaked Borusa, his voice barely above a whisper. 'I see the end of all things, the darkness that cleanses. I see the moment, the very moment, when all things shall cease to be.'

Rassilon bunched his gauntleted fist. 'Then that is what we must change,' he said. 'What of the Tantalus Eye? The Doctor brings us news of a Dalek weapon, a doomsday device that could bring about our destruction.'

For a moment, Borusa didn't answer, but turned his head as if looking away, seeking a vision of the future. 'The Doctor speaks the truth,' he said. 'The

Dalek plan draws close to its zenith. If left unchecked, they will eradicate Gallifrey and all of her children from history.'

'Then we must act,' said Rassilon. 'We are left with no choice.'

Borusa's head turned, and his weird, crackling eyes seemed to fix on the Doctor, who was still lurking in the shadows by the door. The Doctor felt a shudder of nervous anticipation. Had Borusa seen he was here? Would he reveal it?

'There is another here,' said Borusa, answering the Doctor's question. 'Come forward, Doctor.'

Well, he supposed it was too late to make a run for it now. He stepped into the light to see Rassilon twist around, raising his gauntleted hand. The metal fist began to glow, taking on a bright, blue sheen, humming with energy. He held it out, spreading his fingers, as if at any moment he might clench them again, crushing the Doctor. Instead, he lowered it to his side, and the blue glow began to recede.

'I might have killed you, Doctor, for your intrusion. You are not welcome here,' he said.

The Doctor ignored him, looking up at Borusa, lashed to the monstrous device. 'Rassilon, what have you done?'

'A thing of majesty, is it not?' crowed Rassilon, unable to resist the temptation to show off. 'This, Doctor, is my possibility engine.'

'It's appalling,' said the Doctor. 'Monstrous.'

'It is a gift. Borusa brings enlightenment. His reward is to see all the wonders of the universe, in all their myriad forms.'

'And all the horrors, too, by the sound of it,' said the Doctor. 'What have you done to him?'

'His timeline has been retro-evolved,' said Rassilon. 'He is trapped in an iterative regenerative cycle, always changing, always becoming more.'

'More?' said the Doctor. 'It sounds terribly like a prison, to me.'

'You lack imagination, Doctor. This machine – it has freed Borusa of the prison of the flesh. It has unlocked his true potential. He is free to wander all of time and space inside his own mind. Every permutation of reality is his to navigate, every single possibility.'

'And Borusa? What of you?' asked the Doctor.

'I see,' answered Borusa, simply. 'I see everything.'

'It's an abomination,' said the Doctor. 'What you've done here – it diminishes us all.'

'You're wrong, Doctor. Borusa has transcended. He represents the future. He is the lucky one, the first of us to be truly free.'

The Doctor shook his head. 'Can't you see it, Rassilon. What this means? By doing this to Borusa, you're reducing us to the same level as the Daleks. You're altering us, making us something less than we are. It's only one step removed from deleting our capacity for empathy, for emotion. Where will it lead? Soldiers without a conscience? Metal travel units?'

'You're being melodramatic, Doctor,' said Rassilon. 'It's one man.'

'It always starts with one man, Rassilon,' replied the Doctor solemnly.

'I have done only what was necessary,' said

Rassilon. 'What no one else was prepared to do. Borusa understood what was required of him. The possibility engine represents our salvation. With it, we might see the weave of all possible futures. We can choose our own destiny, selecting only the most fortuitous paths. We can measure the potential outcomes of all of our offensives against the Daleks, ensuring our victory at every turn. We can bring an end to the War!'

'Go on, then,' said the Doctor. 'Ask it. Ask it whether there's a way to deploy the Tear of Isha without murdering all of those people.'

Rassilon looked defiant. 'Very well,' he said. He turned to Borusa. 'Borusa, the Castellan's plan to deploy the Tear of Isha into the Tantalus Eye – will it work? Will it put an end to the Dalek threat in that sector, and destroy their new temporal weapon? Will it save us?'

Borusa rolled his head from side to side, emitting a low moan. After a moment, he spoke. 'It will work. The Tear will close the Eye, and the Dalek weapon will be neutralised.'

'Excellent,' said Rassilon.

'The reprieve will be only temporary, however,' continued Borusa. 'The darkness still comes. It will smother all things. The age of the Time Lords draws to a close.'

'You see?' said the Doctor. 'Even your own machine warns you that this is not the solution. The Tear isn't the answer. It's not going to stop them.'

'It'll buy us time!' said Rassilon. 'Valuable time to prepare, to strategise, to further consult the possibility engine.'

'And at what cost?' said the Doctor. 'You claim to be better than the Daleks, that it is our *duty* to survive this war, to bring peace and stability to the universe – and yet you are happy to re-engineer the very essence of your own people to turn them into strategic assets, to obliterate entire civilisations to get your own way. How is that any better? How is it different?'

'You sound as if you prefer the Daleks to your own people, Doctor,' said Rassilon. 'Am I to take you for a traitor now?'

'I hate the Daleks for everything they represent,' replied the Doctor, his voice level. He was trying not to lose his cool, despite the fact that every fibre of his being was telling him to wrestle Rassilon to the ground, to try to knock sense into the idiotic man before it was too late. 'I don't wish to end up hating my own people for the very same reasons,' he added.

Rassilon remained silent, as if contemplating the Doctor's words.

The Doctor glanced up, looking into Borusa's disorientating, shifting face. 'Borusa – is there a means by which the Tear can be deployed into the Tantalus Eye without causing the deaths of the people inhabiting the twelve worlds of the Spiral?'

'No,' said Borusa, without hesitation. 'I see no thread of possibility in which the human colonists survive if the Tear is deployed.'

The Doctor turned to Rassilon. 'Then surely you have your answer?'

'I have only an awareness of the consequences of my actions, Doctor. This changes nothing,' said

Rassilon. His tone was firm, final. 'The decision has already been made. The Tear *will* be deployed. I had thought to spare your precious humans, if Borusa could show us a means to do so. Alas, he has not. The time has come to act.' He crossed to the console and initiated the command to lower Borusa's cradle back onto the tomb.

The Doctor trailed after him. 'You cannot do this, Rassilon. It changes everything. I warn you now – you will never come back from this decision.'

'It is already done,' came the response, stern and final. 'Come. I shall speak again to the High Council.' He made for the door.

With sinking hearts, the Doctor followed Rassilon back to the transmat station.

Chapter Thirteen

Cinder had been pacing the observation lounge for at least half an hour, and with every step her frustration was mounting. She wanted to *do* something. The Doctor had told her to remain here and stay out of trouble, but that simply wasn't Cinder's style. She'd never been comfortable staying still for very long, and she doubted she ever would.

With a groan of irritation she went to the window, peering out over the city.

Night had fallen, and with it, the stars.

The stars. She'd read about them, of course, understood exactly what they were – but she'd never seen them for herself. Not until now. All those years, growing up on Moldox, the night sky had always been tainted by the fluctuating auroras that, to her, described colourful dreams, drifting off into the ether as people slept. Of course, she now knew them to be caused by the temporal radiation leaking from the Tantalus Eye – the very same radiation that the Daleks were harnessing to power their weapons.

Somehow, that made it seem less beautiful. This, in itself, wasn't anything new. Everything she'd ever loved, the Daleks had taken from her. Everything beautiful, they had spoiled. That was what the Daleks did. They took. They pillaged. And now they'd even tainted the sky.

Cinder was done with that, though. She'd found a way off Moldox with the Doctor, and she would no longer allow herself to be diminished, by the Daleks, or anyone else.

She stared up at the twinkling constellations. The stars were like pinpricks of light, holes in the fabric of the sky, through which she could observe the glow of distant universes. She'd never imagined there would be so many of them. She understood, intellectually, that the universe was populated with countless billions of stars, but seeing them shining overhead was something else entirely. It was startlingly beautiful.

She wondered how many people were out there, just like her, looking up to the sky and feeling hopeful. Perhaps she'd get to visit some of those places with the Doctor, once the war was over. She'd like that, and she could tell that he needed it too. It would do him good to get away from it all, to remember who he really was. She could tell that the War was eroding him. He'd become calloused, hardened to it, but she was certain there was much more to him than that – another man, buried away somewhere beneath the curmudgeonly exterior.

She sighed, glancing at the door. How long had he said he'd be? Surely it wouldn't hurt to have a little look around? How much trouble could she really be?

Cinder made her mind up. Perhaps she could even discover something useful, something that might help the Doctor to persuade the Time Lords against deploying their doomsday device. She knew he would. She had to have faith in him. The alternative was unthinkable.

She crossed the door, half expecting it to be locked. It wasn't. She opened it just enough to peer out. The passageway beyond was empty. She didn't want to go far. She could probably find her way back to the War Room or the council chamber, but any further afield she risked incurring the wrath of the Castellan and his guards.

She stepped through the door, closing it behind her, then screamed as a hand grabbed her firmly by the shoulder.

Karlax made a *tutting* sound, and she squirmed, trying to break free. He was too strong, and had caught her off guard.

'Thought you'd go for a little wander, did you?' he said. His breath was hot on the back of her neck. 'Well, we can't have that. What would the Castellan say? Hmmm?' He moved around behind her, pinning her arms behind her back. 'In fact,' he continued, 'I think we should go and find out, don't you?'

'Let me go, Karlax,' she said. 'The Doctor will be back any minute.'

Karlax laughed. 'Oh, I'm afraid that doesn't

trouble me in the slightest, young lady. Not one bit. He's not here now, and that's all that matters. I'll have everything I need by the time he finds you.'

'What do you mean?' she said, beginning to feel frightened. What did the odious little man have in mind?

'Oh, it's nothing to worry about,' he cooed, clamping a hand over her mouth to stifle any screams. 'Just a little test I need to run. The Castellan has a machine, you see, known as a mind probe…'

Panicked, Cinder kicked back, jamming her heel into Karlax's shin. He yelped, but didn't relinquish his grip. In retaliation, he pushed her arm further up her back until it threatened to break and the intensity of the pain made her swoon. As she fell limp and delirious into his arms, he dragged her away into a side room, where the Castellan was waiting.

'Are you sure you want to go through with this, Karlax?' said the Castellan. He was stooped over her, strapping her in to a hard, metal chair, and tightening the straps around the helmet they had forced over her head. 'It's just – she's only human. There's a risk it might kill her.'

'Irrelevant,' said Karlax. 'As long as you get me the information I require, I couldn't care less what happens to her. In fact, it might teach the Doctor a valuable lesson if she *does* die.'

At this, Cinder struggled violently against the bonds, bucking in the chair, but the Castellan had done his job well, and there was no chance of her breaking free. She couldn't even call for help, as they'd gagged her as soon as Karlax had bundled her into the room.

She'd managed to scratch Karlax's face with her fingernails during the ensuing struggle, drawing blood, but it had been only a small victory, a fleeting moment of satisfaction, before the horror of her situation had really set in. She was trapped in the room with these two men and their machine, and no one even knew she was here. Whether she liked it or not, they were going to use their mind probe on her.

Cinder found herself wondering how often they had occasion to use it. Judging by the look of anticipation on Karlax's face, it wouldn't surprise her to learn that he used at any opportunity he could. Clearly, amongst his other virtues, he had a well-developed sadistic streak.

She was strapped into the high-backed chair, facing a bank of glass monitor screens. Presently they showed only static snow, white noise, but she assumed this was where any memories they managed to extract from her mind would play out for the others to watch.

She could see her own reflection in the polished glass. She looked dwarfed by the chair, and the cables rising from the helmet to the ceiling might have been long strands of fibrous hair, standing on end as if charged with static electricity.

It reminded her of the glass incubation chambers she had seen on the Dalek ship, and she only wished she had the same opportunity now to sabotage the machine before they had chance to activate it.

'Get on with it,' said Karlax. He was watching the

door, clearly nervous that the Doctor might burst in at any moment to interrupt proceedings.

'I'm working as fast as I can,' replied the Castellan. 'If I don't get the levels right we'll fry her brain before you get anything out of her head.'

Karlax was pacing, his hands behind his back. He looked imperious, full of self-import, and Cinder smiled at the site of the three angry gouges on his left cheek. With any luck, she'd be able to offer him a matching set for the other cheek when this was over with.

The Castellan stepped back. 'I'm ready,' he said.

Karlax ceased his pacing and moved behind the chair, out of sight. For the first time, the Castellan, standing beside the chair, looked down and met her gaze. 'I'm sorry,' he said. 'This is going to hurt.' He flicked the switch.

At first, nothing happened. She heard a gentle buzzing sound coming from behind her left ear, and all she could feel was a warm tickling sensation at the front of her skull. It was uncomfortable, but not painful. She glanced at the monitors, but they continued to display nothing but dancing static.

She concentrated on the buzzing, as it seemed to grow in intensity. With it, the pressure inside her head began to mount. Pain blossomed, and she bit down on the gag. Still, the heat and the pressure continued to increase, until she was sure that at any moment it was going to cause her skull to crack.

She rocked forward in the chair, her vision blurring. The pain was like a white light, searing and bright, and there was no way of shutting it down or escaping it. She tried to scream, but choked back on the rag in her mouth.

The memories came in a sudden flurry, cascading through her mind as a series of stuttering images. Curiously, they were the devoid of colour, like ancient black-and-white photographs being sorted in her mind's eye. They played out of sequence: a snippet here, a snippet there, fragments of her childhood, of her time with the rebels on Moldox, her recent time with the Doctor.

She forced her eyes open to see these scenes unfolding on the monitors, the story of her life being replayed in a bizarre, looping sequence.

She saw faces, people talking to her, and although she could hear nothing, the tastes and smells were fresh, as if she were experiencing them again for the very first time.

She saw her brother, gambolling about like a monkey, pulling silly faces at her. She watched her mother serving dinner in their homestead, her father reading her a bedtime story. And then she watched them die all over again, exterminated by the metal monsters, who seemed to come out of nowhere, tumbling from the sky in a glowing discs, lighting bonfires with their screaming weapons.

They had burst in through the kitchen wall, five of them, rasping in their oily, mechanical voices, all gold and bronze and barking commands. She hadn't understood a word of it, but when they started firing and her father collapsed on the living room floor, steam rising from his lifeless body, she had understood enough to run and hide.

Just moments before the Daleks had arrived, Cinder's mother had been emptying the kitchen bin, and in the chaos, Cinder snuck onto the porch, quickly overturning it and ducking inside. She cowered in there while the Daleks razed her homestead to the ground.

She'd never seen her family again, not even their corpses.

The memories continued to rise unbidden into her consciousness. Now, they came with startling clarity, and excruciating pain:

– Coyne teaching her how to aim a rifle, targeting the burnt-out shell of a Skaro Degradation he'd destroyed earlier that day in an ambush

– Learning how to pick a lock with Ash, a 12-year-old boy with sandy blond hair, who'd been killed that night during a Dalek raid

– Lying atop a building during a rainstorm, waiting for a Dalek patrol to pass by underneath, so that she might trigger the mine she had buried in the street that morning

– Her first kiss with another girl from the rebel camp, the raven-haired Stephanie, who had taught her things that she could never have imagined

– And Finch, who she had somehow forgotten. Finch, her partner in crime, her friend. Finch who had died during the ambush that had brought the Doctor tumbling from the sky; who'd been erased from existence by the temporal weapon of the new Dalek...

Cinder felt tears streaming from her eyes, running down her cheeks, but they were not tears of pain.

They were tears of sadness.

Images of the Dalek base flickered through her mind – of running through corridors behind the Doctor, of exploding Daleks and obscene hatcheries. Of the laboratory where the Daleks were dissecting the Degradations, and of their flight through the ruins, all the way back to the TARDIS.

Cinder wasn't aware of the Castellan turning off the machine, but she felt the fire in her head begin to quell. The buzzing sound ceased suddenly. She slumped back in the chair, nauseous and dizzy. Her breath was coming in ragged, fitful gasps.

She felt someone check the pulse at her throat. 'She'll survive,' said the Castellan.

'A pity,' said Karlax. 'I was looking forward to seeing the expression on the Doctor's face when I told him the news.'

The Castellan removed the rag from her mouth. She gasped for air. 'He'll kill you,' she said, between shallow breaths. 'He'll kill you for this.'

Karlax laughed. 'Oh no, not the Doctor,' he said. 'The Doctor and I are old playmates. He doesn't like to get his hands dirty.'

Cinder closed her eyes. The world was spinning. She couldn't risk slipping into unconsciousness around these men. If she did, there was every chance that she would never wake up again.

'Water,' she said, her voice a dry croak. She was parched, and there was an odd taste on her tongue, like aluminium.

'Karlax, get her some water while I remove these straps, will you?' said the Castellan. 'You've got what you wanted. You've seen the evidence to support the Doctor's claims, and you know what he was up to on Moldox. It's time to leave the girl alone.'

'If I must,' replied Karlax, with venom, and quit the room.

'Right,' said the Castellan, once the door had closed behind Karlax. 'Let's get you out of here.' He began unbuckling straps. 'Quickly now, help me if you have the strength. I want to get you away from here before he's back.'

Cinder looked up at the man as, red-faced, he hurried to free her. She had no strength left with which to help him. It was all too little, too late. He was clearly the weakest sort of man, complicit in her torture, and now remorseful. She'd known people like this before. On Moldox, they didn't survive for very long.

The Castellan had finished unbuckling her, and bent down, cupping her out of the chair and lifting her into his arms. 'I'll take you somewhere you can sleep it off,' he said, 'while you wait for the Doctor to return.' He staggered towards the door, kicking it open. 'For what it's worth, I think you're right. The Doctor is a different man these days. If he gets hold of Karlax after this, I think he *might* just kill him.'

Cinder, however, heard only a vague mumble, as she finally allowed herself to slip into peaceful oblivion.

Chapter Fourteen

The Doctor and Rassilon returned to the High Council chamber via the transmat, to find Karlax waiting for them. He was sitting at the table wearing an anxious expression, his hands steepled beneath his chin.

'Ah, Doctor. We were concerned for your whereabouts. No one seemed to know where you were.'

'Concerned,' echoed the Doctor. 'Yes, I can believe you were *concerned*, Karlax.'

The man gave a sickly smile. 'I see that we had no need to worry, given that you were in the company of the Lord President.'

Rassilon stepped down from the transmat podium. His face was impassive. 'Karlax, gather the Council. I shall relate my instructions immediately.' He turned to the Doctor. 'Your presence is no longer required,

Doctor. Find your assistant, and leave.'

'You're making a grave mistake, Rassilon,' said the Doctor.

'I am making the only choice I can. I shall hear no more of your insolence. I grow weary of it. Go now, before I am forced to silence you myself.' He fixed the Doctor with an unswerving stare and his fingers tightened visibly around the shaft of his staff, as if to underline his point. The Doctor knew this was not an idle threat. Rassilon was quick to anger, and even quicker to act.

Defiantly, the Doctor met his gaze. Then, with reluctance, he turned his back on the man. It seemed he was running out of options. Clearly, none of the High Council members were prepared to listen to reason. He decided he was going to have to find another approach, another way to stop them. Whatever happened, he couldn't allow them to deploy the Tear, even if it meant acting against them and intervening in their plans.

Without another word, he thundered from the room, heading for the observation room to find Cinder.

'What have you done with her?' growled the Doctor, bursting in through the doors of the High Council chamber. His jaw was set, and he was full of indignant ire. 'Where is she, Karlax?'

The High Council was, once again, in full session, and the assembled Time Lords ceased their chatter to look round at the Doctor as he marched towards them, glaring at Karlax, awaiting an answer.

The aide was standing on the opposite side of the room, his back to the wall, just behind Rassilon's left shoulder.

'Your female companion, Doctor?' said Karlax, with affected innocence. 'Didn't you leave her in the observation room to wait for you while you took your little – and I feel obliged to add, *unauthorised* – jaunt?'

The Doctor slammed his fist down on the table. He'd searched the observation gallery and the surrounding rooms, and Cinder was nowhere to be seen. Something had clearly happened to her while he'd been away at the Death Zone. 'Don't play the innocent with me, Karlax. I know you're up to something. Now tell me – where is she?'

'I can honestly say, Doctor, that I have no idea,' said Karlax, with a satisfied grin. He folded his arms across his chest. 'If you've misplaced her, perhaps you might consider investing in a more effective leash.'

The Doctor drew a deep breath. He knew Karlax was behind Cinder's disappearance. He *knew* it. He was furious with himself for leaving her so exposed, as he'd raced off after Rassilon into the Death Zone. He'd foolishly thought there was less chance of her coming to harm, here in the Time Lord Capitol. They were supposed to be *civilised*. This was why he travelled alone, nowadays. The War had changed everything, changed every*one*, and he didn't want the responsibility. He wasn't sure he could protect them any more.

This, however, was just like Karlax. He was an opportunist. He'll have seen his chance and seized it, whisked Cinder off as a way of getting to the Doctor.

He bunched his fists, so hard that he felt his fingernails digging into the flesh of his palms. 'I'm warning you, Karlax…' he said.

The Castellan hesitantly got to his feet. He coughed nervously into his fist. 'I know where she is, Doctor,' he said levelly. 'I'll show you.' He pushed his chair back, its legs scraping rudely on the marble, and walked around the table until he was standing by the harp. All eyes in the room were on him, and the Doctor noted that Karlax had fixed the Castellan with a particularly menacing stare.

The Castellan paused, glanced at Rassilon – whose features remained impassive – and then reached for the harp. His fingers plucked clumsily at the strings, his hands trembling. He was reading the notes detailed in the painting on the wall, recreating them on the real harp. The Doctor understood what was about to happen – he had seen this before.

After a moment the melody came to an end, and a panel in the wall, just behind the plinth upon which the harp rested, slid open to reveal a hidden control room. Lights winked from an array of dusty old computer panels and consoles. And there, sprawled in a chair, was Cinder.

The Doctor rushed over to her, barging past the Castellan and into the small antechamber. She was barely conscious; her head was flopped across her left shoulder, so that her bright orange hair fell in strands across her face. Her eyes were closed, her breathing ragged.

Gently, the Doctor repositioned her head, brushing the hair from her forehead. She was pale and cold, her skin clammy to the touch. Her eyelids fluttered, trying to open. He checked her pulse, and sighed in relief as he realised it was still strong and regular.

'What happened?' he said, softly. 'What did they do to you, Cinder?'

Her mouth opened, but all that came out was an indecipherable mumble. 'Mm... mmm...'

He leaned closer, putting his ear close to her mouth so that he could feel her warm breath against his cheek.

'M... mind... probe...' she said, with what seemed like a gargantuan effort. She seemed to fold back into the chair, the last of her energy spent.

The Doctor straightened up, turning slowly to face the expectant faces in the other room. He felt the white heat of fury building inside his chest. 'The mind probe!' he bellowed, causing the Castellan, who was still standing by the harp, to wince.

The Doctor stormed from the room, making a beeline for Karlax, who – seeing what was coming – began to circle the table, seeking to put a barrier between himself and the Doctor.

The Doctor was not interested in playing games of cat and mouse with the obsequious fool, and so, rather than attempt to chase him around the table, he tossed the Castellan's chair out of the way and leapt up onto the table, to the startled gasps of the rest of the High Council.

Sending papers fluttering to the floor with every step, he marched across the table top towards Karlax, who was now pinned in the corner, with nowhere left to run. He cowered as the Doctor hopped down from the table.

Two strides put him directly in front of the aide, and without losing his momentum, the Doctor thrust out his hand, grabbed the man by the throat and shoved him back against the wall, hard enough that he squealed in pain as his head struck the plaster.

'Tell me why I shouldn't just throttle you now, Karlax?' barked the Doctor. Spittle flecked Karlax's face, and he flinched, his eyelids fluttering in panic.

'L… Lord… President…?' he stammered, squirming in the Doctor's grasp.

The Doctor glanced round at Rassilon to gauge his reaction. The Lord President appeared entirely uninterested in what was happening, as if he were simply waiting for it all to blow over. This, in itself, only added to the Doctor's rage.

'Begging for your master, eh?' laughed the Doctor, returning his attention to Karlax. 'Now who's straining on a leash? I could kill you before he so much as looked at you again, you snivelling toad.'

'But of course, you won't,' said Rassilon, from behind him. He heard the tap-tap-tap of Rassilon's gauntleted fingers on the surface of the table. A warning, the Doctor knew – that gauntlet held unimaginable power, including the ability to dematerialise a person, just like the new Dalek weapon. Rassilon was reminding him where he was.

The Doctor sighed. 'No. I won't.' He released Karlax by pushing him to the floor, where he sank to his knees, scrabbling at his throat. 'But trust me, Karlax – it wouldn't leave a stain on my conscience.'

'Are you finished with your little rebellion now,

Doctor?' said Rassilon. 'It grows wearisome.'

The Doctor rounded on the President. 'Did you know about this, Rassilon? Did you know what they were going to do?'

Rassilon's lips curled into a thin smile. 'Oh, no, Doctor. That was all down to Karlax and the Castellan here, using their initiative. The results, however, have been most enlightening.'

The Doctor looked at the Castellan, who wouldn't meet his eye. 'You might have killed her!' he said. 'She's human. Her mind isn't strong enough to withstand the probe. What could you possibly hope to gain?'

'It's just as you said, Doctor,' mewled Karlax, climbing to his feet and dusting down his robes. 'Her perspective proved most valuable. We've now been able to corroborate your story. We're fully appreciative of the Dalek threat.'

'What are you saying?' said the Doctor.

'That the High Council have endorsed my recommendation, Doctor,' said Rassilon, rising to his feet. 'You're just in time to see the order given.' He turned to his aide. 'Karlax, you may give the order. The Tear of Isha is to be deployed.'

'Yes, Lord President,' said Karlax, eyeing the Doctor.

'Castellan, tell Commander Partheus to ready his fleet,' continued Rassilon. 'He is honoured this day. He shall carry the Tear deep into the Tantalus Eye, and with him, the hopes of all Time Lords, living, dead and still to be. We will strike a hard blow to the Daleks this day. They shall know the fury of the Time Lords.'

'And you shall know mine,' said the Doctor quietly.

He could not – *would* not – allow this to happen. So many lives, on so many worlds. There had to be a better way.

'Doctor?' said Rassilon. 'You have something to add?'

'I'll stop you,' he said. 'Understand that, Rassilon. I refuse to allow you to deploy the Tear of Isha.'

'You *refuse*?' said Rassilon, his tone incredulous. 'You will directly disobey a decision of the High Council, of the Lord President?'

'It's nothing I haven't done before,' said the Doctor. 'It means nothing.' He looked at them each in turn. 'You're all mad,' he said, exasperated. 'You've forgotten who you are. You've allowed the War to make you desperate and blind. Look at you all, hiding up here in your robes and fancy headdresses, pretending you know what's really going on out there, telling yourselves you're so damn important. Well, let me tell you the truth: you're wrong! You're just *wrong*.'

He jabbed his finger at Rassilon. 'If you allow him to do this, to commit genocide on this scale, then we're every bit as bad as the Daleks. Can't you see that? You're so obsessed with your own, petty survival that you've lost sight of the bigger picture. If this is what the Time Lords have become, then we don't deserve to survive.'

The room was silent for the moment. The Doctor tried to regain his breath. Rassilon was the first to speak. 'Am I to understand, Doctor, that you intend to move against us?'

The Doctor met his gaze. He could feel all the eyes in the room on him. He glanced at Cinder, still semi-conscious in the chair. 'Yes,' he said, with steely determination. 'If that's what it takes. I do it for your own good, for the good of the Time Lords. I'm trying to save you from yourselves. The path you are taking, Rassilon – it doesn't lead to victory. If you do this, it will be the end of the Time Lords. Ask Borusa if you doubt me,' he added, bitterly.

He marched across the room towards Cinder. It was time to leave Gallifrey, and he doubted he'd ever return. There was no looking back. He'd had enough.

'Seize him,' said Rassilon. 'Him and the girl. Throw them in a cell and impound his TARDIS.'

The Doctor felt hands grab him from behind, twisting his arm up behind his back. He struggled, but to no avail. The Castellan was younger, and stronger, and adept at carrying out orders, no matter how unsavoury. 'Better still,' continued Rassilon, 'scrap it. It's a decrepit old thing and of no use to us. The Doctor is a renegade and he will not be allowed to interfere with our plans. Once the Tear of Isha has neutralised the Dalek threat, he will be tried and found wanting.'

The Doctor heard Karlax calling for more guards. It was useless putting up a fight – for now, at least. His chance would come. He had to believe that.

As the Castellan dragged him off to the sound of Karlax's sniggering laugh, the Doctor took one last look at Cinder. He hadn't wanted the responsibility, but he'd assumed that mantle now, regardless. Not just for Cinder, but for the entirety of her race, all those billions of people being held prisoner on the occupied worlds of the Spiral. Judging by the current state of affairs, they were better off with the Daleks than with his own people.

The Time Lords were about to cross a line they could never come back from, and there was only him, an old, tired warrior, standing in the way.

He wasn't going to be able to do very much from the inside of a cell.

Chapter Fifteen

Cinder stirred. The side of her face was pressing against something cold and hard. Her head throbbed as if someone were using her skull for a bass drum, *bang, bang, bang,* and for a moment she had no idea where she was, or what she had been doing to get there.

Had she been at the grain alcohol again? She was sure there hadn't been a party last night. She'd been out on an ambush, but then something had happened, and –

She sat up with a start, and, moments later, when the world came with her and she swooned, she wished she hadn't. Lights danced before her eyes like sunspots, obscuring her view. She took a deep breath, which encouraged a painful, racking cough. She blinked away the fog.

She was sitting in a cell, on a low bunk formed from a slab of rough stone. Across from her, the Doctor sat slumped against the wall, his feet jutting out in front of him. He peered at her myopically. 'Hello,' he said.

'Where are we?' she said. Her mouth was dry. She rubbed the back of her neck.

'In a cell,' he said, redundantly.

'A cell?'

'Yes, beneath the Capitol on Gallifrey. Do you remember…?'

'The mind probe,' she said. 'How could I forget?'

The Doctor sighed. 'I'm sorry,' he said. 'I shouldn't have left you. I shouldn't even have brought you here, to Gallifrey, and got you mixed up in all of this.'

Cinder massaged her temples. 'Like I told you, back at the Dalek base on Moldox, we're in it together,' she said. 'Although I admit, I hadn't imagined we'd end up in a cell.' She considered for a moment. 'Why *are* we in a cell?'

'Ah,' said the Doctor. 'Now that's a bit of a long story.'

'You told Rassilon where to shove it, didn't you?' she said. She grinned. 'Where he could go and stick his Tear of Isha.'

The Doctor laughed. 'In as many words,' he conceded. 'Perhaps with a little less vulgarity.'

Cinder shrugged. 'Perhaps a little vulgarity was what he needed. Well, perhaps a lot of it.'

'You're not wrong,' said the Doctor.

Cinder studied the cell. It was very much a *cell*. No plumbing, heating, monitor screens, books or data slates – just four stone walls, a raised stone slab, and a door. The floor was dressed in uneven flagstones, and covered in a grimy layer of dust. The Doctor was sitting in it. The only light came from a small panel in the ceiling, dim and watery.

'Nice place you've got here,' she said. 'I like what you've done with it.'

The Doctor winced. 'It's positively mediaeval,' he said.

'Meddy-what?' said Cinder.

'Barbaric,' replied the Doctor. 'Unimaginative. Primitive.'

Cinder's head was still spinning. To her, the whole situation seemed somewhat surreal. 'How long was I out?' she said.

'Two or three hours,' replied the Doctor. 'You did well to withstand the effects of the mind probe. Better than well. I've seen it unravel the minds of those with far superior intellects.'

'Oh, thanks,' she said.

'It was a compliment!' said the Doctor.

'Sounded like one,' said Cinder.

The Doctor laughed again. 'You know, you're quite remarkable, Cinder,' he said. 'You know your own mind. You're aware of what you want, and you go out and get it. It's an enviable quality.'

'Now *that's* a compliment,' said Cinder. 'See the difference?' She stretched, yawning and arching her back. She got to her feet. 'So – and I want a straight, honest answer here – are they going to deploy the weapon?'

The Doctor nodded. 'I'm afraid so,' he said. His voice was grim. 'I tried to stop them, but Rassilon had already made up his mind.' The way the Doctor said his name made it clear he'd lost all respect for the Time Lord President – if indeed he'd had any in the first instance.

'Well, it's not over yet,' said Cinder. 'How long have we got?'

'Until they're ready to deploy?' The Doctor appeared to do a quick calculation in his head. 'No more than a couple of hours,' he said.

Cinder stood over him, offering him both hands. 'What are you doing sitting down there, then?' she said. 'You're not going to save everyone wallowing in the dust and grime.'

The Doctor took her hands and allowed her to help him up, but his expression was telling. 'I wish it were that simple,' he said. 'We're in a Time Lord prison cell. Despite its primitive aesthetics, there's no way out. They've impounded the TARDIS and they're not going to let us out of here until the Tear has been deployed and the Tantalus Eye has been neutralised.'

Cinder fixed him with her best incredulous look. 'Sounds like a lot of excuses to me,' she said. It was pure bravado. She knew that. Inside, her heart ached at the certainty of the Doctor's response. Her chest felt tight and she could feel the panic welling up, threatening to overwhelm her. She simply didn't want to believe that he was right, that this stranger she had grown to trust had been defeated, and that everyone she knew – everyone even remotely like her, on twelve inhabited worlds – was going to die.

The Doctor looked pained. He was still holding her hands. 'It's all right,' he said. 'I understand.'

'No!' she said. 'No, you don't understand. You don't get to be kind. You don't get to hold my hand while everything I've ever known is obliterated. That's not how this is going to work.' She sucked at the air. 'You're going to find a way out of here and you're going to go and *stop* them.' She pulled her hands free of his grip and struck him forcefully in the chest with both fists. She felt tears welling in her eyes. 'Do you understand?'

The Doctor looked at her with sad, haunted eyes. 'If there was a way…' he whispered.

She shook her head. 'When we first met, you told me that you used to have a name, that you were no longer worthy of it. Today's your chance to prove that you are.'

Cinder walked to the cell door. It was made from heavy wooden beams, banded with wrought iron. There was a large mechanical lock. 'Here, look,' she said. 'You can use your screwdriver thingy to open it.'

The Doctor came to stand beside her. He put a hand on her shoulder. 'I'm sorry, Cinder,' he said. 'I've tried. Remember what I said. This is a *Time Lord* cell. The lock is immune to the effects of sonic devices. That's why they didn't even bother to take it off me when they threw us in here. I spent the first hour and a half looking for ways out. I simply can't find one. If we could get out of this cell then maybe we'd stand a chance. As it is, we're stuck.'

Cinder kicked the door. It didn't even move in its frame. Her foot flared with pain. Miserably, she sank to the floor, rubbing at her smarting toes through her boot.

The Doctor, clearly deciding it was best to leave her to her own devices for a few minutes, walked back to where he'd been sitting against the wall and made himself comfortable.

Cinder glowered at the lock. It didn't *look* that sophisticated. In fact, it was just like the human locks back on Moldox, a simple lever tumbler affair, opened with a key. Were the Time Lords really so arrogant that they thought adapting a simple, mechanical lock to be immune to sonic manipulation was going to be enough to keep their prisoners in?

She felt a glimmer of hope. She glanced at the Doctor, who had taken his sonic screwdriver from the hoop on his ammo belt, and was fiddling with the settings, presumably in an attempt to override the protocols on the lock.

She slid the sleeve of her jumper up her arm, hooking it over her elbow. She hardly dared look. *Maybe…*

It was still there. She breathed a sigh of relief. The bracelet she'd brought with her from Moldox, the one her brother had made for her when she'd been a child, twisting a hoop from strands of thick copper wire. It had been too big for her, then, but she'd held on to it all the same, and when Coyne and his crew had found her in the burned-out ruins of her homestead, it was the only thing she'd been able to save.

She plucked at it with her fingertips, considering. If she uncoiled it, maybe the wire would be strong enough to make two lock picks. There was a part of her that didn't want to do it, that wanted to pull the sleeve of her jumper back down over her arm and curl up, pretend she'd never had the idea, but she knew she couldn't. Too many lives were at stake. Her brother would have understood.

'I'm sorry, Sammy,' she whispered, as she slipped the bracelet off and slowly began teasing apart the metal strands. They were stiff with age, and for a moment she thought they were simply going to snap in her hands, but as she worked at them they gradually began to come free.

Within moments the bracelet had separated, unfurling into two separate strands. She straightened them as best she could and laid them out before her on the ground.

The Doctor was still intent on his screwdriver, a look of deep concentration on his furrowed brow.

Cinder got to her knees, leaning close to the lock, closing one eye so that she could peer through the keyhole. She could see little of the passageway outside, other than another door across the hall. There was no sign of any guards.

She retrieved her makeshift tools from the floor. Cautiously, she inserted them into the lock, half expecting to receive a violent electric shock, or at the very least to trigger an alarm, but nothing happened. Slowly, deliberately, she set to work, using the metal rods to gently force the mechanism, turning the tumblers so that the lever slid out of the hole in the wall.

She heard the mechanism click. She'd only been at it for seconds. Could it really be that simple?

She realised she'd been holding her breath and let it out. Then, getting to her feet, she jammed the lock picks into her pocket and, hand trembling, tried the door.

The handle turned, and the door opened a fraction of an inch. Her pulse was thrumming in her ears. Quietly, she pushed it closed again, and turned to see if the Doctor was watching. He was still fumbling with his screwdriver.

'Doctor?' she said, her voice wavering slightly.

'Hmmm,' he replied, only half listening. 'You said that, if we could get out of this cell, you thought we still stood a chance of stopping the Time Lords from deploying the Tear?'

The Doctor peered up at her, narrowing his eyes. 'Yes, he said. 'But I've to—'

Cinder waved him quiet. She reached behind her, turned the handle and allowed the door to swing wide open. 'Time to make good,' she said.

The Doctor glanced at the lock, and then at Cinder. 'I'm impressed,' he said.

She shrugged. 'Clearly, they weren't expecting a measly human girl with a lock pick.'

'No,' laughed the Doctor, scrambling to his feet. 'I don't think any of us were.' His waistcoat was rumpled beneath his jacket and his boots were spattered in dried mud. He looked somewhat bedraggled. But then, she supposed, they'd both been through the wars in the last few days – quite literally.

Without further ado, they slipped from the cell.

'Which way?' said Cinder.

'Left, I think,' said the Doctor, lowering his voice to a whisper. 'Thankfully, I've never spent a great deal of time down here, but I think we have to go down.

There should be a sloping passageway up ahead, on the left.'

'Down?' said Cinder. 'I thought we were in the dungeons? They certainly *look* like dungeons.'

The Doctor nodded. 'There's an under croft that stretched right beneath the main citadel. It's where they send TARDISes to die.' His voice cracked as he spoke. 'That's where she'll be.'

Trailing one after the other, the Doctor led the way along the passage. It was dimly lit and dank, and the four or five other cells they passed were all empty, the doors hanging open. The walls were roughly hewn, chiselled from the bedrock beneath the citadel, and were largely unadorned, save for the occasional lumen sconce. Either this particular wing of the prison had been reserved just for them, or the Time Lords didn't make a habit of taking prisoners. Cinder pointed this out to the Doctor as they walked.

'It's my understanding that Rassilon favours execution as a means of punishment these days,' he said darkly.

Cinder frowned. 'Then why shove us in a dirty old cell?' she said. 'Not that I'm complaining, or anything.'

'He knows I might yet prove useful,' said the Doctor, 'and he can use you as leverage, despicable as it is.'

Cinder didn't very much like the idea of being used as leverage, but at least it gave her some comfort to know that the Doctor was looking out for her, and that he wouldn't simply abandon to save his own skin, or leave her somewhere to die.

They reached the end of the tunnel and turned

left, straight into the eye line of a waiting guard, who was sitting on a stool, leaning back against the wall and casually perusing a data tablet. She was a tall, muscular woman, dressed in the familiar red and white uniform of the Castellan's Guard. Cinder couldn't help but notice the pistol jammed in her belt.

Slowly, the woman got up from the stool, placing the data slate on the seat behind her. 'Stop there!' she said. She hurried toward them, her footsteps echoing in the confined passageway.

The Doctor stepped forward to greet her, extending his hand. 'Hello,' he said.

'Now look, what are you doing down here?' said the woman. 'The prison is strictly out of bounds.'

'Ah,' said the Doctor. 'I'm sorry. Must have taken a wrong turning somewhere back there. It's clearly just a misunderstanding. Don't mind us. We'll be on our way.' He turned around on the spot, making as if to leave.

'Hold on a moment,' said the woman. 'You look familiar. Aren't you…?' Her eyes widened. 'You're the Doctor!' she said. 'You're supposed to be in that cell. How did you get out?' She fumbled for her pistol.

'Now listen,' said the Doctor, holding out his hand in an effort to calm her. 'As I say, it's just a simple misunder—'

Cinder stepped forward, drew back her fist and delivered a neat right hook to the woman's jaw. She crumpled to a heap on the floor, her pistol skittering away.

'Now really!' said the Doctor. 'Was there any need for that?'

Cinder rolled her eyes, nursing her painful hand. 'Something tells me you've got the dynamic of this situation all wrong,' she said. 'This is a prison break. She's a guard. We're supposed to be running away.'

The Doctor seemed to weigh this up for a moment, and then shrugged. 'Well, when you put it like that…' he said. He looked down at the unconscious form of the guard. 'Let's at least make her comfortable.'

Cinder sighed, while the Doctor dragged the woman to the tunnel wall and propped her up in a sitting position, resting her hands upon her lap. 'There,' he said, dusting his hands. 'She'll thank us for that when she comes round.'

'I really think she won't,' said Cinder. 'Now let's get a move on.'

The end of the tunnel dipped as the Doctor had predicted, turning into a long, gentle slope that led further underground. 'This way,' he said, waving her on.

Cinder heard voices behind them – two men, shouting to one another in alarm. Clearly, they'd discovered their unconscious colleague. 'They've found her,' she said. 'Come on, we'd better run.'

Abandoning all hope of remaining inconspicuous, the Doctor and Cinder started off at a run, charging down the slopes toward the depth of the under croft. Moments later, they heard footsteps starting out behind them.

The passage continued to delve down for what seemed like miles, winding back on itself until Cinder was utterly disorientated. She was dog tired, the muscles in her thighs aching from all the running, her head still pounding with the after-effects of the mind probe. She was driven on, however, by the sound of the accompanying footsteps, which seemed to be growing louder, gaining on them with every second.

'It's just down here,' gasped the Doctor, breathlessly.

Up ahead, the tunnel widened abruptly, the floor levelling as it disgorged into the mouth of an enormous cave.

The Doctor skidded to a halt, and Cinder almost ran into his back, forced to catch hold of his arm to slow her momentum, and almost pulling them both over in the process.

The under croft was immense, just as the Doctor had described, stretching out beneath the entire city. The ceiling was high and vaulted, clearly built in millennia long past, and softly glowing strips criss-crossed the brickwork, providing a measure of weak illumination. The walls were roughly cut stone, which disappeared away into the horizon, absorbed by the shadows.

The floor of the cave was littered with the carcasses of dead or dying TARDISes. There were thousands of them, tens of thousands, even. It was impossible to estimate.

She stood in the mouth of the cave, looking out upon a sea of TARDISes in all their myriad forms, all manner of different shapes and sizes. Some of them were plain white lozenges scarred with the sooty streaks of battle, others silver and grey capsules, their surfaces pitted and cracked with age.

One of them, close by, had cracked open like an egg, its interior folding out to create a higgledy-piggledy landscape of geometric weirdness. Cinder could make no sense of it – the walls were on the ceiling; the ceiling was on the floor. The console room stood perpendicular to a fragment of outer casing, which in turn bisected an empty pine bookcase. It was like staring at a weird dreamscape rendered in steel and wood.

In the distance, she could see some that had bloated to massive proportions; their outer forms swelling to press against the cavern roof, like asymmetric pillars, supporting the city above.

To her left was one that looked like a damaged Dalek saucer, lying on its side; another that resembled an ancient oak tree, sitting upon a tangle of gnarled and knotted roots; still more that had taken the form of a neoclassical pillar, a circus tent, a scuttled galleon, listing against the wall. There were others, too, describing strange and unusual objects that she could not recognise, presumably derived from alien civilisations.

There was something terribly forlorn about the place, that these vessels should be abandoned here in such a fashion to end their days.

'It's a graveyard,' she said.

The Doctor nodded. 'The final resting place of old friends,' he said. He stroked his beard. 'They were once alive, you know.'

Cinder frowned. 'But they're machines.'

The Doctor shook his head. 'No. They're much more than that. You should try running away with one of them.'

Behind them, the footsteps of the guards were

approaching.

'How are we going to find her amongst all of these?' asked Cinder, with a sudden sense of urgency. They were wasting time. 'Your TARDIS. There are too many.' She waved her hands to encompass the breadth of the cavern. 'It would take weeks to search this place.'

Her statement was punctuated by a short, electronic bleep, which seemed to come from beneath the lapel of the Doctor's leather coat. He raised an eyebrow. 'Oh, she's good,' he said. 'Clever, clever girl.' He reached for his sonic screwdriver. The tip had come to life, lighting up, but he hadn't done anything, and there was no annoying whirring sound. After a second it emitted another bleep.

'She's calling to us,' he said. 'She knows we're here. She wants to be found. Come on!'

Holding the sonic aloft like a flaming torch, the Doctor hopped down from the small ledge, disappearing amongst the forest of broken TARDISes. Cinder jumped down behind him, following the glow of the sonic.

'That's far enough!'

Behind them, the guards emerged into the mouth of the cavern. Cinder didn't pause to look at their faces, but darted for cover behind the scorched shell of a Battle TARDIS.

'Come back to the cells now,' bellowed one of the guards, 'and we won't shoot.'

'Fat chance!' came the Doctor's muffled reply, causing Cinder to splutter with laughter. It only lasted for a moment, however, as an energy bolt from one of the guard's pistols zipped past her ear, striking the galleon and sending a shower of sparks streaming into the air.

So, they weren't out to stun.

She could hear the Doctor's sonic bleeping ahead of her, the pips increasing in frequency as he moved deeper into the warren, and presumably closer to his TARDIS. 'This way!' he called, waving his sonic over the top of a TARDIS that looked like a canal barge, and eliciting another shot from one of the guards.

Keeping her head down, Cinder scuttled after him. More shots whizzed over her head as the guards, clearly deciding that accuracy was not a virtue, began to fire indiscriminately in their general direction.

The broken TARDISes formed a haphazard maze full of jagged edges and disorientating geometry.

As the guards split up, coming after them in a pincer movement, the Doctor and Cinder followed the insistent bleeping of the Doctor's sonic screwdriver, rushing chaotically from place to place, stumbling upon dead ends, backtracking, circling around.

A well-timed shot from one of the guards fizzed into the pale outer skin of a Battle TARDIS, which was lying on its side just beside her, and she dived for cover, ducking behind what looked like a greenhouse. Half of its panes were broken and it was covered in creeping vines.

The Doctor was running on ahead. 'Come on, we're close now!'

She took off after him, her feet slipping on the dusty floor. She almost went over, wheeling her arms, and catching sight of the red and white uniform of the guard in hot pursuit. He was closing on them.

Up ahead, the Doctor was veering right, and she charged after him, grabbing hold of what looked like a torpedo chute, and using it to propel herself around the corner.

'There she is!' cried the Doctor jubilantly. Cinder caught sight of the now familiar blue box, nestled amongst a pile of fragments and broken interior walls, bearing the same, strange roundels as the inside of the Doctor's console room.

As they ran towards it, the door opened for them, welcoming them inside. They charged in, the Doctor leaping up onto the dais and banging his fist against a large red button on the console. The door swung shut behind them.

'That's it,' he said, breathless. 'Ha! They'll not get inside now.' He laughed boyishly. 'Thank you, old girl.' He stood with his hands raised to either side, turning on the spot and looking up, as if speaking to the ship. 'You've never let me down.'

He glanced at Cinder. 'This isn't the first time I've had to steal away with her from Gallifrey,' he said. 'Sometimes, I think she wanted to go on an adventure just as much as I did.'

On the monitor screen, Cinder saw the two guards just outside the TARDIS door. They kicked at it, trying to break it down, and when it didn't give, stood back, took aim, and fired simultaneously at the lock.

The noise inside the TARDIS was tremendous, but the energy bolts rebounded, flashing off into the darkness of the graveyard, and the doors did not give. She watched as one of the men – a swarthy-looking fellow with a full, black beard – spoke into his wrist communicator. She imagined alarms going off elsewhere in the prison complex.

The Doctor was adjusting the flight controls. 'Something tells me we're not welcome here any more,' he said sarcastically. He pushed a sequence of button, twisted a dial and cranked a lever.

The glass column at the heart of the console stuttered to life, emitting a bright, ethereal light. Inside, the cluster of glass tubes began to slowly rise and fall, accompanied by the wheezing groan of the ship's engines.

Cinder grabbed for the railing, finally allowing herself a sigh of relief.

The ship gave a sudden judder, the engines coughing as if stalling.

'Oh, no, no, no,' said the Doctor, his fingers dancing over the controls. He followed the same sequence again, cranking the lever. The central column began to rise once more, but then stuck, stalling. The engines choked, as if straining to get away.

The Doctor stepped back from the controls, glancing at Cinder. 'They've changed the security protocols,' he said. 'They're not going to allow us to dematerialise.'

A voice boomed out over the comm-link, causing Cinder to start. 'It's time to give up on this rebellion of yours, Doctor, and come quietly.' It was the Castellan, speaking from somewhere within the citadel, Cinder presumed. 'Your TARDIS no longer has access to the correct protocols to leave Gallifrey. Give yourselves up to the guards and you can return to your cell.

There'll be no more said about it. That's the most I can do for you.'

'No!' bellowed the Doctor, full of rage. 'You're going to let us go.'

The Castellan laughed. 'I'm afraid that's more than my life is worth,' he replied.

'That may be so,' said the Doctor, his tone grave, 'but for once in your life you're going to do the right thing. Because you know what they're doing is wrong, don't you, Castellan? You're not yet sure how you're going to live with billions of lives on your conscience, once this is over with.' The Doctor had begun pacing back and forth before the console, lost in his argument. 'Deep down in your hearts, you know that I have to prevent them from deploying the Tear, and so you're going to transmit the correct protocols to my TARDIS console.'

'But…' the Castellan faltered, and Cinder could hear in his voice that he couldn't object to what the Doctor had said. 'But Karlax?'

'This is bigger than you and Karlax,' said the Doctor. 'It's bigger than me, than any of us, Rassilon included. You heard what I said in the council chamber. If you allow this to happen, then you're no better than a Dalek.'

There was a chime from the console, and a button began to blink.

'Thank you,' said the Doctor. 'I understand what you have sacrificed.'

'Don't let it be in vain,' said the Castellan, before cutting the link.

Once more, the Doctor adjusted the controls and

the TARDIS wheezed out of existence, leaving the two guards standing in the under croft, staring at each other in bemusement.

Chapter Sixteen

Karlax had always detested travelling via the transmat device, the way it made his fingertips tingle for an hour afterwards, the quickening of his hearts when the particles of his body began to disentangle, unweaving him at the molecular level. Even the very concept of it troubled him, and he recalled lying awake all night in the aftermath of his first trip, many lifetimes ago, wondering whether he was still the same person, or if the process had irrevocably changed him somehow.

Of course, all of this was long before his first regeneration, when the concepts of change and identity had effectively become irrelevant to him. He realised now that change was inevitable, just another weave in the long tapestry of life. The key was in ensuring that you managed that change to get what you wanted, encouraged it, even, in a particular direction. Some might call that manipulative, he supposed. Karlax simply saw it as pragmatic. So far, it was an approach that had paid great dividends for him, and he saw no reason to stop now.

So it was that he'd come here, to the Lord President's tomb, to speak with him. He was anxious to be the first one to deliver the news, so that he might influence any decisions that came after. Karlax knew exactly what he wanted, and he would do everything in his power to get it. The time was ripe for revenge. The Doctor would get what he richly deserved.

Karlax had visited the tomb once before, and he knew what Rassilon was keeping here – they all did. Every member of the High Council had sanctioned the creation of the possibility engine. The work had been carried out in the Capitol, behind closed doors, and the Council had been kept abreast of progress. When the time had come to unveil the remarkable new device, however, none of them had been able to look upon it. They'd shunned it, calling it an abomination, and Rassilon had been forced to have it moved to his old tomb in order to keep it out of the way.

Now, it was barely acknowledged. The High Council knew that Rassilon spoke with an authority bestowed by the machine, but it remained unstated, and Borusa's name was never uttered.

That was one thing about which the Doctor was absolutely correct, Karlax begrudgingly admitted – they were all hypocrites, prepared to make the necessary decisions and reap the rewards, just so long as they never had to face the consequences.

He'd implied as much to Rassilon earlier that day, whispering in his ear that the Castellan was beginning to develop a conscience, that he didn't have the necessary detachment to be able to properly fulfil his duties. The incident with the human girl had been evidence enough of that, and now Karlax suspected he'd had a hand in the Doctor's escape. There would be repercussions.

He'd reached the entrance to the Tower. He stepped inside, bowing his head, mindful of showing due reverence.

Rassilon was standing at the foot of the tomb, speaking with the possibility engine, demanding that Borusa show him a pathway through the fluctuating chaos of the timelines; that he predict the most effective time to deploy their weapon. 'Tell me, Borusa, of the Tear of Isha. What is the true path to victory? How do I ensure its deployment strikes at the very heart of the Dalek cause?'

Karlax cringed at the sight of the possibility engine, cranked up on its metal bed so that Rassilon might look upon it. To Karlax it was like a pale corpse, reinvigorated with life; emaciated, yet filled with a vitality that was not its own. The Time Vortex was running through its head, filling it with wonders and terrors beyond imagining. In the dim light of the tomb, it glowed with the aura of oscillating regenerative energy.

'The timelines are no longer clear to me,' mumbled Borusa. 'There is no true path. Every outcome is in flux, and possibilities bloom. A random factor has been introduced which… unsettles things.'

'A random factor?' echoed Rassilon. 'What is it? The Dalek weapon?'

'No, my Lord. Something else. A knot of potential, moving unchecked through the timelines, weaving patterns in the future and the past.'

'You speak in riddles,' cursed Rassilon. 'Riddles and ciphers. I cannot understand you!'

Karlax hovered by the entrance, unsure how to proceed. He didn't wish to incur his master's wrath, but all the same – there was news that he need to impart. 'Lord President?' he called, tentatively.

Rassilon turned. He looked annoyed to see that it was Karlax who had come to disturb him here, in his haven.

'What is it, Karlax?' he snapped. 'Can't you see that I'm busy?'

'My apologies, Lord President,' said Karlax, 'but I bring grave news from the Capitol. Our plans could be at risk. I thought to inform you immediately.'

Rassilon waved him closer.

Karlax crossed the mausoleum, hesitant to be so close to the creature that had once been Borusa. Despite his disdain for the manner in which the members of the High Council had insisted on Borusa's removal from the Capitol, Karlax had grave misgivings about being in such close proximity to the thing. It looked down at him with its weird, flickering eyes, and grinned knowingly. Karlax shuddered. He wondered what it was thinking, what it might be *seeing* when it looked at him.

'Well?' said Rassilon. 'Get on with it.'

'It's the Doctor,' said Karlax. 'He's escaped.'

Rassilon's jaw worked as he ground his teeth, evidently attempting to retain his composure. 'Escaped?' There was a steely edge to his voice. Karlax had to choose his next words very carefully.

'Clearly, he was assisted in some way,' he said. 'We have a traitor in our midst. It should be a simple matter to trace the data logs and see who granted the Doctor's TARDIS access to the security protocols.'

'Do it,' said Rassilon. 'I'll have someone's head for his.'

Karlax had a feeling the High Council would be looking for a new Castellan in the coming days. He suppressed a smile. 'What of the Doctor?' he ventured. 'He might yet attempt to prevent Commander Partheus from deploying the Tear.'

'Yes,' said Rassilon. 'The random factor.' He glanced up at Borusa, momentarily lost in thought. Then, after a moment, he appeared to make a decision. 'I see it clearly now, Karlax. The Doctor is a wildcard, a renegade, and he has made his position abundantly clear. He intends to act against us. He must be prevented from influencing the outcome of events. There is only one recourse.'

'My Lord?' said Karlax.

'The Doctor must die, Karlax,' said Rassilon. 'Only then can we be sure.'

Karlax couldn't help his smile from spreading to his lips.

'You, Karlax, are the only one I can trust with such a significant task,' continued Rassilon.

'Me?' said Karlax, suddenly panicked. This was not at all what he'd expected. He was not a man of action.

He'd built his career through the manipulation of others. He'd barely ventured out in a TARDIS since his days in the Academy. 'Are you sure that I'm adequately equipped for such a pivotal role, my Lord?' said Karlax.

'Uniquely so,' said Rassilon. 'You, more than any of us, want him dead.'

So Rassilon was more perceptive than he looked. Karlax could see there was no way of changing his mind. He'd walked right into it, and now he'd have to see it through. Still, he mused, at least this way he'd get to see the look on the Doctor's face as he died. That would be some measure of consolation. 'Very well, my Lord,' he said.

'Excellent. Time is of the essence. Engage the assistance of the Celestial Intervention Agency. If you are to be the bullet, Karlax, they shall be the gun.'

'Immediately,' said Karlax. He turned and walked towards the door, his head spinning.

'Oh, and Karlax?' called Rassilon, as he was just about to step over the threshold.

Karlax stopped and looked back. 'Yes, my Lord?'

'If you fail, do not bother coming back.'

Karlax swallowed. There were no words for how terrified he felt at that moment. 'My life or the Doctor's,' he said, with a nod of his head. 'I understand.'

So, it had come to this. Karlax knew one thing for certain: whatever happened, he was going to make the Doctor suffer.

Part Three
Into the Eye

Chapter Seventeen

The TARDIS hung still in the Time Vortex amidst a swirling chaos of purples and blues. Cinder could see the colours raging through the clear ceiling of the console room, like a tempestuous storm, bruised clouds pregnant with crackling energy. For all she knew, the outer shell of the ship was being buffeted and battered, but inside, everything was calm.

She was perched on the edge of the central dais, the ship's console at her back. It seemed odd to her not to be running about, chased through meandering corridors or desperately trying to escape from a Dalek ship, a ruined city, or a Time Lord prison. From *anywhere*. She considered that for a moment. All of her life she'd been trying to escape from wherever she was, always working on the assumption that if only she could get away there'd be a better place, waiting for her somewhere out there in the cosmos. A place she could call home.

Now, she wasn't so sure. She couldn't help wondering, while she watched the billowing storm of the Time Vortex, blowing all around them, whether the entire universe was this angry, this violent. It certainly seemed that way.

All the same, it felt strange to be sitting still.

The Doctor was bustling about the console room like he'd lost something.

'What are we going to do now?' asked Cinder. She rested her chin on her upturned palm. 'We can't go back to Moldox, and we can't go back to Gallifrey. We're not very popular, are we?' she mused.

The Doctor stopped what he was doing for a moment. 'We're going to stop the Time Lords from deploying the Tear of Isha,' he said. 'That's what we're going to do.'

No mean feat, thought Cinder, for two renegades in a blue box. She realised she was being maudlin and decided to cheer herself up. 'Assuming we're successful,' she said, 'and that we're able to prevent the Time Lords from collapsing the Tantalus Eye…'

'Yes,' said the Doctor.

'Then what about the Daleks? What are we going to do about them? Surely you're not going to allow them to finish what they've started, to wipe Gallifrey from existence?'

'Shouldn't I?' he said, but she could tell his heart wasn't in it. He was furious at his people, and justifiably so. Not only had they refused to listen to him, they'd turned on him when he was trying to help them, when they'd needed him most. They'd shown him their true colours.

Everything she'd heard about the Time Lords, all the rumours – she now supposed they must be true, that there really wasn't that much difference between them and the Daleks.

All except one, she thought, with a smile. He wasn't so bad. And she didn't believe for one minute that he was going to stand by and watch them be obliterated.

'Ah, got it!' the Doctor exclaimed, and Cinder shuffled round to see what he was up to, bringing her knees up to her chest and curling her arms around them.

The Doctor was on his knees, worrying away at something beneath the mushroom-shaped console. 'What is it?' she asked.

'Hold on…' came the muffled response. He was wearing a look of intense concentration and his tongue was sticking out comically from the corner of his mouth. 'There!' he declared. A small black pod, which had evidently been fixed beneath the control panel, came away in his hand. He tossed it in the air and caught it again. 'That'll teach them,' he said, getting to his feet.

'What is it? What have you found?'

The Doctor got to his feet and crossed to where she was sitting. He held out his hand. The black object was a thin ovoid, made of what appeared to be glossy ceramic. It didn't give much away. 'A tracking device,' he said. 'I knew they wouldn't be able to resist. The Castellan's men must have planted it before they moved the TARDIS to the scrapyard.'

'So you think they'll come after us, then?' asked Cinder. That was all they needed. She'd had enough of the Time Lords to last her a lifetime. Maybe two.

'Nothing would surprise me,' said the Doctor, resignedly. 'If they can find us, that is. They'll know we're going after the Tear. They'll probably send a strike force to try to stop us.'

Cinder sighed. When would it all end? 'So, about the Daleks, then,' she said.

'What about them?'

'Well, I know you weren't serious. But what *are* we going to do to stop them?' she said. 'If they use their weapon on Gallifrey, it'll only be a matter of time before they use it somewhere else, too. There'll be no one to stop them.'

'Yes, I haven't quite worked that bit out, yet,' said the Doctor. His bushy eyebrows twitched.

'Then have you considered the alternative?' she said. She hated herself for even bringing it up, but it had to be said.

'There is no alternative,' replied the Doctor.

Cinder shook her head. 'You could let the Time Lords deploy the Tear. What if Rassilon's right? The lives of a few billion human slaves to ensure the safety of everyone else in the universe…'

The Doctor looked furious. 'That's not how this works, Cinder. We don't get to make that choice. *No one* should wield that sort of power.'

'But if we don't, aren't we handing that same power to the Daleks?'

'I'll find a way,' said the Doctor. 'I always do, in the end. But I certainly won't allow the Time Lords to commit genocide to do it.'

Cinder nodded. Idly, she picked up the Dalek cannon, which was lying on the floor by her feet. There was nothing aesthetically pleasing about the thing. It was a weapon of pure hate, functional and deadly.

'Where did you get that?' said the Doctor. He sounded suspicious.

'Just here, where you left it,' replied Cinder.

The Doctor dropped to his haunches beside her and put his hand out. She passed it to him. 'I left this on Gallifrey,' he said. 'In the council chamber.'

'They must have decided to return it,' said Cinder.

'Mmmm,' mumbled the Doctor, turning the weapon over in his hands. 'Yes, as I thought.' He turned it around to show her the little black nodule that had been secreted beneath the barrel. He wrenched it free.

'Seems they weren't taking any chances,' he said. 'I do have a reputation for being difficult to keep in a cell.'

He stood, leaving the two tracking devices side by side on the floor. He then stomped on them repeatedly, crushing them beneath his heel until there was nothing left but a pulp of broken ceramic and diodes. 'There, that should see to that,' he said.

He offered her his hand, hauling her up. 'Now, it's time you got some rest.'

Cinder rubbed her eyes. 'No, I'm OK,' she said.

The Doctor shook his head. 'You need sleep.'

Now that he had mentioned it, she realised how close to exhaustion she really was. Her eyes were hot and heavy and there was a dull ache at the back of her skull, which had been there ever since her experience with the mind probe. Her limbs were leaden. 'All right,' she said. 'For a little while.'

'Up those steps,' said the Doctor. 'First door on the left. You'll find somewhere to get some sleep.' Cinder smoothed her tunic. It was filthy. 'There should be some fresh clothes in the wardrobe, too. Take whatever you want.'

'Thanks,' she said. She crossed to the stairs. Perhaps for the very first time in her life, she felt peaceful. Yet she couldn't help wondering if this was the calm before the storm, the eerie silence on the night before battle. Either way, she would take a while to muster her strength.

'Do you know what you're going to do yet?' she said. 'How you're going to stop them. The Time Lords, I mean.'

The Doctor smiled. 'I've always been one for just… well, winging it,' he replied.

Cinder laughed. 'Me too.'

She climbed the steps in search of a bed.

Cinder came hurtling down the steps to find the Doctor still standing at the console, tinkering with the controls. 'I've been asleep for hours,' she said. 'Why didn't you wake me?'

The Doctor looked up, unperturbed. 'You needed the rest,' he said.

'But the Tear! Won't we be too late?'

The Doctor laughed. 'This is a *time* machine,' he said. 'Out here in the Vortex we're one step removed from what's going on.'

'I don't understand.'

'Think of it like a river,' said the Doctor, 'always flowing, always rushing by. That's time, and the TARDIS is hovering above that river. Follow it upstream and we can dip into the future, back in the opposite direction, and although we're swimming against the tide, we can find our way to any point in the past.'

Cinder shook her head, hopping down the last of the steps. 'I'll take your word for it,' she said.

Navigating the TARDIS hadn't been as simple as 'the first door on the left', which had actually led to a palatial courtyard, filled with olive trees and park benches and complete with a marble fountain sculpted to resemble a naked woman, pouring water from a jug. Here, at least five other doors led off to adjoining rooms. She'd tried them each in turn, discovering all manner of bizarre environments: a squawking jungle, heady with the scent of fresh rain; a vast aviary filled with colourful, chirping birds; a chemistry lab with old-fashioned wooden benches, gas taps and Bunsen burners, and bookcases lined with innumerable phials. Finally she had found a bedroom, evidently still filled with the clutter of a previous occupant. Cinder hadn't taken most of it in, but simply collapsed in a heap on the bed and drifted off into a long, luxurious sleep.

Upon waking, she'd found a pair of skinny black jeans and a Greenpeace T-shirt in the wardrobe, although she had no idea what the slogan meant.

'So what's the plan?'

'Head to the Tantalus Spiral,' said the Doctor. 'The

Time Lord fleet is going to have to get close if they intend to deploy the Tear. That's where we'll find them.'

'And then?' said Cinder.

'And then we make it up as we go along,' he replied. 'Hold on!'

She did as he said, grabbing hold of the edge of the console as he stirred the TARDIS back to life. The engines roared as they plunged toward the Tantalus Spiral. Towards the place she had once called home.

The Doctor had left the ceiling de-opaqued, and Cinder watched as the swirling mists of the Time Vortex shifted suddenly, giving way to a crisp star field.

'Now, we just have to hope we don't attract the attention of any Dal—' The Doctor stopped short, as the TARDIS shuddered, as if caught by a glancing blow.

'What was that?' said Cinder.

The Doctor grabbed a knob on the console and twisted it in a circle, causing the view through the canopy to slide dizzyingly, offering them an alternative perspective of local space. Five white Battle TARDISes, similar to the ones they had seen in the graveyard, but bristling with an array of brutal-looking armaments, had formed a ring around them.

'An ambush,' said the Doctor, grimly. 'They were waiting for us, the moment we materialised. There must have been another tracking device.' He looked at Cinder. 'Of course!' he said, dashing the heel of his palm against his forehead. 'I should have seen it.'

'Seen what?' said Cinder, eyeing the array of

TARDISes on the screen.

'You! It's you!'

Cinder stepped back, feeling uncertain. 'What? What have I done?'

The Doctor shook his head. 'No, they must have planted the tracker on you during that business with the mind probe.'

Cinder wasn't sure 'that business' adequately described the torturous episode to which she'd been subjected by Karlax and the Castellan. Nor did she like the implication that they were somehow still using her to get to the Doctor. She didn't have time to consider it, however, as a familiar voice crackled over the comm-link.

'Most perceptive of you, Doctor,' said the thin, reedy voice.

'Karlax,' spat the Doctor. 'I might have known. With a few friends from the CIA, no doubt?'

'Naturally,' replied Karlax. 'I must say, Doctor, we were all very impressed with the way in which you were able to give our guards the slip. I understand it's always been very difficult to keep you in a cell.'

The Doctor glanced at Cinder with an expression that said 'I told you so.'

'Still, it matters little,' continued Karlax. 'Commander Partheus will soon deliver the Tear of Isha to the Eye. You and your companion, alas, will be counted amongst the billions of the dead.'

On the monitor Cinder saw one of the Battle TARDISes extrude what looked like a torpedo chute. It was pointed directly at them. 'Doctor,' she said.

'I know.' He had his back to her.

'No, Doctor, I really think you need to—'

'I *know*,' he said, more forcefully.

'Then *do* something!'

There was a burst of light from the end of the torpedo chute as the other TARDIS fired. In response the Doctor fell against the controls, and the TARDIS dropped, plummeting straight down and leaving the five Battle TARDISes hanging in a neat circle.

The torpedo swam away into the void, trailing light. Moments later there was a flash as it detonated harmlessly in the vacuum. Above them, the ring of TARDISes stirred.

'Find something to hold on to,' said the Doctor. 'This is going to be a bit of a bumpy ride.'

There was a sudden jolt as the Doctor manipulated the controls and the TARDIS ceased its freefall and spun sideways, twisting in a corkscrew which left Cinder feeling as if her heart was in her mouth and her stomach was in her chest cavity. She closed her eyes, but it didn't make the spinning feel any better.

They flipped, dropping again – this time upside down – to avoid the trajectory of another torpedo. The Doctor yanked a lever and they lurched into a loop, climbing upwards in an effort to shake one of the Battle TARDISes that had fallen in behind them, riding hard on their tail.

'You know you're wasting your time,' said Karlax over the comm-link. 'Think about it. Isn't it better to go gracefully, with dignity, knowing that your time is up?'

'That sounds like you, Karlax,' replied the Doctor. 'Always willing to give up when things gets tough. If

I'm going, I'm going out fighting.'

'So be it,' said Karlax, cutting the connection.

The Battle TARDIS behind them was gaining on them. It was well within range to fire its weapons, but the Doctor was weaving from side to side, clearly making it difficult for them to get a lock.

'Fire!' bellowed Cinder.

'I can't!'

'What do you mean, you can't?' she called, incredulous.

'We don't have any weapons,' shouted the Doctor. The noise of the squealing engines was drowning everything else out.

'Why not?'

'The TARDIS, she doesn't like them,' replied the Doctor. He was hanging on to the console with both hands, but leaning back, as if trying to physically pull the ship in a different direction.

'Doesn't *like* them!' Cinder would have put her head in her hands if she hadn't been hanging on for her life. 'What can I do?' she called. 'Tell me!'

'Just hold on,' said the Doctor. 'I'm going to attempt to dematerialise and get away, buy us a little time.' He jerked the controls, just as the trailing TARDIS set loose another torpedo.

This time the Doctor didn't have chance to slide out of the way, and the thin, silver cylinder slammed into the side of the police box, detonating in a halo of intense white light.

The console room shook, causing Cinder to drop to one knee, and then suddenly, everything stopped. The engines sighed, the lights dimmed, and she could tell from the vibration of the floor plates and the view through the ceiling that they'd come to an immediate and complete stop.

'What was that?' she said.

The Doctor banged his fist against the console. 'Time torpedo. We're temporarily frozen in a stasis bubble. We can't move.'

'Perfect,' said Cinder. 'I wish I'd stayed in bed.'

As they watched, one of the Battle TARDISes slid into view, drawing closer with the clear intent to board them. 'This'll be Karlax,' said the Doctor. 'Wanting to crow.'

'Can't we stop him coming aboard,' she asked.

'We can try,' said the Doctor.

Cinder sensed movement out of the corner of her eye, and a split second later the Battle TARDIS bloomed, detonating suddenly, as if struck by a shot from behind. The console room shook with the aftershock of the blast. She couldn't see anything, any sign of what had caused the explosion, as she hurriedly searched the view.

The ruined TARDIS seemed to unpack in space before her eyes, its interior unfolding like the ones she had seen at the graveyard, swelling until it filled their entire view. Objects drifted away into the vacuum: broken monitors, spacesuits, chairs.

The Doctor wiggled the knob on the console and the view shifted. A formation of sleek, black vessels had engaged the four remaining TARDISes, and the two sides were pitched in battle, trading shots as they circled each another in a fast and violent dance.

The black ships seemed to have come out of

nowhere. 'What are they?' asked Cinder.

'Dalek stealth ships,' said the Doctor. 'They don't show up on any Time Lord monitoring systems. They lie in wait in the Time Vortex like hunters stalking prey, then strike at the most opportune moment.'

One of the TARDISes appeared to land a missile on the flank of one of the stealth ships, and it detonated in a shimmering burst, rolling over the black carapace of the vessel. The TARDIS tried to capitalise on its strike, swinging around for a second shot, but another of the Dalek vessels swept past, unleashing a volley of super-charged energy, which shredded the TARDIS, annihilating it in a matter of seconds.

'We're sitting ducks, here,' said Cinder, with rising panic. 'Can't you do something?'

The Doctor shook his head. 'We have to hope that they're happy to deal with the moving targets first,' he said, although she noticed his hands had not strayed far from the controls.

One of the stealth ships erupted in a ball of flame, caught in a volley between two of the remaining Battle TARDISes, but it was never going to be enough. There were simply too many of the Dalek ships. Cinder hadn't been able to count them, but the number was in double figures, more than twice those of the Time Lords. They were outclassed in every respect.

Almost simultaneously, she watched the remaining TARDISes die, their interior dimensions suddenly, dramatically exposed.

Cinder's palms were sweating. She knew what was coming next. The stealth ships would converge on the Doctor's TARDIS, and in a moment, it too would be reduced to nothing but a bloated carcass, drifting in the void.

She watched one of the Dalek ships glide overhead. The Doctor flicked a switch on the console and the engine hissed to life.

'I thought you said we were frozen in a temporal bubble,' she cried.

The Doctor shrugged. 'I'm not falling for that old chestnut again,' he said. 'I upgraded the shielding.'

'Then… you were just stalling for time?'

'Precisely,' said the Doctor, slamming his fist into the controls. The TARDIS corkscrewed up at an incredible velocity, slamming into the underside of the stealth ship.

The Doctor's aim hadn't been quite true, and they caught the side of it, rending a massive hole as they burst through. On the monitor she saw the other ship spin out of control, a twisted mass of tortured metal. Jets of gas billowed into the void, freezing instantly to form drifting clouds of ice.

'Quickly! Get us out of here,' bellowed Cinder. 'Dematerialise. There are too many of them.'

The Doctor tapped the monitor with his index finger. 'There's someone still alive down there.'

She moved round, still holding the railing. On the monitor she could see the carcass of one of the devastated TARDISes. A tiny figure writhed in agony in the ruins of a console room.

'Surely you can't be thinking…'

'Oh, but I am,' replied the Doctor. He yanked a lever and the TARDIS dematerialised for the briefest of seconds, forming again amongst the wreckage of the downed Battle TARDIS. Stealth ships were closing in from all directions.

Cinder tried to make sense of what was happening. Suddenly, there was wreckage all over the floor: bits of broken coral pillar, fragments of a dark grey wall, half a shattered console, still fizzing and popping as the electrics discharged. Amongst them all, nestled in a pit of cables, lay a Time Lord.

He was dressed in scarlet robes and skullcap, and was clutching at his throat with both hands, struggling to breathe. Bright blood bubbled from his eyes, nose, and lips, dribbling down his chin. His flesh was burnt and blistered, but his features were unmistakable. 'It's Karlax,' she said.

'Make him comfortable,' said the Doctor.

'But I—' she started.

'Just do it!' he bellowed, cutting her off.

The TARDIS trembled as they pirouetted out of the way of another Dalek volley. 'Damn it!' said the Doctor. He mashed the controls and the engines whined, phasing them into the Vortex. 'Damn it!' he said again.

Cinder was on her knees, cradling Karlax's head in her hands. He was in a bad way. His breath was coming in short, wheezing gulps. Exposure to the vacuum had almost killed him, and even now, she wasn't sure he was going to make it. His skin had taken on a strange glow, which seemed to fade in and out, as if the light was somehow shifting about beneath the surface of his flesh.

She had no idea what to do. She didn't even know if Time Lords had the same physiology as humans.

Cinder sensed the Doctor over her shoulder. 'The Daleks?' she said, without looking round.

'They won't find us here,' replied the Doctor. He crouched down beside her, putting a hand to Karlax's throat, feeling for a pulse. 'We're too late,' he said. 'He's already started to regenerate.'

Karlax coughed, and a gout of thick, dark blood spilled from his mouth, dribbling onto his robes.

'Help me with him,' said the Doctor. He slid his hands beneath Karlax's arms and hauled him into a sitting position, instigating an explosive round of coughing. 'Take his feet.'

Cinder did as the Doctor asked, and they hauled him up, shuffling awkwardly towards the steps. Karlax was limp and heavier than he looked. 'Where are we taking him? A medical room?'

'No,' said the Doctor. 'The Zero Room.'

'The Zero Room?' asked Cinder, breathless, as she struggled to keep Karlax's hindquarters from banging against the floor. The Doctor mounted the steps backwards, lifting Karlax's head and shoulders higher.

'A place where he can regenerate in peace,' said the Doctor, 'and perhaps more importantly, where he'll be out of the way. It has a lockable door.'

'Why are you helping him?' said Cinder. 'After everything? He was trying to kill us. He doesn't deserve our help. We should have left him to die.'

'When we first met, back on Moldox,' said the Doctor, 'do you remember what you were doing?'

Cinder frowned. 'Fighting Daleks,' she said.

'No, after that, when I arrived.'

'I didn't know whether to trust you,' she said. 'I threatened you with my gun.'

'Precisely,' said the Doctor. 'And I didn't leave you to die.'

Cinder sighed. 'You're not seriously telling me he's misunderstood? Doctor, he *actually* tried to kill us.'

'Be that as it may, Cinder – everyone deserves a second chance. And Karlax here is about to get an entirely new perspective.' They'd reached the top of the steps, and the Doctor led them along a passageway to a door. He kicked it open, and they carried Karlax inside.

The room was empty, devoid of any furniture. The walls were covered in the same glowing roundels that decorated the console room. 'Just set him down here,' said the Doctor. They laid him out on the floor. Disconcertingly, his pale skin was now glowing even more intensely than before, his hands and his face.

'Is that the regeneration?' said Cinder.

'Yes, it's coming,' said the Doctor. 'We'd better leave him to it.' He ushered her out of the door, producing a key unexpectedly from his trouser pocket and locking the door behind them. 'There,' he said. 'That'll keep him busy for a while. Now, where were we?'

'About to prevent a Time Lord flotilla from committing genocide,' said Cinder.

'Ah, yes!' said the Doctor, as if she'd just reminded him where he'd left his reading glasses. 'Better get back to it!'

Chapter Eighteen

Cinder whistled as she stood beside the Doctor, peering at the display on the monitor. 'That's a *lot* of TARDISes,' she said.

They'd emerged from the Vortex on the outer limits of the Tantalus Spiral, and the image on the screen was magnified to provide them with a view of the massive Time Lord flotilla that was crawling steadily towards the Eye.

The scale of it was simply too much for Cinder to comprehend. How many ships were there? Five hundred, a thousand – it was impossible to tell, but they filled space on the monitor like a flock of gulls, determinedly following their leader.

On the edges of the vast formation flitted Dalek saucers in squadrons of five or ten, darting in and out, picking off the occasional TARDIS but failing to make any significant dent in the armada. She watched as a handful of TARDISes broke free of their formation, darting away to engage the enemy vessels.

'It looks as though they've decided brute force is the answer,' she said. 'They're just going to wade on in there, aren't they? Right up to the Eye, with a complete disregard for how many of them will fail to make it back.'

'They're soldiers,' said the Doctor, as if that in itself was enough of an explanation.

'I hesitate to ask this,' she said, 'but how the hell are we going to stop them? I mean – we don't even have any weapons, except an old Dalek neutraliser and a single temporal cannon.'

The Doctor was leaning forward, peering closely at the monitor, his nose almost touching the screen. 'That one there,' he said. He tapped the screen with his fingernail, and in doing so, utterly obscuring the object from view. 'That's Partheus's TARDIS. I'd wager that's where we'll find the Tear. He wouldn't trust it to anyone else.'

He leaned back. The TARDIS he'd been pointing to was surrounded by a cluster of at least twenty other Battle TARDISes, each of them heavily armed. 'We're not going to get anywhere near it!' said Cinder.

The Doctor tapped at the controls and the image on the screen switched to a series of scrolling icons. He studied them intently for a moment. 'We're not going to get near it,' said the Doctor. 'We're going to get *in* it.'

Commander Partheus stood on the bridge of his

TARDIS, surveying his route to the Eye. He'd de-opaqued the walls and the ceiling, so that he had the impression he was standing on a large grey platform, drifting through the void.

Around him the other TARDISes flocked, holding their battle formation, while further afield the halo of a raging firefight showed where the ships on his left flank were holding the enemy at bay. Ahead, the Tantalus Eye itself seemed to glare angrily at him, warning him not to proceed.

This far into the Spiral, the radiation from the Eye was affecting the flight systems of their TARDISes, meaning they were unable to simply dip in and out of the Time Vortex, and had to make their final approach in real space. It left Partheus feeling exposed and uneasy, and vulnerable to attack.

He glanced at each of the three men stationed at the consoles. 'How is it looking?' he said.

'We have a clear path, Commander,' replied one of the men, his lieutenant. 'Another few light years and we'll be within range to deploy.'

'Excellent,' said Partheus. 'Hold the line.'

More and more Daleks were streaming out of the Vortex, stealth ships and saucers both, and around them, the battle raged.

Partheus's TARDIS, however, nestled at the heart of a defensive huddle, and remained unmolested. He stroked his beard, willing the ship on.

He was just about to put a call out to for a report from the other ships, when the sound of a shrill klaxon drowned out his thoughts. 'What the devil?' he bellowed. 'Report, now!'

His lieutenant turned, his expression panicked. 'I don't know, Commander. It says we have an incoming.'

'An incoming *what*?' boomed Partheus. 'A missile?'

'No,' replied the lieutenant. 'A time ship.'

To Partheus's right the air seemed to shimmer, as the interloper attempted to materialise, its appearance accompanied by a deep, wheezing groan. Partheus fumbled for his pistol.

'It's a TARDIS, Commander,' said one of the other men. Partheus couldn't remember his name. He had trouble remembering *any* of their names. They never survived for long enough to make it worthwhile.

'A TARDIS? But that's insane! He'll tear us both apart. Annihilate us.' The other ship was clearly struggling to get a lock, stuttering as it tried to emerge from the Time Vortex. 'Can't you stop it?' he barked.

'I'm trying, Commander,' called the lieutenant. 'The shields are set to maximum power.'

There was a sudden, clanging chime, and a tall blue cabinet marked 'POLICE BOX' was standing in Partheus's console room.

'Too late,' he said, his voice full of ire. 'They're here.'

'This is it, then,' said Cinder.

'This is it,' replied the Doctor, heading for the door. He stopped and looked back. His expression was stern. 'Bring your gun,' he said, 'but under no circumstances are you to actually use it.'

Cinder swept it up from the floor as she trotted after him.

Her first thought, when she emerged from the TARDIS, was that something had gone horribly, inexplicably wrong, and that instead of landing inside the other TARDIS as the Doctor had intended, they were drifting in the open vacuum of space.

Panicked, she glanced from left to right, searching for a way to take cover, but all she could see was the open vista of space and the raging inferno of the battle between the Time Lords and the Daleks.

She gasped, and then realised she was still breathing, and that gravity of some description was still holding her to the floor. They *were* inside a TARDIS.

After the initial shock, her mind began to process the rest of what was going on. They were standing in the console room of the other vessel, but it was so fundamentally different to the Doctor's that at first it hadn't registered. There were three squat, hexagonal consoles, dark grey in colour and seemingly identical in appearance. Unlike the Doctor's they were not covered in all manner of makeshift levers and contraptions, and looked smooth and manufactured, rather than organic. Boring, was the word for it, thought Cinder.

The room itself was cavernous, bigger than the Doctor's by a magnitude of three or four times. The walls and ceiling had been rendered transparent so that Commander Partheus might better see how his fleet was faring against the Daleks.

There were three male Time Lords, one in attendance at each of the consoles. They were dressed in the same red and white uniform as the Castellan's guards at the Capitol.

Commander Partheus himself stood on a raised

platform, glowering at them. He was clutching a pistol in his left hand. He was a tall, portly fellow, with a bushy black beard. He was wearing black robes with a red skullcap. 'You!' he said. His voice was thunderous. 'What do you think you're doing? That little trick of yours might have resulted in a Time Ram, annihilating us both.'

The Doctor shrugged. 'Come now, Partheus. Do you really think I'd be that reckless?' He beamed.

Partheus offered the Doctor a look of sheer disbelief. 'I think you're the only one who might,' he said. 'I thought you were in a cell on Gallifrey?'

'So did Rassilon,' said the Doctor, 'but even the Lord President can't get his way all the time.'

Partheus raised his pistol. 'I'm sorry, Doctor. I don't want to do this, but you're putting me in a terrible position.'

'Not as terrible a position as those you're about to murder,' replied the Doctor.

'If you try anything…' continued Partheus.

Cinder coughed. 'I don't think so,' she said, waving her gun from her hip.

The three other men were looking decidedly uncomfortable, but remained where they were standing by their consoles. The Doctor walked to the first of these, glanced at the controls, and then shook his head. He walked around the man and over to the next console, repeating the procedure. Evidently he saw what he wanted there, as he reached over and began pressing buttons.

The other man, whom Cinder guessed was a pilot, looked outraged. 'What are you doing?'

'Setting a new course,' said the Doctor. 'This is, after all, a hijack.'

'But you can't!' The man turned, trying to intercept the Doctor.

'Step away,' said the Doctor. 'This doesn't concern you.'

The man continued to try to push the Doctor out of the way.

'Believe me when I say that I'm truly sorry for this,' said the Doctor resignedly.

'Wha—'

He turned and delivered a smart right hook, which connected with the man's jaw and dropped him to the floor in an unconscious heap. The Doctor shook his hand and wiggled his fingers, pulling a pained expression. 'Oh, I really don't like that bit,' he said. 'I wish people would just *listen*.'

He ducked suddenly, dodging to the right, as a bolt of energy fizzed past his left hand, burning a dark, smouldering depression into the console. Cinder turned to see Partheus holding his weapon outstretched. 'A warning shot, Doctor,' he said. 'To let you know that I'm serious.'

The Doctor crossed to Partheus and snatched the pistol from his grip, tossing it away so that it clattered to the floor near the foot of his own TARDIS.

'I'm trying to help you, Partheus. Believe me – this is a burden you don't want to live with.'

'In the corner,' Cinder said to the other two, waving her gun, but keeping Partheus covered.

'Don't worry,' said the Doctor. 'This isn't going to take very long. Just a short glimpse into the future.' He began turning dials and manipulating the controls, his fingers dancing over the keys. Cinder heard the distant groan of the engines responding to his ministrations. It was a different sound entirely to that made by the Doctor's TARDIS – more of a subtle burr than an elephantine roar.

'Well, I can't say I think much of your TARDIS, Partheus,' said the Doctor. 'It lacks… character.'

'You'll pay for this with your life, Doctor,' said Partheus. 'You know that, don't you?'

The Doctor shrugged. He didn't even turn to look at the man. 'My life in exchange for billions of others,' he said. 'Not bad odds, I suppose. I've lived long enough.' He glanced over his shoulder at the Commander. 'Have you even considered what it is you're about to do?'

'Don't patronise me,' snapped Partheus. 'Of course I'm aware of the gravity of the situation. As I see it, though, we have little choice. The Daleks must be stopped.'

'There's more than one way to skin a cat,' said the Doctor. He pulled a face, looking at Cinder. 'I've never liked that expression. Why would anyone want to do *that*?'

He was in his element again, Cinder realised. She could see it in the child-like gleam in his eyes. He was enjoying himself. She wondered if this was what he would be like all of the time, if it weren't for the weight of the War bearing down on him. Being around him when he was like this – she couldn't help but smile.

The view all around them had altered. No longer were they anywhere in the vicinity of the Tantalus

Eye, or the fleet of Battle TARDISes, locked in combat with enemy saucers.

Here, they hung alone in the void. Around them the darkness was all-consuming, with only a handful of stars still twinkling in the still night of space. All except for the massive, swollen carcass of a red giant, a dying sun, which filled the forward view screen. The core of the star burned gently; a dying flame in the last embers of a fire that had burned for millennia. The outer envelope was pale and thin, near transparent.

'Where have you brought us?' asked Cinder.

'To the end of the universe,' said Partheus, 'to the last, lingering moments before the final stars wink out and the universe contracts.'

'I see you have at least some poetry in your soul,' said the Doctor. 'Perhaps you're not irredeemable, after all.'

'I can't let you do this, Doctor,' said Partheus. 'The Tear is our last hope.'

'We'll find a way,' said the Doctor. 'It's not over. It *cannot* come down to this.' He moved to one of the other consoles and tapped in a sequence. 'There. The Tear is primed.'

'You're going to shoot it into the heart of that star?' said Cinder.

The Doctor nodded.

With a sudden roar, Partheus launched himself from the platform toward the Doctor. Cinder fought the urge to squeeze the trigger of her gun. The Doctor had, after all, told her not to fire it under any circumstances, and if she did, she risked hitting the Doctor. All the same, she kept it trained on Partheus as he collided with the Doctor at the console.

Both men fell forward across the controls and the TARDIS listed to the right in response.

'Get away from the controls!' Partheus bellowed. He grabbed the Doctor around the waist and hauled him bodily away from the console. With immense strength, he tossed the Doctor onto the floor, where he landed on his backside, wearing an outraged expression.

He scrambled to his feet and without missing a beat, charged at Partheus, his head down and to one side, taking the other Time Lord in the chest with his shoulder and sending them both barrelling over in the other direction. Partheus pounded at the Doctor's back with his fists, and the Doctor rolled off him, struggling free.

Cinder glanced up at the two other Time Lords, who were still cowering in the corner. She showed them her gun, just to remind them to keep out of it.

The Doctor sprung to his feet while Partheus was still struggling to shift his considerable bulk from the floor.

'Look, Partheus. This is all terribly unseemly. Why don't we ju—' The Doctor stopped short as Partheus kicked out at his ankles, taking his feet out from under him. He went down again, barely avoiding smashing his head on the edge of the console. He groaned as he rolled into a sitting position.

Cinder had had enough. She stormed forward. 'Which button is it?'

'The red one,' gasped the Doctor.

Cinder shrugged. She supposed that should have

been obvious, really. She slammed her fist against the button.

'You *stupid* girl!' roared Partheus. Both men were getting to their feet, dusting themselves down.

There was a mechanical *clunk* from beneath their feet, followed by a series of sounds like clamps being released. Partheus lurched to the console, jabbing at the buttons. 'It's too late. The sequence has been initiated. The Tear is being deployed.'

There was a rumble of ignition and then, as they watched, a rocket blazed silently, seemingly from beneath their feet, towards the heart of the Red Giant.

The rocket was small and Cinder couldn't help thinking that what had been described to her as such a devastating weapon, was, in fact, somewhat anticlimactic. Perhaps, like a TARDIS, the Time Lord weapon was bigger on the inside.

All of them stood in stunned silence, waiting to see what would happen when the Tear fell into the star and began to unpack itself.

'I'd suggest we make a strategic withdrawal,' said the Doctor.

Partheus, still standing by the controls, tapped out a series of commands and the TARDIS began to slowly back away from the star.

The rocket was now a tiny speck, barely visible against the bloated aurora of the celestial giant.

'Nothing's happening,' said Partheus.

'Keep watching,' said the Doctor, and a second later Cinder noticed the slight hint of a shadow at the centre of the star. As she watched, it began to grow steadily in size, swelling like an oil spill. The black stain continued to spread, gaining momentum, drawing in and consuming the faint red light from the outer rim of the star.

'It's collapsing the star,' said the Doctor, 'dragging it all towards a gravitational singularity.'

'You're a fool, Doctor,' said Partheus. 'You've thrown away the best chance we had of defeating the Dalek threat.' He'd stopped, and was helping his lieutenant up from the floor as the man had blearily started to come round. 'They'll make you pay for this.'

'I don't doubt it,' said the Doctor levelly. 'But that doesn't make me wrong.'

The last of the red light had now faded to black, and the collapsing star was now beginning to drag at the surrounding matter. The floor of the TARDIS began to vibrate as the engines fought against the pull.

'Time to go,' said the Doctor.

Partheus had retrieved his pistol and was pointing it at the Doctor. 'I should kill you now,' he said, 'for all the lives you've just condemned.'

The Doctor met his gaze, his eyes challenging. 'Well, then,' he said. 'Do it if you're going to. I've just prevented you from becoming a murderer, but if you're that set on the idea…'

Partheus's resolved seemed to falter. The end of the weapon dipped. 'Go,' he said. 'Get off my ship.'

Wordlessly, the Doctor turned his back and walked toward his own TARDIS. Cinder followed, keeping her weapon trained on Partheus, but she could tell the fight had gone out of him.

The Doctor unlocked the TARDIS door and they both stepped over the threshold.

Cinder breathed a sigh of relief, dropping her gun, as the door closed behind them. 'We did it,' she said. 'We really did it.'

The Doctor smiled. 'Yes, I suppose we did. But I'm afraid our problems aren't over yet. There's still the Daleks to deal with, not to mention a bunch of furious Time Lords, baying for my blood.'

'What are you going to do about it?' said Cinder.

'There's only one thing *to* do,' said the Doctor. 'We're going back to Gallifrey.'

'What!' said Cinder. 'You really *are* insane.'

The Doctor laughed. 'I like to think so.'

Chapter Nineteen

The TARDIS materialised on a bluff above a desolate, wild landscape.

After a moment, the door opened and Cinder emerged, bracing herself against the sharp bite of the wind. Her hair whipped up into her face, her eyes streamed, and she found herself wrapping her arms around her body, trying to retain the warmth.

She heard the Doctor close the TARDIS door behind her and looked round to see him standing there, surveying the moorland below them. As far as the eye could see, fields of straw-like grass and heather, punctuated by the occasional clump of trees, dominated the view. The sky was a crisp, pale blue, shot through with wisps of cloud.

'I thought you said we were going back to Gallifrey?' she said.

'Ah,' replied the Doctor. 'Yes, I should explain.'

Cinder raised an expectant eyebrow, putting her hands on her hips. 'Well?'

'This *is* Gallifrey,' he said. 'At least, in a sense. It's a small pocket of Gallifreyan wilderness, cordoned off in a temporal bubble. The Time Lords know it affectionately as the Death Zone.' He grinned. 'Pretty inhospitable place, really,' he said.

'Wonderful,' said Cinder. 'The Death Zone.' She stamped her feet, feeling exposed up there in the hillside. 'Remind me why we're here again?'

'The Death Zone used to be the place where unlucky participants were co-opted to play the Game of Rassilon, pitted in a life or death battle against a variety of alien species, forcibly scooped from their natural habitats,' said the Doctor, ignoring her question.

'And here's me thinking the Time Lords were the good guys,' said Cinder sarcastically.

'It was a long time ago, back in the first Age of Rassilon. He built his tomb here.' The Doctor turned on the spot, pointing to a black spire in the distance, jutting from the earth at the foot of a mountain. 'There,' he said. 'The Dark Tower.'

'His tomb?' said Cinder. 'But he's not dead. I met him. As much as I wish I hadn't.'

'It's complicated,' said the Doctor. 'Rassilon is essentially immortal. In ancient times he gave up corporeal form, and for millennia resided here in his tomb, worshipped as a once-and-future king. He was resurrected back in the early days of the War, however, when the Time Lords realised they needed a different sort of leader.'

'I can see it's done them the world of good,' said Cinder.

'Quite,' replied the Doctor. He looked downcast.

'You still haven't answered my question?' she said.

'What question?'

'Why we're here?'

'We're here to commit a jailbreak,' said the Doctor. 'Rassilon has… someone trapped in the Tower. Someone whose help we need. His name is Borusa. We're going to help him to escape.'

'Couldn't you have parked us a bit closer?' said Cinder, blowing into her cupped hands.

The Doctor shook his head. 'That's the problem with the Death Zone. Unless you have access to the transmat device in the chambers of the High Council, you have to make the trek through the wilderness to get anywhere close to the Tower. It's a hangover from the games, but it also serves as excellent protection for Rassilon and whatever he wants to get up to in his old tomb.'

Cinder nodded. 'Well, let's see if we can climb down over there,' she said, walking to the other edge of the bluff and looking down. When she saw what was at the foot of the bluff, she emitted a sound that was somewhere between a scream and a terrified squeal.

'What is it?' called the Doctor, running to her side.

'*That*,' she said, pointing the thing at the base of the hill. A massive, lizard-like creature was lounging in the heather, merrily chewing on the local flora. It was at least twenty metres long, with four stumpy, elephantine legs and a long snaking neck. Its hide was green and its back was adorned in scales of thick, chitinous armour. The head was small, with black, beady eyes and a jaw full of sharp, serrated teeth. Its tail swished nonchalantly from side to side, tearing up the undergrowth. 'What is it?'

'A primitive beast,' said the Doctor, 'from Gallifrey's dim and distant past. The Time Lords stopped scooping up unwary aliens many years ago, but it clearly hasn't prevented them from interfering with their own past. This is a creature out of time, a long-extinct species from before the Time Lords ever walked the planet.'

Cinder looked at the giant lizard, which was still chomping sedately on the bushy leaves of a fallen tree. 'As long as he doesn't have any bigger, carnivorous siblings,' she said.

'Ah…' said the Doctor again.

Cinder rounded on him. 'Seriously?' she said.

'You shouldn't trouble yourself unduly,' he replied. 'They're big enough that we'd see them coming in plenty of time. It's the carnivorous ants that you need to watch out for. Now *they* really can give you a nasty bite.'

Cinder glanced at her boots, nestling amongst the heather, and immediately began to scratch at her legs. The Doctor laughed, and she turned and hit him crossly on the arm. 'You're incorrigible,' she said, allowing a smile to creep onto her face. After everything, a little levity was precisely what she needed.

*

'So, what's so special about this Borusa character? How is he going to be able to help us against the Daleks?'

The Doctor looked sheepish. 'Borusa can see the future,' he said, 'and the past. The web of all-time. Each and every possibility, how they interrelate, how every decision causes a fracture in the universe, opening up new pathways through time. The Time Vortex flows through his mind. Rassilon uses Borusa to navigate the timelines, to discern the most effective course of action for their offensives against the Daleks.'

'Was he born that way?' said Cinder.

They were trudging across an empty field, her boots catching in the long grass with every step. The occasional gust threatened to tip them over, but so far there had been no signs of any carnivorous beast and, thankfully, no ants.

'No,' said the Doctor. 'He was made that way. His timeline was retro-engineered. He was forged by Rassilon in an attempt to find a solution to ending the War.'

Cinder didn't quite understand the implications of this, so kept her own counsel. How do you retro-engineer a person? Time, she supposed, would tell. 'So, this friend of yours, he's going to tell us how to defeat the Daleks?'

'In a manner of speaking,' said the Doctor. 'We're going to take him into the Tantalus Eye. He's going to help us change the future.'

'Right,' said Cinder, 'of course. Into the Eye. That makes *loads* of sense.' She glanced up at the Tower, looming in the distance.

From somewhere close by there was a sound like a foghorn – the trumpet of a massive, forlorn beast. Cinder's eyes widened in panic.

'Don't worry,' said the Doctor. 'It's just another of the friendly ones, a herbivore like the one we saw before, calling to its kin.'

Cinder breathed a sigh of relief. 'Why would it be doing that?' said Cinder. 'A mating call?'

The Doctor shook his head. 'No,' he said, with a shrug. 'Probably more of a warni—' He stopped short, glancing at Cinder, realisation in his eyes. 'Ah. I suppose it was rather close, wasn't it?'

There was a thunderous roar that seemed to shake the earth beneath their feet. Cinder felt her legs tremble. The hairs on the back of her neck prickled.

From behind them came the *clomp* of a tremendous footstep, followed by another, then another, increasing in pace. Cinder swallowed, rooted to the spot. The expression on the Doctor's face was one of startled surprise.

Slowly, she turned her head.

The creature was like something born out of a child's nightmare. It was titanic, twice the size of a hab-bloc back on Moldox, and even more ugly to look at. It stood upright on two stocky hind legs, with a short, fat tail dragging along the ground for balance. Where she might have expected two front legs to protrude from either side of its chest the beast had wings – short, flightless wings, covered in downy feathers of purple and white. Its massive head was mostly teeth, contained in a yawning chasm of a mouth. Above this, a row of four beady eyes blinked in rapid succession. Presently, all four of them were fixed on Cinder and the Doctor as it came charging across the field towards them.

'I thought you said we'd see it coming in plenty of time,' said Cinder.

The Doctor shrugged. 'I was trying to make you feel better,' he said. He grabbed her by the arm. 'See those rocky cliffs over there?'

Cinder nodded.

'Run!'

Cinder ran for all she was worth. Her thigh muscles burned as she plunged across the uneven earth towards the cliff face. She was strides ahead of the Doctor, who, despite his surprising agility, was simply unable to keep up.

The lolloping beast charged after them, its bizarre, flightless wings flapping excitedly as it ran. Strands of drool dripped from its terrifying jaws.

Cinder's foot caught in a root or an uneven clump of grass and she went over, throwing her hands out and slamming into the hard, dry loam and jarring her wrist. She immediately broke into a roll, refusing to allow it to halt her momentum, and in one lithe movement sprang back up onto her feet and continued her frantic dash for cover.

Behind her the beast roared, a primal, rumbling cry that hit her like a punch in the belly. Any number of times in the past she'd heard the sound of a gunshot or an exploding mine described as 'deafening', and she'd never really given much thought to what a deafening sound might actually be. The noise that came out of the beast, however, was – quite literally – that. It left her ears ringing, as if someone had just stuffed balls of cotton wool in them, and drowned out the world.

Everything felt hyper-real, dream-like. Was she really running across a field on a distant planet, pursued by a carnivorous creature analogous to a dinosaur?

The cliff face was coming up at her, black and slab-like, a wall across the world. She realised with horror that she had no idea what she was supposed to do when she got there. She was effectively running toward a dead end. The creature would have them pinned against the wall with nowhere to go.

'Doctor!' she wailed, knowing full well that she'd be unable to hear his response.

The creature's footsteps were getting closer, physically bouncing her into the air with every thunderous step. Her hearing was beginning to return in a series of stuttering, disorienting episodes. She began to slow.

She reached the very foot of the craggy mountainside, glancing from left to right. All she could see was a lone boulder, sitting amongst a heap of loose rocks. Had the Doctor intended for them to take cover behind that?

She felt him suddenly grab at her wrist and, surprised, allowed him to pull her away, running parallel to the wall. The creature tried to slow its pace and, unable to halt its momentum, skidded sideways into the rock face.

Cinder glanced over her shoulder as she ran and saw that it had not been dissuaded, however, as it continued to stagger after them, swaying its head from side to side.

'In here!' called the Doctor, pointing to a narrow fissure in the rock. 'Get inside!'

'In *there?*' cried Cinder.

'Just do it!' bellowed the Doctor, releasing his grip on her arm and shoving her in the direction of the large crack. She ran towards it, turning sideways so that she could wriggle through, hoping that it would widen out once she was inside to create a space in which they could shelter until the monster had gone.

The rocks were jagged and scratched painfully at her back and hands as she forced her way in. Through the narrow opening she could see the Doctor, backing up towards her, waving his sonic screwdriver at the creature. It didn't appear to be having any effect. 'Doctor!' she shouted.

'I'll be right there,' he called over his shoulder.

He disappeared from view for a moment, and then he was at the entrance, forcing his way in after her.

The creature roared again, butting its head against the cliff face, as if trying to smash its way through to get at them. Snorting, it lowered its head to the crevice, peering in with its multiple, winking eyes. It could see them squirming into the crack in the rock, and it wasn't happy. It snorted again, sending gobbets of spittle deep into the crevice, spattering Cinder's face and hair. She made a disgusted sound as she tried to wipe it away, and succeeded only in smearing it across her cheek. It growled at them, and the backwash of its breath was hot and rank with the stench of rotten meat.

'We'll be safe here,' said the Doctor. 'We can wait

here until it's gone.' He put a reassuring hand on her shoulder. She glanced at him. He was standing at least a metre away, still trying to negotiate his way into the cave, his shoulders heaving with every breath. So whose was the hand…?

Cinder twisted frantically, catching her other shoulder on a sharp outcrop of rock and screaming in frightened surprise at the man standing behind her. A man whom she was not entirely sure was a man at all.

He appeared to be dressed in roughly woven linen robes, and was thin and pale-skinned. His face, however, was almost impossible to focus upon. The features flickered and altered as she watched, as if one face was morphing into another, and then another, and then another, locked in a constant cycle of change. More, it seemed to glow with a soft amber light, as if impregnated with weird, flickering energy, similar to the manner in which Karlax's face had begun to glow, just before the Doctor had explained the Time Lord was about to regenerate.

This was different, however. It was like the man wasn't really there, like his features were ghostly and incorporeal, despite the face she could feel the weight of his hand on her shoulder. She couldn't read any expression on his faces. Everything was too fluid. She had no idea whether he meant her harm or not.

'It's all right,' said the Doctor from behind her. 'He won't hurt you.'

The newcomer withdrew his hand and inched back the way he had come, deeper into the cave. Now he had their attention, he soundlessly waved for them to follow.

'What is he?' whispered Cinder.

'He's a Time Lord,' said the Doctor, his voice heavy with sadness.

'A Time Lord?'

'Yes. Remember I told you about Borusa?'

Cinder nodded. 'Is that him?'

'No, that's not him, but that is what he's like now. This poor soul must have been one of Rassilon's earlier experiments, cast out into the Death Zone when the experiment failed.'

'What experiment? You're not making sense,' said Cinder.

'Rassilon, just like the Daleks, has been toying with Time Lord evolution, picking subjects and retro-evolving their personal timeline, tampering with their genetic make-up so that they evolve into something else. Into that.' The Doctor waved her on down the tunnel, urging her to follow the strange half-man.

'What's the matter with his face?' she said.

'Those are all of his past and future incarnations,' said the Doctor. 'The different faces he would have worn. They're trapped in a cycle of constant flux. He's neither one nor another of the people he could have been. He's locked in a state of constant metacrisis between faces, his mind exposed to the raw energy of the Time Vortex.'

Cinder didn't know what to say. It sounded awful, and she was still unsure if she could trust the strange Time Lord mutant, offering to lead her deeper into its cave. Her choices, however, appeared to be between him and the angry behemoth that was still pacing outside, hoping to eat her. She supposed it was no choice at all. She went after him, the Doctor following up behind.

Within a few metres the cavity widened, and the cloying sense of claustrophobia that had been threatening to overcome Cinder began to dissipate. She was able to turn and walk normally. In the distance, guided by the gentle glow of the half-man's flesh she could see that the crevice in the rock opened up into a fully fledged cave system, linked by a network of tunnels. It was like a warren, carved deep into the underside of the mountain.

As they wound their way deeper into the mountainside, Cinder caught the thick scent of wood smoke drifting through the tunnels, and wrinkled her nose. She realised this probably meant that the half-man was leading them to his camp, hidden in one of the nearby caves. Hopefully that meant there'd be a chance for her to take a short rest – her thigh muscles were killing her – although the idea of being trapped in a confined space with this strange individual didn't particularly appeal to her, despite the Doctor's reassurances.

She supposed he must have been living rough in here. Cast out into the wilderness of the Death Zone, he'd probably found this place while seeking shelter from the monsters, just as she and the Doctor had, and had taken up residence. Cinder would probably have done the same, she considered, if presented with a choice between a dank, dark cave system and the slavering jaws of a hungry dinosaur.

The smell of the fire grew steadily stronger, leading them on like a beacon. The passage through the caves forked and twisted, and she realised they must have passed deep under the mountain. They didn't appear to be travelling downward, however, so she assumed they had to be passing *through*, and that perhaps at some point it would become clear that there was another way out on the opposite side. She certainly hoped so – she didn't fancy their chances retracing all these steps without getting lost. And, of course, there was still the monster to consider.

They trudged on in silence for a short while, until, eventually, the crackling sound of the fire became audible above their echoing footsteps. The half-man rounded a bend, disappearing suddenly from view, and Cinder hesitated, hanging back in the passageway, unsure whether to go on. The Doctor put a hand on her shoulder and silently urged her on.

Around the kink in the tunnel she found a large, irregularly shaped cave. Two further passages ran off into the shadows, and a fire blazed in a shallow pit in the ground. The half-man was standing facing them, as if welcoming them to his home, and two further people sat on boulders by the fire, warming their hands. One was a woman, the other a younger man, and both of them shared the same condition – or affliction – as the first man. Their faces shifted in constant, flickering patterns, cycling disconcertingly through their lost incarnations.

The first man – the one who had led them here – beckoned for them to enter the cave and take a seat by the fire pit.

'Go on,' said the Doctor. When she hesitated again, he gently pushed past her, smiling at the two new figures, and circled the fire, searching out another boulder. He sat, stretching his neck and shoulder muscles.

Deciding she had nothing to lose, Cinder joined him, taking a seat beside him, while the half-man busied himself piling more logs onto the fire.

'Do you see the way the smoke is curling?' the Doctor said.

She watched for a moment, as the thick, oily smoke swirled from the fire, as if swirled by a breeze. 'There must be another way out,' she said, relieved. They'd clearly passed under the mountain and were close to an alternative route out. Closer to the Tower.

'Precisely,' said the Doctor. 'But let's sit for a while and get our breath back, shall we?'

Cinder eyed the curious, unspeaking Time Lords. She couldn't tell if they were watching her or not. 'Yes,' she said. 'Just not for too long.'

The Doctor nodded his understanding.

Cinder glanced around the cave. There was little here to mark it out as a home. A few straw mats and clay pots. No sign of any food. She wondered if these people even needed to eat, trapped as they were in a weird cycle of life and death.

She peered curiously at the wall. There appeared to be streaks of colour on the bare rock, but it was difficult to discern in the dim light. Was it lichen or mould?

'What's that?' she said, nudging the Doctor and pointing at the wall.

The Doctor followed her gaze. 'Oh... they're paintings,' he said, his eyes suddenly lighting up.

He got to his feet, started over toward the wall, and then came back, reaching for a stick from the fire. He selected one and yanked it out, hoisting it up before him like a torch. Cinder, getting to her feet, dodged out of the way of its flaming tip as he swung it around. He crossed to the wall, holding the torch aloft. 'They're marvellous,' he said. 'Utterly marvellous.'

She joined him, conscious of the three half-people, who remained seated impassively around the fire.

The paintings were primitive and clearly rendered by fingers daubed in vibrant pigments. They covered an entire wall of the cave, spilling onto another – a series of small, apparently self-contained scenes, each one representing a different story. They looked to Cinder like pictograms inside an ancient tomb, speaking to her across untold centuries. There was no indication how old they actually were.

She trailed behind the Doctor as he paced back and forth, holding the torch aloft. In the warm, orange glow, the pictures seemed to take on a life of their own, shifting beneath the flickering shadows. She barely knew where to look. There were so many of them. She traced one with her finger, trying to interpret what she was seeing.

In it, a figure that was clearly intended to be the Doctor, with a shock of grey hair and dark leather jacket, was standing beside a blonde woman in rags. A tall, red flower stood between them.

In another, five Daleks formed a loose circle around a sixth, larger Dalek silhouette.

A third showed a massive eye and a blue box which, Cinder realised, was intended to represent the

TARDIS in flight around the Tantalus Eye.

There were others, too: a thin figure with long, curly hair; a lanky man in a blue suit; a third with bouffant white hair and a cape being chased by a silver robot; a red-headed woman lying still on the ground beside what appeared to be the TARDIS console.

Cinder swallowed. She didn't want to even imagine what that one might mean. 'What are they? Who are these people?' she said.

'They're me,' replied the Doctor. He looked utterly bewitched by the primitive paintings, tracing them across the wall with his fingertips, moving the torch back and forth in order to see. He leaned closer, studying them intently. 'At least, I think they are. I don't recognise them all. Some of these things haven't happened yet. I might have changed faces.'

Cinder frowned. *Haven't happened yet.* Then if the woman in the picture *was* supposed to be her, that didn't bode well. She considered pointing it out to him, but decided against it. There was a risk that if she did, she might somehow make it real. Better to ignore it, she decided. 'Why are there paintings of you on a cave wall, out here, in the middle of nowhere?'

'They're painting what they see,' said the Doctor. 'And for some reason, they see me. Past, present and future. This is my story.'

'Then you shouldn't read it,' said Cinder. 'No one should know their own future.' She felt a shiver pass unbidden down her spine.

'No,' agreed the Doctor. 'You're right.' He didn't turn away, however, but continued to stand there, studying the pictures.

'Doctor?'

'Oh, all right,' he said, reluctantly stepping away from the wall. 'It's just so tempting to have a little peek, to see what my future selves might look like.'

'I'm not sure how much you're going to glean about that from cave paintings,' said Cinder, 'and suppose you saw something you shouldn't, like how you were going to die? What would you do then?'

He eyed her suspiciously. 'Nothing's fixed. No matter what I saw, if it hasn't happened yet, it can be changed.'

She breathed a sigh of relief. Well, that was good to know, at least. 'We should go,' she said. 'We'll need to get back from the Tower before it gets dark.'

The Doctor looked a little crestfallen; as if he'd much rather stay here in the cave, studying the paintings. 'Do you always have to be so sensible?' he said.

'I'm afraid so,' she replied. 'On Moldox you learn not to sit still. You've got to keep moving to stay ahead of the Daleks.'

'When this is done,' he said, 'I'm going to teach you about some of the finer things in life. Books, marshmallows, Earl Grey tea, the view from the banks of the Rhine, the ash oceans of Astragard, the pleasure of Cleopatra's court.'

'I'll hold you to that,' she said, with a grin. She glanced at the painting of the red-headed woman, and then cleared her throat. 'All the more reason to get on with finding this Borusa character. Come on!' She crossed to the passageway on the left, and felt a light breeze against her cheek. 'This way.'

A glance back over her shoulder told her that the Doctor and the three half-people were following her.

The Tower stood dark and foreboding ahead of them. Cinder felt an involuntary shudder run down her spine at the sight of it. 'It doesn't look much like a tomb,' she said to the Doctor, who was trudging along beside her. 'More like a fortress.'

'Mmmm, hmmm,' mumbled the Doctor, noncommittally.

Close by, the three half-people from the cave trailed behind them. Cinder kicked herself for continuing to think of them like that. Of course, these were *not* half-people. Interstitials? It would do for now.

She wished she knew how to communicate with them, whether they were able to understand her. She wasn't quite sure how to act around them.

The Doctor saw her looking. 'They want to help,' he said. 'They've foreseen all of this. They're prepared for the storm that's coming.'

Cinder nodded but said nothing, wondering what else they had foreseen. That was the real root of her discomfort. She didn't know if the Doctor had seen the painting on the cave wall of the red-haired girl, lying on the ground of what looked like the TARDIS console room. Was it Cinder, or some other flame-haired girl from the Doctor's future or past? The painting was too primitive to tell, but something about it troubled her. She couldn't get the image out of her head.

As they approached the Tower, she could see that burning braziers flanked the lofty entrance. She'd half expected the place to look abandoned, or to be in a state or ruin or disrepair, but the braziers showed it was clearly still inhabited.

'Stay back,' said the Doctor, waving her towards a nearby copse of trees. She skipped over to them, noting that the Interstitials had come to a stop, but remained where they were on the path in plain view, ignoring the Doctor. She had no idea if this was dumb obstinacy, or simply because they were already aware that there was nobody else inside the Tower.

The Doctor, however, was taking no such chances, and Cinder watched him creep towards the entrance. He hovered there for a moment, evidently listening for any noises from within, and then stepped through, disappearing from view.

A moment later he returned, waving both arms to indicate the all-clear.

Cinder and the Interstitials trotted up to join him.

'We need to work quickly,' said the Doctor as he led them into the dimly lit interior of the Tower. 'Rassilon could return at any moment, and that would make things exceedingly difficult.'

Cinder considered this for a moment. 'Oh, I don't know. One of him, two of us…' she said.

The Doctor shook his head. 'That gauntlet he wears? It has the same effect as the Dalek's temporal weapons, amongst other things. It wouldn't do to get into a tangle with him.'

Cinder frowned. The more she discovered about Rassilon, the more she decided the universe would be better off without him.

She looked around, trying to get a sense of the

place. In here it did look more like a mausoleum – a cavernous hall, with tattered banners drooping from the roof, a stone pedestal that looked for all the world like a font, and the tomb itself, resembling a vast four-poster bed devoid of its canopy.

The whole place had an aura of abandonment about it, a depressing air that made her want to get out of there as quickly as she could.

'He's over here,' said the Doctor, leading her to the short flight of stone steps that led up to the tomb. The Interstitials were waiting silently in the doorway.

'Borusa?' said the Doctor. 'Are you there?'

There was a whirring sound, as of gears turning, and the metal platform that rested on top of the tomb began to pivot up on ratcheting spokes. To her horror, Cinder realised there was an emaciated person strapped to the frame. His feet and hands were bound, and cables seemed to pour from his chest cavity and the back of his skull, trailing off down the far side of the tomb.

'Doctor,' said the man-thing. Like the Interstitials, his face was in constant flux, flitting between that of a pale, elderly man, to a bronze, olive-skinned youth, to a middle-aged woman and more besides. His eyes, however, were unlike those of the others, and flickered with dancing blue lights, as if an electric current was running through his head and his eyes were tiny windows, allowing her to peek inside. It was the most appalling thing she had ever seen.

'Borusa, I'm here to help,' said the Doctor. 'But first, I need you to help *me*.'

Borusa laughed, and it was a wet, wracking choke.

'The random factor,' he said. 'The knot of possibility. You always were a difficult one to pin down, Doctor. Lord Rassilon will not be amused.'

The Doctor ignored him. 'Borusa, I'm going to cut you free and take you with me to the Eye. I have a plan to defeat the Daleks.' He hesitated. 'Can you see it? Can you see that future unfolding?'

'I can,' said Borusa.

'Then you'll help me?'

There was a long pause, as Borusa seemed to consider the Doctor's request. Cinder wondered if he was, in fact, attempting to look ahead, to see what might become of them all if he did.

'I will help you,' he said after a moment, 'but there is a condition.'

'Name it,' said the Doctor.

'That afterwards, when it is done, you will end my suffering. You will set me free.'

The Doctor bowed his head, clearly pained by the notion.

'The Time Vortex,' said Borusa. 'It unravels inside my head. It is beautiful, exquisite. I see the map of all-time, every moment, every delicate decision that is made, and how it alters the course of the future, changes the possibilities. But it hurts, Doctor. It is more than I can bear. No living thing should have this burden.'

Cinder looked at the Doctor. His eyes were downcast.

'Will *you* help *me*?' said Borusa. 'Will you free me of the possibility engine?'

'I will,' said the Doctor, his voice cracking.

'Then we are in agreement,' said Borusa. 'Cut me free. Sever my ties to the Matrix. I will join you in your TARDIS for one final trip.'

'Help me,' said the Doctor to Cinder, as he mounted the steps. 'We need to free him.'

The Doctor scampered up to the raised platform and edged around the metal frame upon which Borusa was bound, until he was able to crouch awkwardly behind Borusa's head. He set to work, popping cables from sockets in the back of Borusa's skull. White fluid oozed from the open ports. Cinder decided not to watch.

'What do you need me to do?' she said. 'Are we cutting him off the metal frame?' She poked at the knotted ropes that bound Borusa's left foot. She could see where they'd bitten into his flesh, rubbing sores around his ankle.

'No!' said the Doctor, urgently, popping his head around the frame in panic. When he saw that she hadn't yet started, he visibly relaxed. 'No, don't do that. I very much doubt he could support himself after all this time tied down. We just need to loosen the frame from its housing.'

Cinder nodded. She dropped to her haunches, peering underneath the frame. It was a primitive mechanism, really, as if it had been constructed at the last minute as an afterthought, once the real work – the 'retro-engineering', as the Doctor had called it – had been done.

Borusa moaned as the Doctor pulled the last of the wires from the back of his skull, shutting down his interface to the Matrix – whatever that was. 'Over here,' she called to the Doctor. 'I've found the right bolts, but you're going to need your sonicky-do-dah.'

'My *what?*'

'Oh, you know what I mean.'

The Doctor edged round to join her. 'Under there,' she said, indicating the first bolt.

'All right,' said the Doctor. 'Secure the frame while I see to it.'

Cinder stood, considering how best to do as the Doctor had asked, only to find the three Interstitials had joined them and were each holding onto a corner of the frame, steadying it as the Doctor depressed the button on his sonic and the bolts began to loosen and drop free.

Moments later, the possibility engine was free of its housing, and the three Interstitials were carefully lifting it down, holding it level above their heads. From her vantage point atop the tomb, Cinder could see his face. His electric eyes seemed to stare directly into her soul.

'Right,' said the Doctor. 'Let's get back to the TARDIS before Rassilon realises his favourite toy has been appropriated.' He hopped down from the tomb, stuffing his sonic screwdriver back into his ammo belt. He offered Cinder his hand, and she took it, jumping down beside him.

'Ask him if we're going to meet another one of those dinosaurs,' she said, nodding toward Borusa. 'Because if we are, I'm staying right here, Rassilon or not.'

The Doctor laughed, heading for the door.

'I'm not joking,' she called after him. 'Doctor? Doctor!'

The three Interstitials bore the possibility engine on their shoulders like the men of old, carrying their king on a litter. Borusa lay still atop the steel frame as they marched across the wilderness towards the TARDIS, Cinder and the Doctor trailing behind in quiet contemplation.

For nearly an hour they trudged across windswept fields, and all the while, Cinder nervously kept watch for any signs of the beast that had previously come after them, or any of its infernal kin.

As they approached the bluff, following the Interstitials, who seemed instinctively to know which route to take, Cinder saw the TARDIS perched on the hillside. The sunlight was beginning to fade, and as she peered ahead, she saw that scores of tiny lights had been laid out in a track, leading from the base of the hill to the TARDIS itself.

'What are those?' she said.

The Doctor grinned. 'You'll see,' he replied, laughing to himself.

As they drew nearer and the view properly resolved, she gasped at the sight of fifty or more of figures; all lined up like a bizarre procession, showing them the way to the TARDIS. They were all Interstitials, every single one of them. She counted dozens of them, rows deep, before she gave up, realising it was a fool's errand.

The lights she had seen from a distance were the soft glow of their flesh, shining in the gloaming.

'They're here to wish us well,' said the Doctor. 'To guide us on our way.'

'There are so many of them,' said Cinder. A thought popped into her head. 'How come they're not attracting the carnivorous beasts?'

'They can see the *future*, Cinder,' said the Doctor.

'Ah, yes. I suppose that would be helpful,' she replied.

They'd reached the foot of the bluff, and the three Interstitials ahead of them began the slow climb to the top, hoisting the possibility engine high above their heads in order that the others might see. As they passed, the members of the crowd bowed their heads in reverence.

Feeling a little sheepish, Cinder followed behind, unsure quite how to act, and whether she was supposed to do or say anything. In lieu of any forthcoming guidance, she simply copied the Doctor, who kept his eyes down and slowly followed behind the litter bearers.

When they reached the TARDIS the three Interstitials stood to one side while the Doctor unlocked the door. Then, with a quick glance over his shoulder at Cinder, he ushered them all inside.

Cinder watched as they disappeared through the small doorway, and then, pleased to be getting as far away from the Death Zone as possible, she hurried on in behind them.

Chapter Twenty

Cinder eyed the possibility engine uncomfortably.

The Doctor had directed the Interstitials to prop the frame upright between two stone pillars on the other side of the console, and in what she considered a bit of a surprise move, had yanked two of the dangling cables from their sockets in the ceiling and used the ends of them to secure the frame in place. She hoped they weren't supposed to be doing anything important.

Now Borusa hung upright, his wrists and ankles still bound to the frame. His chin had sunk forward to rest on his chest, but she could still see the flickering blue light dancing behind his eyes.

The Interstitials had retreated after depositing Borusa in the TARDIS, making no attempt to join them on their journey. Perhaps they already knew how this was going to end, she considered, and wanted nothing more to do with it. The thought wasn't particularly comforting.

They'd parked in a temporal orbit and the Doctor was busy running cables from underneath the console, attaching them to the empty sockets in the undercarriage of the possibility engine. He appeared to be reading diagnostics on the monitor, his sonic screwdriver clenched between his teeth.

He saw her watching, and grabbed the screwdriver out of his mouth. 'Almost ready,' he said.

'You, or Borusa?' she asked.

The Doctor gave a weak smile. 'Both.'

He'd seemed different after leaving the Death Zone. Part of it, she supposed, could be down to the fact they were heading into battle, and he was preparing himself for the coming conflict, adopting a more contemplative mood. There was something else there, though, something bothering him. She'd seen him watching her when he thought she wasn't looking, and he'd had that same, haunted expression on his face, the one he'd been wearing when they'd first met on Moldox. It was as if he was scared of her, somehow, and she couldn't quite fathom why.

She wondered if she'd done something to worry him. It was noticeable how he'd avoided telling her his plans as he'd worked on hooking Borusa up to the console, feigning concentration.

She watched him circle the console now, double-checking his links. He mumbled something quietly to Borusa, who didn't appear to respond, and then walked over to the dematerialisation lever, and cranked it. The TARDIS trembled, and slid noisily out of the Vortex.

Holding on to the rail, Cinder looked up. The Doctor punched a sequence of buttons, and the ceiling, which until then had been the same, muted grey material as the walls, seemed to clear suddenly, revealing a wide vista of space.

Before them was the familiar sight of the Tantalus Spiral, the planets weaving in a single, twisting helix around the roiling anomaly of the Eye.

In the distance, the tiny specks of Dalek saucers flitted through space like clouds of insects, swarming around a hive.

'What are we going to do?' she said. The Eye looked so distant from here, on the outer reaches of the Spiral, with the threat of thousands of Dalek saucers between them and their goal. How were they going to get anywhere close to the Eye, let alone inside it?

The Doctor began tapping buttons and flicking switches on the control panel. Lights blinked off in the console room. The engines sighed. The rotor dimmed and stilled. 'We're going to surrender,' he said wearily.

For a moment they stood in near darkness, with only the eerie, crackling lights of the possibility engine for illumination.

'Surrender?' said Cinder, incredulous. 'After all this? You're just going to power down the ship and let the Daleks come for us?' She glanced up. Overhead, the Tantalus Eye peered down at them through the TARDIS canopy, a baleful, watchful presence. Countless Dalek saucers skimmed across the star field, flitting around the vast spiral of occupied worlds. Surely they'd already noticed the arrival of the TARDIS? It couldn't be long before the Daleks ships began to converge on their position.

'That's exactly what I'm going to do,' said the Doctor. He had his back to her, acting as if she wasn't there.

'You can't! You can't stop now. We've come too far. If we don't find a way to stop them, the Daleks will just keep on going for ever. They'll destroy everything. They'll murder every last one of your people—'

'*My* people!' bellowed the Doctor, cutting her off. 'My people would have done the same to you. I'm not even sure they're worth saving any more.'

'Yes, they are' said Cinder, quietly. 'Despite everything, they're worth saving. I know you believe that. Otherwise, why are we here?'

The TARDIS gave a sudden jolt and its engines sputtered to life. The lights flickered and dipped, and the central column began to steadily rise and fall with its familiar, gentle sigh.

The Doctor shook his head. 'No, old girl. We've no choice. We have to do this.' He cranked a lever on the console, his expression pained.

The TARDIS shuddered again, the engines burring. Somewhere deep in the bowels of the ship, a bell began to clang repeatedly, echoing through the warren of ever-shifting corridors and rooms. It filled Cinder's head like an incessant metronome, a cry for help. She fought the urge to press her hands over her ears.

'She knows, doesn't she? The ship knows what

you're planning to do, and she's trying to stop you?' said Cinder. 'She's trying to take you far away from here. Perhaps you should listen to her...'

The Doctor spun around, waving his hand at Cinder dismissively. 'Oh, just get out!' he barked, angrily. 'Get *out!*'

Cinder took a step back, quelled by the sheer ferocity of the Doctor's response. Her back encountered the metal railing that ran around the central dais. She grasped at it for support, steeling herself. 'Why did you allow me to come? If you're so keen on being alone, why did you encourage me? Why are you keeping me around?'

'To remind me of who I'm not,' said the Doctor.

'You're angry, about what we saw in the Death Zone, about what the Time Lords have done to their own people,' she said. 'And you're scared about what saving them might mean. I understand.'

The Doctor shook his head. When he spoke, his voice was tinged with sadness. 'That's not it,' he said. His shoulders slumped. He turned around, and she saw the weight of centuries, resting heavy on his shoulders.

'It's me, isn't it?' she said. 'You're worried about what I might do, that I'm going to go and get us both killed.'

The Doctor sighed. 'No, Cinder. I'm worried that I won't be able to protect you. I've lost so many people, so many friends. I...' he faltered, and then drew himself up tall. 'I don't know how I could bear to lose another.'

She crossed to where he was standing. 'Remember

what I said, back on Moldox. I'm in. I made a choice to come with you. We're in this together, one way or another. I want to stick it to those Daleks as much as you do. Don't try to stop me now.'

'Very well,' he said.

'So, about this surrender?'

'If I show myself, they won't be able to resist gloating. They'll take us prisoner; get us closer to the Eye. They know me of old,' he said.

Cinder frowned. 'It doesn't sound like the safest of pl—'

'Predator.'

The metallic scrape of a Dalek voice resonated throughout the console room. Cinder froze, her hackles rising. The sound of those things, those cold, metal demons, seemed to scratch at her very soul.

She turned about on the spot, fearful that, with the shields lowered, one or more Daleks had teleported themselves aboard the ship. She was convinced that, at any moment, she'd feel the excruciating burn of an energy weapon, boiling her flesh from her bones.

But there was nothing there. The voice had been broadcast from deep within the Spiral, picked up by the TARDIS's communications systems.

The Doctor stepped away from the console, gingerly removing his hands from the controls. Even the TARDIS herself seemed to understand that the moment had passed, that now was the time to stop fighting. The central column sighed, and stilled. The clanging bell ceased its deafening peal.

'I'm here,' said the Doctor. His voice was low and gravelly, weighted with the gravitas of centuries.

'Doc-tor,' said the Dalek. 'Dalek killer. The Great Scourge. The Living Death. The Executioner.' The Dalek paused. Cinder watched the Doctor, gauging his reaction. His face remained impassive, his jaw set tight. 'These are the names awarded you by the Daleks, Doctor. I wonder if you feel proud. I wonder if you revel in the deaths of your enemies?'

This was like no Dalek that Cinder had ever heard. The voice was the same, but there was a different quality here, an unfamiliar intelligence, perhaps even a hint of reverence.

'I have never revelled in death,' said the Doctor. 'I value life above all else. I am not like you. I am no Dalek.'

'Yet you exterminate us with impunity. Allow me to assure you, Doc-tor, that Daleks also value life.'

The Doctor laughed, but it was tinged with regret. 'You value only Dalek life. You exist only to destroy, to consume. You are parasites, living off the carcass of creation.'

'Daleks are the superior life form in the universe,' said the Dalek. 'All other life is irrelevant.'

'Ah,' said the Doctor, with a sigh. 'Now you're beginning to sound more like the Daleks I know. Now you're telling me what you *really* think.'

'Yet you, Doc-tor. You are *admired* by the Daleks. You are revered. Your mere presence invokes terror amongst our kind. There is no greater honour. I would meet the creature that can terrify an entire species. We would learn from you.'

The Doctor grimaced at this most horrific and unwelcome of compliments.

Cinder swallowed. She wanted to tell the Doctor to switch it off. To silence the monster, power up the TARDIS engines and take her as far away from the Tantalus Spiral as possible. To use his time machine to take her somewhere where there *were* no Daleks, and no Time Lords, and no War.

But she knew that she could not. The Doctor was right. They had no choice. If there was even the slightest chance that his plan might work, that they might find a means of getting close enough to the Eye to deploy the possibility engine, to somehow defeat these monsters, then they had to take it.

'I'm here to parlay,' said the Doctor.

'The Daleks do not parlay,' said the Dalek. 'We do not negotiate. We do not bargain.'

'No,' said the Doctor. 'I didn't really think you would.'

Cinder tensed in concern. Had he misjudged? They were sitting ducks out here. The Daleks could easily destroy them before the Doctor could ever bring the power back up. It was a hell of a gamble he was taking.

'Yet we would look upon you, Predator, before you are ex-ter-min-ated,' said the Dalek. 'You will be granted an audience with the Eternity Circle. You will speak with us before you die.'

'How kind.' The Doctor glanced at Cinder, and she couldn't help but catch the impish 'I told you so' expression he was wearing. Childishly, she succumbed to the urge to stick her tongue out at him.

The TARDIS gave a sudden, unexpected shudder, and Cinder was forced to steady herself against the rail. She felt the ship move jerkily, rocking her onto the balls of her feet. The Doctor was steadying himself at the console, clinging on to a nearby lever.

'What…?' she started, but stopped when she saw the Doctor was staring intently up at the ceiling. She followed his gaze. Through the transparent roof she saw a large escort party of about ten Dalek saucers had gathered around the stationary TARDIS. Hoops of flickering blue light emanated from the base of the nearest saucer, encircling the TARDIS in what she assumed to be a tractor beam. They were slowly being dragged toward the Eye, and the beating heart of the Dalek operation.

'Where do you think they're taking us?' she asked, her voice barely above a whisper.

The Doctor reached over and pushed a button on the console before answering, presumably to ensure the Daleks would not overhear their conversation, although Cinder could see no actual microphone in the console room. 'There's a station orbiting the Eye,' he said. 'The seat of this so-called Eternity Circle. That's where they're taking us.' He pointed up at the ceiling, to a tiny black speck, hovering close to the heart of the Eye.

'The Eternity Circle?' she said. 'I thought the Daleks only took orders from their Emperor?'

'The Dalek Emperor is experimenting,' replied the Doctor. 'Sanctioning the creation of new types of Daleks, hoping that they might provide them with an edge, a means to win the War. As far as I can tell, the Eternity Circle is a select group of Daleks charged with developing new weapons, and coordinating the Dalek war effort throughout time.'

Cinder shrugged. 'Just like the Time Lord council,' she said.

The Doctor pulled a face, as if he'd just swallowed something distasteful. 'Yes,' he said. 'I rather suppose you're right.'

She looked over at Borusa, still lashed up into the framework of the Time Lord machine. She could barely stand to look at the thing, or to even consider it a being. She felt disorientated just trying to focus on Borusa's ever-changing face, stuck in that dreadful, regenerative loop. His eyes, electric blue and all seeing, seemed to burrow into her from across the console room. She wondered if he could see into *her* future, if he knew whether or not they were going to survive this.

A sudden thought occurred to her. 'Hold on a minute,' she said. 'Did you *know* the Daleks were going to fall for your plan? That they were always going to be unable to resist the temptation to watch you die in person?'

The Doctor grinned. 'I didn't need Borusa to tell me that,' he said.

The Dalek command station looked more like a vast, floating city than the sort of modular, habitable satellite that Cinder had imagined. Domed structures nestled amongst clusters of bristling spines and transmitters, and whatever substance it was constructed from – Dalekanium, she supposed – gleamed like burnished bronze in the reflected light of the Eye. Hundreds, if not thousands, of Dalek saucers and stealth ships buzzed around it like bees dutifully attending to a queen.

Behind it, though, dwarfing even the massive station into insignificance was the Tantalus Eye itself. This close, through the de-opaqued ceiling of the TARDIS, Cinder could clearly see the fissure at the heart of the anomaly: an immense, crackling nucleus of raw energy, a ragged wound in the fabric of time and space, fizzing with ruby-coloured light.

She could see now, more than ever, why the anomaly had come to be known as the Eye – this nucleus was its pupil, surrounded by the swirl of softly glowing gas that formed its kaleidoscopic iris. Within that expansive region, time ran amok, accelerating and decelerating, reversing itself and generally behaving so unpredictably that the laws of physics had no way of explaining its existence.

Cinder watched as stars burst to life with sudden, intense ferocity, only to evolve into bloated, dying giants within seconds. Meanwhile, others collapsed and reignited, resurrected from the verge of death, blooming once more into vibrant life. She wondered what had become of the many explorers who had flown into the Eye, and whether they explored it still, trapped in an intermediary space somewhere between life and death. Is that what would become of her and the Doctor if their plan was successful? Or might the TARDIS protect them somehow?

All such thoughts were forgotten, however, at the sight of an even bigger Dalek structure hanging above the Eye – the immense cylindrical barrel of their planet killer, the weapon she and the Doctor were supposedly there to prevent them from firing.

DOCTOR WHO

Cinder swallowed. She didn't even know where to start. The cannon was the size of three moons – or rather, it was actually *comprised* of three moons – which had been lashed together in a massive latticework of struts and nodes, and segmented by vast, shimmering discs of metal. At the front, three spokes came together to form a massive tip, from which she assumed the energy blast would be fired.

Swarms of Daleks tended to it, thousands of them, *hundreds of thousands* of them, like worker ants, crawling all over its surface.

A stream of ruby-coloured light was being siphoned from the Eye itself, channelled into two crackling antenna towards the rear of the weapon. She could see at the business end of the gun – if it could even be called a gun – the ruby light was beginning to flicker, as if it were building up for a discharge, just like the smaller temporal weapons she'd seen the Daleks using on Moldox.

This, then, was the weapon they would use to obliterate Gallifrey, and any other planets that stood in the way of their terrible ambition. Cinder could see now, for the first time, the true scale of the threat. She could see what had terrified Rassilon and his council.

This was engineering on an epic scale. With it, she had no doubt the Daleks would be able to end the War and claim dominion over the entire universe. It was in equal parts one of the most terrifying and impressive things she had ever seen, and worse, it looked to her as if it were almost ready to fire.

She stepped back from the console, averting her gaze.

The Daleks had been silent since the Doctor had severed the connection, but now the communications system crackled to life again, picking up a transmission from the command station.

'Report,' demanded an abrupt Dalek voice. Cinder jumped at the sudden intrusion.

'Target acquired,' replied another, near-identical voice, presumably from onboard one of the escort vessels.

'Proceed,' came the economical response.

Cinder and the Doctor watched in silence as they were dragged toward the station. She couldn't help but marvel at the sheer size of the structure, as they drew closer and the true scale of the Dalek operation dawned on her. There must have been *billions* of them there in the Spiral, when she considered how many of them had been on Moldox, and must have spread across all of the other inhabited worlds. And this was only *now*, in this particularly time period, in this one specific region of space.

The thought of a universe teeming with Daleks filled her with dread. Had she been wrong? Had the Doctor? Perhaps they should have allowed the Time Lords to proceed with their plan to deploy their Armageddon device. Perhaps the loss of human life would have been worth it.

As if understanding her mounting sense of terror and the darkness that was beginning to creep into her thoughts, the Doctor moved over to stand beside her, taking hold of the rail. 'It'll be all right,' he said, quietly. 'Just stay by my side and you'll be fine.'

She wanted to ask how he could be so sure, so

confident, but the moment had passed. He'd already returned to watching their approach. The station now filled their entire view, and the escort ships were starting to peel away, spinning off into the void. The Daleks were clearly under the impression that they'd managed to cage the Doctor; that he and his TARDIS were entirely at their mercy. Cinder couldn't shake the feeling that, somehow, the reality of the situation was quite the opposite.

The TARDIS, anchored to the Dalek saucer like the swinging pendulum of a clock, slid through the cavernous mouth of the station's docking bay, and deep into its maw.

She barely had time to gain an impression of what the interior of the station looked like before, with a sudden jolt, the TARDIS was released from the tractor beam and crashed to the floor of the loading bay. She was flung forward, and was only prevented from stumbling head-first into the console by the Doctor, who swung out an arm to catch her around the waist, maintaining his own grip on the railing all the while. Breathless, she thanked him, finding her footing again a moment later. She brushed her hair out of her eyes.

'So,' she said. 'We're just going to waltz out of here like we own the place, into the waiting arms of a billion Daleks?'

'Something like that,' said the Doctor, distracted. He'd returned to the console and was fiddling with the dials and switches again.

Cinder gaped at him. 'I mean... I... I was only being sarcastic,' she mumbled. 'That's not *really* the plan? Is it?'

The Doctor glanced at her over his shoulder, moving smoothly around the console to crank another lever. 'Parking brake,' he said, as if that answered everything. 'Best not to leave that on if we think we might need to make a quick getaway.'

'Oh, I don't think there'll be any need for that,' said Cinder, incredulous. 'I think we'll be too busy getting unequivocally exterminated for that to make much of a difference.'

The Doctor shook his head. 'You do have a way with melodrama,' he said. 'Now come along. Bring your coat.'

Cinder emitted an exasperated gurgle, but did as he said, fetching her old, scorched jacket from where she'd tossed it on the floor after fleeing Gallifrey. She shrugged it on. 'I can't quite believe we're going to do this,' she said. She turned to see the Doctor was no longer there. Twisting about, she spotted him, coming down the short flight of steps from the upper level. Cinder frowned. She hadn't even seen him leave. He must have stepped out while she was collecting her coat.

'A little late for regrets now,' he said, striding confidently toward the door. He pushed it open and stepped out into the harsh, electric light of the Dalek command station.

'Hello,' she heard him say. 'What is it that one's supposed to say in such situations? Ah, yes, that's right. Take me to your leader!'

With a heartfelt sigh, Cinder rushed out behind him.

Chapter Twenty-One

A clutch of Daleks led them at gunpoint through the quiet, cavernous passageways of the command station. The walls here were similar to those aboard the Dalek saucers on Moldox: a hexagonal crystal lattice, pulsing with the passage of coloured gases and fluids.

They passed branching corridors and rooms that formed hubs, like nexus points in a strange, otherworldly labyrinth. Sealed doors suggested rooms and cells, but none of them were open. Other Daleks glided silently along the hallways, like solemn monks in the corridors of an abbey, not even greeting one another as they passed by. All of the Daleks here appeared to be of the typical brass and gold variety. None of the mutants or Degradations appeared to be present.

Soon after, their Dalek guards came to a halt before a large, open archway.

'Wait,' said one of them in a deep, mechanical monotone, before sliding off into the chamber beyond.

Cinder couldn't see much from where she was standing behind another of the Daleks, other than the fact the walls inside the room changed in appearance, becoming white and opaque. The floor, too, appeared to be made from panels of smooth, white metal.

The Dalek returned a few moments later, clearly having checked ahead. 'Proceed.'

'Glad to see you're feeling conversational,' muttered Cinder.

The Doctor, who had so far kept his own counsel as they'd been led through the station, turned to her. 'Right, let's see what we're up against, shall we?' He stroked his beard nervously, tugging on the corner of his moustache.

Cinder gave a startled yelp as one of the Daleks prodded her between the shoulder blades with its manipulator arm, jostling her forward. 'All right, all right,' she said. 'I'm going.'

The Doctor glared at the Dalek and caught her arm, pulling her to his side. Together – arm in arm – they strolled into the room to meet the Eternity Circle.

Cinder and the Doctor found themselves entering a large audience chamber, arranged around a hexagonal concourse.

On each side of the hexagon, excluding the entrance, was a raised plinth, and atop each one sat a Dalek, looking down imperiously upon the auditorium.

They were similar in size and appearance to the bronze Daleks she had seen elsewhere on the station and so frequently on Moldox – the same manipulator arm and energy weapon, the same menacing eyestalk – save for the colouring, which, Cinder supposed, marked them out as unique. The casing of all five of these 'Eternity Circle' Daleks was a deep, metallic blue, with silver sensor globes and domed heads. They appeared to be identical to one another, although she knew from examining the casings of dead Daleks on Moldox that they usually carried small markings beneath their eyestalks to make them easier to identify.

Two other passageways fed into the room, and a series of shadowy alcoves existed between each of the Dalek's pedestals.

'Welcome, Doctor,' announced the Dalek on the central plinth.

'So this is the so-called Eternity Circle,' said the Doctor with a smirk. 'You do realise it's not actually a circle, don't you?' He traced a circle in the air with his finger to emphasise his point.

The Daleks regarded him in silence. Cinder noticed the guards had retreated to stand in the shadow of the archway, watching from the side lines.

'So you're the ones responsible for all of this? For harnessing the power of the Tantalus Eye?' said the Doctor. 'I'll grant you, it's certainly original.'

'It is a weapon worthy of the Daleks,' replied the Dalek on the central plinth. Cinder decided it had to be the leader.

'Is that what you do, then?' said the Doctor. 'Sit there on your pedestals feeling superior and dreaming up new ways to torture any of the other life forms in the universe?'

'That is, indeed, our purpose,' said the Dalek, and again, Cinder got a sense of a deep and disturbing intelligence at work. This was the Dalek they had heard over the TARDIS's communications array. It was different from the others, and not simply by virtue of the colour of its casing. It appeared to have a sense of irony. 'We of the Eternity Circle are charged with securing the proliferation of the Dalek race throughout time. We undertake the invasion of history in order to secure the future, and the eradication of all other forms of life.'

'Creatures born of hate,' spat the Doctor in response. 'You disgust me.'

'Such fury. Such pure, burning rage. It is a thing of rare beauty to behold. You are every bit as worthy as we hoped, Doc-tor.' The Dalek sounded impressed.

'Worthy?' said the Doctor. 'Of extermination? I was under the impression that one simply had to have the temerity to be alive in order to warrant such a response from your kind.'

The Dalek made a sound as if it were choking – a strange, strangled cry that Cinder realised, with disgust, was in fact a rasping cackle. The Dalek was actually *laughing*.

'You're even more deluded than I'd imagined,' said the Doctor, pointing to each of the five blue Daleks in turn. 'Sitting here in your ivory tower, hatching schemes and constructing your super-weapons.'

'The Temporal Cannon is but one small component, Doctor. A means to an end. Gallifrey will be destroyed regardless. The Dalek ambition knows far greater bounds.' The Dalek paused, as if weighing its words. 'You, Doctor. You will be our saviour. You will ensure the survival of the Dalek species.'

The Doctor narrowed his eyes. 'I will *not*,' he said. 'I made that mistake once before, back on Skaro, when I failed to put an end to the work of your creator.'

'Ah,' said the Dalek. 'The beginning of the Time War. The moment that you, Doctor, taught the Daleks their most valuable lesson of all – that emotion is a weakness that must be eradicated. That mercy has no place in victory.'

'Not a weakness,' said the Doctor, 'but a strength.'

'If it had not been for your hesitation,' said the Dalek, its tone derisory, 'for your inability to do what was necessary, then the entire War could have been prevented. The Daleks would have ceased to exist.'

'Is that true?' said Cinder, astonished. 'That you had the chance to kill them all and you let them live?'

'Continue,' said the Dalek. 'Tell your companion. Tell her how you failed.'

'It's true,' said the Doctor, hanging his head. 'Long before the War began, in a different life, I had the chance to prevent the advent of the Dalek race, to murder them in their cradle before the universe ever knew of their terror.' He sighed. 'But I hesitated. I still hoped that they might be saved. I was wrong, and when I went back, when I realised my mistake and *did* try to destroy them, I was too late. They'd already started the production line.'

Cinder didn't know what to say. The thought that he might have prevented all of this, what had happened to her family, her friends, the trillions of lives that had been lost throughout the cosmos – how could he have allowed it all to happen?

The Doctor had held that power in his hands. Yet he had also spoken to her about responsibility, about how it should never be the burden of one person alone to wield such power. Did he really have the right to destroy a race in its infancy, before he truly understood what it was capable of, how it might evolve? Of course he didn't. There could be no blame on him for that. 'Not wrong,' she said, quietly. 'Only human.' It was the greatest compliment she could think to offer him. He smiled appreciatively.

'I see, Doc-tor, that you understand,' said the Dalek. 'And now we shall offer you a gift, a role in the coming dawn of the new Dalek empire. You will become our instrument of extinction. You will conceive of new and inventive means by which to spread your gift of death throughout the cosmos. Your rage shall reignite the flames of war, leading the Daleks to victory on a billion worlds. It shall be a beautiful and terrifying reign, and the Daleks shall worship you for it.' The Dalek fell silent, awaiting the Doctor's response.

'I will die before I lift a finger to help you,' replied the Doctor.

'The entity known as the Doctor will, indeed, be exterminated,' said the Dalek. 'The emotion centres of your brain will be neutralised. All thoughts of your prior lives will be excised. Your mind, however, will be harvested. Your creativity will be put to wondrous use supporting the Dalek cause.'

'You don't get it, do you?' said the Doctor, laughing. 'You have no idea. It's *because* of my emotions that I am who I am. Without them I'd be nothing more than a drone, like the rest of your pathetic race.'

'We shall see, Doctor,' said the Dalek. Its eyestalk shifted suddenly to the right. 'It is time. Commence the procedure.'

'I obey,' came a metallic response from somewhere out of sight.

Cinder sensed movement in one of the alcoves beneath the Eternity Circle, and something began to emerge from the shadows. It was the silhouette of a Dalek, only far larger.

'Behold, Doctor – the Predator Dalek.'

Cinder watched in horrified awe as new Dalek rolled forward into the light. It was twice the size of a standard Dalek casing, although constructed to that same, familiar design. Its skirt was a deep, metallic vermillion, with black sensor globes and grilles, and although mostly inanimate, its appearance nevertheless filled Cinder with dread. The Daleks had clearly been planning this for some time, and she was beginning to get the sense that the Doctor had unwittingly stumbled into their trap.

'This is our true victory, Doctor,' said the Dalek on the plinth. 'The weapon that will win the war. The Tantalus Eye is but a means to an end, the removal of the Time Lord distraction. The Predator Dalek will be the herald of a new age. The time of the Daleks approaches.'

The casing of the Predator Dalek hinged apart like doors being simultaneously opened outward, revealing a large cavity within.

Inside, there was a burnished metal seat surrounded by dials and monitors, resembling the cockpit of a small vehicle. It was clearly empty and awaiting an occupant, but unlike the standard Dalek casings she'd seen on Moldox, this one wasn't designed to house mutant Kaleds, but a humanoid figure in the chair.

Fibrous wires and clusters of needle-like probes fought for space on either side of the chair, and a sharp metal spike, fixed to the back of the headrest, glistened with lubricant. This was clearly the Dalek version of a neural interface, to be inserted into the soft tissue at the base of the occupant's skull.

More vicious-looking needles were fixed to the inside of the hinged doors like an iron maiden, waiting to be embedded in the occupant's flesh once they were in situ.

Once entombed, there was clearly no escape. The engines of the casing would merge with the biology of the occupant, fusing to become a single, symbiotic entity. A Dalek.

'This, Doctor, is your future,' said the leading Dalek.

From the doorway, the three Dalek guards whispered forward, forming a loose circle around Cinder and the Doctor.

'Doctor?' she said, concerned. He looked at her, and she saw real terror in his eyes. He hadn't anticipated this, the true agenda of the Eternity Circle. What was more, it didn't appear as if they were going to draw matters out or offer any chance of escape – the casing of the Predator Dalek stood waiting to accept its new host.

'Come on!' bellowed the Doctor, looking around frantically. 'Come on!'

'Do not fight it, Doctor,' said the Dalek.

'Cinder… I…' he didn't seem to know what to say.

'Your companion will have the privilege of being the first human to be exterminated by the Predator Dalek.'

The guards inched closer, their manipulator arms raised like cattle prods. Cinder wanted to scream. She wished she had her gun, had *anything*, but there didn't seem to be any way to fight back, and nowhere to left to run. The Doctor had unwittingly led them into a trap.

She rushed forward, clutching frantically at the lapels of the Doctor's leather jacket. He wrapped his arms around her, kissing the top of her head. 'I'm sorry, Cinder,' he said.

'Doc-tor, it is time,' rasped the Dalek.

There was a sound like the distant rumble of thunder. At first, Cinder thought the Daleks had done something, had activated the Predator Dalek somehow. As the sound grew louder, however, she recognised the familiar, grating wheeze. It rent the air in the audience chamber.

'Explain!' shouted the Dalek. 'Explain!'

Cinder felt the Doctor clutching her even tighter around the shoulders. 'Hold on!' he cried.

'No!' bellowed the Dalek, as the world around Cinder suddenly began to change. She saw illuminated roundels flickering into existence, replacing her view of the white walls and the Dalek guards.

'Exterminate!' The Dalek's voice sounded distant, and she flinched at the sound of an energy weapon firing close by.

The shot never reached her, as the walls of the TARDIS miraculously closed in around them, plucking them neatly from the clutches of the Dalek guards.

Chapter Twenty-Two

Cinder took in her surroundings with an astonished, sweeping glance. Then, doubtfully, she patted herself on the chest to make sure she was real, and that this wasn't, in fact, a bizarre but highly credible dream.

She was standing in the TARDIS beside the Doctor, just inside the door. One minute she'd been surrounded by Daleks, preparing herself to die; the next, the ship had simply materialised *around* them, plucking them from the Daleks' grasp. From where she was standing she could just make out the view on the monitor, which showed Daleks milling about outside, no doubt barking angry commands at one another as they tried to ascertain precisely what the Doctor had done.

She started as she realised that an unfamiliar man was standing at the console. He was dark skinned and muscular, with close-cropped hair and startling blue eyes. He was dressed in the robes of a Time Lord, but they were ill fitting and stained with dark patches of blood.

'But… but… *how?*' she said, looking round at the Doctor.

'Karlax,' replied the Doctor.

The man at the console sneered.

Karlax? Then *this* was Karlax? She knew about Time Lord regeneration, of course, but to see it for herself, to see evidence of such a profound change – her mind reeled. She gaped at him. 'Then it was *you* who saved us?' She wondered if perhaps the change had been deeper than merely cosmetic. Had this new Karlax developed a conscience, as well as a new face?

'Not out of choice,' said Karlax, immediately dispelling that theory.

'I unlocked the door to the Zero Room before we left the TARDIS,' said the Doctor. 'I knew that, given half a chance, Karlax would try to escape. So I made sure the flight path was set to home in on the tracking device he'd planted on you back on Gallifrey. As soon as he started her up—'

'She swooped in to our rescue,' finished Cinder.

'And now it's time to finish the job,' said the Doctor. 'To take Borusa into the Eye.' He started forward, but stopped when Karlax circled around from behind the console, clutching a pistol.

'That's not how this is going to end, Doctor,' he said.

The Doctor's shoulders slumped. More than anything, he looked crestfallen, as if he'd been expecting more of Karlax, as if he'd hoped that perhaps things weren't going to play out this way.

'He saved your life, Karlax,' said Cinder. 'He dragged you from the wreckage of your damaged TARDIS when he could have left you there to die.'

'He always was a sentimental old fool,' said Karlax. 'Never able to understand when he had the tactical advantage.'

'Karlax. Put the gun down,' said the Doctor, reasonably. 'I have a plan to stop the Daleks. We can finish this once that's out of the way.'

Karlax shook his head. 'You're a wanted criminal,' he said. 'You've betrayed the Time Lords. A traitor. I can't trust anything you say.'

Cinder could hear it in Karlax's voice – he'd utterly lost it. Whether it was a symptom of his recent regeneration, or simply that he finally had the opportunity to enact his revenge on the Doctor, she couldn't be sure. Either way, the high-pitched tremor in his voice, the excited way his eyes were darting about, the beads of sweat standing on his forehead – they all pointed to the fact he wasn't in his right mind. Which, to Cinder's mind, made him even more dangerous than usual. He was unpredictable.

'Hoping to please your master, are you?' said the Doctor, his voice dripping with cynicism. 'Hoping he'll pat you on the head and tell you how well you've done? I'll let you into a secret, Karlax – he doesn't care. He's not interested in you and your snivelling little existence. He finds you useful. That's all. When you're gone, he'll replace you without a moment's hesitation. He probably already has.'

'Shut up,' said Karlax bitterly.

The Doctor wagged his finger at Karlax, as if telling him off. 'Besides, even if you do get what you want, it'll be a hollow victory. The Daleks are coming for Gallifrey. Rassilon won't thank you for allowing them to deploy their planet killer.'

Cinder saw Karlax's finger twitch on the trigger of his pistol. She could see what the Doctor was trying to do, to undermine Karlax's resolve, but it wasn't working. He was already too far gone.

'I think that's enough talk for now,' said Karlax, waving his gun.

'Good,' said the Doctor. 'Time to get on with it.' He made a move toward the console. Cinder saw the look of sheer hate in Karlax's eyes, the sudden, jerking movement as he raised the pistol and squeezed the trigger.

'No!' she bellowed, diving at the Doctor and bowling him over, so that he sprawled awkwardly to the floor, cursing in surprise.

The energy bolt from the pistol caught her just below the ribs and she fell heavily to the floor, screaming at the searing pain. She rolled onto her back, scrabbling at the wound with both hands, attempting to apply pressure. Blood pumped, hot and wet, spurting through her fingers as she tried her best to hold it in. She gasped, and then winced at the lancing pain. Her right lung was filling with blood.

The Doctor scrabbled up onto his knees and suddenly he was at her side, cradling her head in his lap. 'Cinder! Cinder! Hold on. It'll be OK. Everything will be OK.'

Cinder opened her mouth to speak but blood bubbled from her lips, dribbling down her chin. The pain was all-consuming. She bit down hard, clenching her teeth, forcing herself to stay awake, to fight back the creeping darkness that limned her vision.

She heard Karlax laughing, and looked up to see him standing over them, his pistol now dangling limply from his fingers. 'Oh dear, Doctor. Your pet seems to have gone and injured herself. You always were over-fond of these human creatures.'

The Doctor growled in inarticulate rage, and Karlax took a step back in surprise, looking momentarily uncertain, before recovering his poise. 'Well, I suppose I've started the job,' he said. He raised his gun, peering at it, as if entranced by its power.

'Why, Karlax?' snarled the Doctor.

'Because I have my orders,' replied Karlax.

The Doctor shook his head. 'That's not good enough,' he said. Looking up, bleary-eyed, Cinder saw the Doctor glance at the console, just a few metres away.

Cinder's breath was shallow now, and every intake wracked her body in pain. She could feel herself fading.

'It's good enough for me,' said Karlax.

What happened next seemed to Cinder to occur as a series of frozen, stuttering images. Karlax raised his gun to take aim, while the Doctor lurched to the left, his fingers reaching for the TARDIS controls. He twisted, slamming his fist down on the dematerialisation lever, just as Karlax managed to take his second shot.

The engines howled and central column pulsed

with light. The energy beam from Karlax's weapon struck the console, showering the Doctor in sparks and causing him to stagger back, cursing as the tiny, glowing stars stung the backs of his hands.

Cinder's vision was swimming in and out. She couldn't be certain what was happening. The pain was withdrawing now, becoming a distant fog. She felt numb, and cold, but Karlax seemed to be… *fading* somehow, as if *he* were the one dematerialising, instead of the TARDIS.

'No, Doctor! You can't leave me here! Not the Daleks!' Karlax's voice was reedy and pleading. He dropped his gun, and it clattered onto the floor of the TARDIS.

'It's no more than you deserve, Karlax,' said the Doctor.

With a shock, Cinder realised what was happening – the TARDIS was dematerialising *around* Karlax, leaving him there in the midst of all those angry Daleks. Leaving him to die.

Karlax stepped forward, his expression filled with dismay. The flesh of his face had taken on a strange, pulsing translucency. He opened his mouth, but no sound came out. He lifted his hands up, staring around him in horror at the sight of the Daleks only he could see. Lights flashed all around him as the Daleks opened fire, his face twisting in pain, and then, as suddenly as if he had never been there at all, he blinked out of existence, left behind on the Dalek station while the TARDIS slipped away into the Time Vortex.

With a grunt the Doctor staggered across to where

Cinder lay, and dropped to his knees beside her.

He brushed hair from Cinder's face. 'Hold in there. I'll find a way.' His voice was a gentle whisper, like the wind ruffling the branches of trees in the spring.

'No,' she croaked, with some effort. Her words were soft and mumbled, and the Doctor had to lean closer to hear her. 'It's too late.'

He stared down at her. 'Don't give up,' he said. His moustache twitched. 'You must never give up.' He looked worried, and there were tears forming in the corners of his eyes.

'The cave wall. The painting,' she said, between short, shallow gasps.

The Doctor shook his head. 'No. That was just one of many possib—' He stopped himself from offering platitudes. 'Keep still,' he said, brushing her cheek. 'It'll hurt less.'

'You said I'd only get in the way,' she said, forcing a smile.

'Oh, Cinder. But you did it with such style.' He took her hand and squeezed it. 'Thank you.' He turned away for a moment, but then forced himself to look back, meeting her gaze. 'Why did you have to do that? Why did you have to go and be so damn… *human*?'

Cinder tried to shrug, but the gesture hurt too much. 'My life in exchange for billions of others,' she said, echoing the Doctor's earlier words. 'I'll take those odds.'

She coughed and her mouth filled with blood. She closed her eyes. She was feeling so tired, and the Doctor stroking her forehead was so soothing. Perhaps if she just allowed herself to sleep for a moment…

When she opened her eyes again a moment later, she was back on Moldox. She was a 6-year-old girl, frolicking in the gardens outside of her homestead. Her brother was playing on the swings close by, whooping with delight as he pushed himself higher and higher. Through the kitchen window she could see her mother and father preparing a meal.

The sun streamed down on her face, warm and reassuring. For the first time in years, she felt happy.

Chapter Twenty-Three

The Doctor emitted a wail that was halfway between an anguished howl and a furious war cry.

Tenderly, he lowered Cinder's lifeless head to the ground and folded her arms across her body in restful repose. Her eyes were closed and she looked peaceful, as if she were simply sleeping.

He got to his feet and hurried over to the console, his vision blurred by tears that refused to roll down his cheeks.

'Doctor?' said Borusa. His voice was dry and husky.

The Doctor didn't look up. He was busy setting a new flight path.

'Doctor?' repeated Borusa. 'It is time.'

'Don't you think I know that?' snapped the Doctor in reply. 'Don't you think I'm aware of what has to be done?' His fingers danced over the ship's controls.

On the monitor the view of the Dalek audience chamber had been replaced by the whirling storm of the Time Vortex.

The Doctor glanced at the prone body of his companion. Perhaps there was still time. Perhaps, with Borusa's help, he could still find a way to save her. He wasn't ready to give up on her yet.

He clutched on to the console as the TARDIS hurtled through the outer envelope of the Tantalus Eye, buffeted by the temporal storms that spilled out from its apex.

Deep in the bowels of the ship the Cloister Bell began to toll again. The engines howled, stuttering and screeching in protest as the Doctor forced them on into the anomaly. The ship's integrity was being tested to the very limit as she tried to stay on course, plunging deeper and deeper toward into the Eye.

Something on the console exploded, sending a burst of sparks showering into the air. The tiny, burning fireflies rained down on the Doctor's jacket, scorching the leather where they fell. He ignored them, clutching the rim of the console as the room began to judder violently. Trailing cables detached themselves from their sockets in the ceiling, swinging loose like jungle vines. A roundel on the wall to his left detonated, flames licking hungrily inside the shattered casing.

The Doctor knew the TARDIS couldn't take much more, that he risked her breaking up in the storms, withering away to nothing. Yet he had no choice. It was the only way he could think to get Cinder back.

She'd died on his watch, protecting him. She was

his responsibility, and he couldn't allow it to happen again. Not now. Not Cinder.

He glanced over at Borusa, who was still lashed to the metal frame of the possibility engine, wedged between two stone pillars on the far side of the console. Just as the Doctor had anticipated, Borusa was beginning to absorb the temporal radiation from the anomaly. His eyes burned like hot coals as he observed the warp and weft of time itself. The cycle of his regenerations was coming faster, his face a flickering blur, shifting in its ever-changing cycle. His flesh now glowed vibrantly with an inner light. His proximity to the heart of the storm was altering him.

Still, the TARDIS plunged on, diving ever deeper into the spatial rift.

The Doctor staggered around the console, barely able to keep his footing as the ship bucked. He stood before Borusa, hanging on to the stone pillars for support. 'Can you see it?' he shouted, above the rending sounds coming from outside of the ship. 'Can you see a thread of possibility in which she still lives?'

Borusa issued a low moan, as if the very act of speaking was itself too much to bear. 'I can see it,' he said. His voice had changed, separating so that now, with every word, each of his regenerations spoke in chorus. It was beautiful and discordant. 'I can see it *all.*'

The Doctor could see, however, that Borusa was beginning to burn up. The temporal disharmony of the Eye was overloading him, as he attempted to channel all of its power, to open his mind and allow it all to flow through him.

The Doctor only had one shot. He could save Cinder now. He could tell Borusa to select that thread in which she survived, tell him to pull it so that it unravelled and became reality, so that history rewrote itself to a point where Cinder lived and Karlax died. That was the true potential of the possibility engine. Harnessing this much power, this much sheer *potential*, Borusa could do anything. He could choose a timeline and forge reality around it. He could weave the universe into a different shape, breathe life into those who had died, or take it from those who weren't worthy. He was life and death incarnate, the bringer of the apocalypse, the herald of oblivion.

This was his chance to bring her back, to resurrect her. He had always done what was necessary, what no one else would do. He had never allowed himself that single, selfish moment, that second of weakness, in which he chose the future *he* wanted, and not what others needed of him. Perhaps it was only fair that he should get to do it now, in the heart of the storm. He would tell Borusa to do it, to use the possibility engine to bring her back to him.

'Then…' The Doctor stopped. What was it she had said to him as she'd lain in his arms? *My life in exchange for billions of others.* That's what she'd given her life to ensure. They'd come here with a single purpose: to stop the Daleks from wielding the might of the Tantalus Eye, from bending its power to their own will, to liberate her people and end the threat to the Time Lords and the cosmos at large.

If he used it for this, was he any better? Did he have the right? He knew, in his hearts, that he did not. If she were here, now, she would never allow him to do it, to give up their chance for the sake of one life.

He stumbled as the console room lurched and another roundel exploded, showering them with fragments of broken glass. Borusa roared with pain as the energy running through his mind grew in intensity. He was becoming a conduit for the power, a focal point for all of the temporal energy boiling at the heart of the Eye.

There was no choice. He had to finish the job and free Borusa of his burden. 'Borusa, it's time. One final job for the possibility engine, and then you can be free. We have to destroy the Daleks. You must find a thread of possibility in which they no longer hold sway over the Tantalus Spiral, and their Temporal Weapon progenitors are never dispersed. Destroy the Eternity Circle and their weapon with the power of the Eye. Wipe them from the universe as if they never existed. Do it now.'

Borusa threw his head back and screamed in all his many voices. It was a sound the Doctor knew would echo through all of time and space, and would haunt him for the rest of his days.

Around them, the storm seemed to abate momentarily, and then a wave of light crashed out of the Eye – a temporal pulse; a single, massive burst of energy that swept out to encompass the entire Spiral. In its wake the threads of possibility were rewritten.

Entire fleets of Dalek saucers and stealth ships dissolved as the ruby-coloured light crashed over them, burning them up into nothingness.

Aboard the Dalek command station, the Eternity

Circle, still resting on their pedestals, whispered out of existence, shimmering into non-life like fragments of a fading dream, only half-remembered.

On Moldox and a dozen other worlds, the last of the Dalek patrols and their hoards of Degradations were overcome, washed away into fragments of light before the eyes of their human prisoners.

Within seconds, it was over.

The TARDIS, ravaged by the storm, limped from the Eye under its own volition, drifting into a loose orbit around Moldox. Inside, the remains of the possibility engine fizzed and popped, where once Borusa had been lashed, but now there was nothing.

The Doctor lay unconscious on the floor beneath the console, within an arm's reach of the body of his dead companion.

Chapter Twenty-Four

It had taken the Doctor three days to find the homestead. Three days of asking questions in the tumbledown human camps, travelling between them like a nomad. It wasn't easy uncovering a trail that had gone cold a decade and a half earlier, but persistence had put him on the right track.

He'd found mouldering records in an abandoned municipal building, and Coyne had helped as much as he could, filling in some of the blanks. For the rest he'd had to rely on the word of strangers, but in their dazed and jubilant state, they didn't seem to mind lending a hand to an unfamiliar face. He supposed they took him for what he was – another lost soul, drifting from place to place, searching for answers, for a home. Only, it wasn't his own home he was looking for.

He was encouraged to see that the humans on Moldox were slowly beginning to find each other. The scrappy groups of resistance fighters and travellers who had eked out an existence during the occupation had begun to merge, finding strength in numbers, and were tentatively taking steps to move back into the towns and cities. Their resilience was uplifting.

All evidence of the Daleks themselves was gone – the saucers, the patrols, the shells of defeated mutants – everything, save for the damage they had caused and the wreckage they had left behind.

The humans he spoke with seemed confused. They understood there had been a war, that terrible hardship had been forced upon them, but the enemy seemed distant and forgotten – a symptom of the temporal excision performed by Borusa and the possibility engine.

Time would serve as a reminder, the Doctor supposed. Time, and the ongoing threat of the war still raging in the heavens. No matter what Borusa had done, the horrors faced by the people here were simply too wretched to be forgotten for long. Those memories would eventually surface, and they would share in their grief. In the meantime, however, people would get on with rebuilding their lives.

The homestead, when he eventually found it, was nothing but a burnt-out husk. The walls had been reduced to rubble, blackened like the stumps of rotten, uneven teeth. Decaying remnants of furniture were strewn about the place, and it was clear the site had long ago been looted for anything valuable or useful. Weeds poked inquisitively through the fractured earth, ropey tendrils encircling fragments of shattered lintel, broken chair or rusted bed head.

It was a solemn job, unearthing the remains of the other three humans – Cinder's mother, father and brother – which had long been covered by the dust and detritus of the Dalek occupation. Now, they were just bones and rags, scattered by scavenging animals. Yet it felt *right* to reunite this lost soul with the family who had once loved her, who had been taken from her by a war for which she held no responsibility.

In the records he had found evidence of her true name. It was a beautiful, human name, and in death he had restored it to her, carving it into the wooden post he'd found to serve as a marker for her grave. He wondered if, when the time came, there might be someone to do the same for him.

The Doctor stood in the ruins beside the grave of his friend and looked up. Night was closing in, and the auroras danced hypnotically across the heavens, their exotic colours mingling like oil separating in water. Behind them, the Tantalus Eye cast its all-seeing gaze upon him. He felt as if he were being somehow singled out, as if he alone stood at the eye of a storm, the only one able to clearly see the chaos that was engulfing the universe around him. He'd come to Moldox feeling maudlin, but now he felt nothing but burning rage.

He stared back at the Eye, defiant. The War had gone on too long. There were too many victims, too many casualties. He couldn't stomach what his people had become. The war had changed them. Their desperation to survive at any cost, their arrogance and sense of entitlement had combined to lead them down the bleakest of paths. Somewhere down the line they had ceased to value the things they should have held sacred, the lives of those fledgling races that the Time Lords should be shepherding into the future, rather than casually consigning to the past.

Their conflict with the Daleks was going to destroy everything. All of creation cowered in their wake, and the only thing that either side could see was the war itself, and their unending crusade for victory. They had to be stopped before anyone else was caught in the crossfire.

The Doctor turned up the collar of his jacket. He would make a vow, to Cinder, and to what was left of the universe. He would bring an end to the War. Whatever it took. He would put a stop to it now. This was it. This was the day he drew the line.

A blackbird was picking at the freshly turned earth in search of worms, and he watched it flutter away into the darkening sky, finally admitting defeat.

Then, alone at last, he quietly uttered his promise. Just two simple words, but leaden with the weight of his resolve:

'No more.'

Acknowledgements

My thanks go out to Justin Richards, Albert DePetrillo and the *Doctor Who* production team for bringing me back into the *Doctor Who* fold, and for giving me the opportunity to send the War Doctor on a brand new adventure.

Also to Cavan Scott, for his constant support and encouragement. His messages helped me to keep going when it looked like I still had a mountain to climb.

Finally, I couldn't have done this without the patience and support of my family, who made time in our busy lives to accommodate the writing of this book. I love you all.

Coming soon from BBC Books:

BBC

DOCTOR WHO

Silhouette

JUSTIN RICHARDS

ISBN 978 1 849 90772 9

'*Vastra and Strax and Jenny? Oh no, we don't need to bother them. Trust me.*'

Marlowe Hapworth is found dead in his locked study, killed by an unknown assailant. This is a case for the Great Detective, Madame Vastra.

Rick Bellamy, bare-knuckle boxer, has the life drawn out of him by a figure dressed as an undertaker. This angers Strax the Sontaran.

The Carnival of Curiosities, a collection of bizarre and fascinating sideshows and performers. This is where Jenny Flint looks for answers.

How are these things connected? And what does Orestes Milton, rich industrialist, have to do with it all? As the Doctor and Clara join the hunt for the truth, they find themselves thrust into a world where nothing and no one are what they seem.

An original novel featuring the Twelfth Doctor and Clara, as played by Peter Capaldi and Jenna Coleman

Coming soon from BBC Books:

B B C

DOCTOR WHO

The Crawling Terror

MIKE TUCKER

ISBN 978 1 849 90773 6

'Well, I doubt you'll ever see a bigger insect.'

Gabby Nichols is putting her son to bed when she hears her daughter cry out. 'Mummy, there's a daddy longlegs in my room!' Then the screaming starts… Kevin Alperton is on his way to school when he is attacked by a mosquito. A big one. Then things get dangerous.

But it isn't the dead man cocooned inside a huge mass of web that worries the Doctor. It isn't the swarming, mutated insects that make him nervous.

With the village cut off from the outside world, and the insects becoming more and more dangerous, the Doctor knows that unless he can decode the strange symbols engraved on an ancient stone circle, and unravel a mystery dating back to the Second World War, no one is safe.

An original novel featuring the Twelfth Doctor and Clara, as played by Peter Capaldi and Jenna Coleman

Coming soon from BBC Books:

BBC DOCTOR WHO

The Blood Cell

JAMES GOSS

ISBN 978 1 849 90774 3

'Release the Doctor – or the killing will start.'

An asteroid in the furthest reaches of space – the most secure prison for the most dangerous of criminals. The Governor is responsible for the cruellest murderers. So he's not impressed by the arrival of the man they're calling the most dangerous criminal in the quadrant. Or, as he prefers to be known, the Doctor.

But when the new prisoner immediately sets about trying to escape, and keeps trying, the Governor sets out to find out why.

Who is the Doctor and what's he really doing here? And who is the young woman who comes every day to visit him, only to be turned away by the guards?

When the killing finally starts, the Governor begins to get his answers...

An original novel featuring the Twelfth Doctor and Clara, as played by Peter Capaldi and Jenna Coleman

Coming soon from BBC Books:

BBC

DOCTOR WHO

The Official Quiz Book

JACQUELINE RAYNER

ISBN 978 1 849 90769 9

For over fifty years, *Doctor Who* has been one of the nation's
favourite television programmes. Now you can discover just
how much you know about it.

Straightforward or fiendish, easy or horrendously difficult, all
3,000 questions in this book have one thing in common – a
certain traveller through time and space. From Ace to Zoe and
Axons to Zygons, it covers every single one of the almost 250
Doctor Who stories that have been broadcast since 1963.

So put on your brainy specs, pour yourself a nice glass of carrot
juice and prepare to discover if you have the knowledge to
graduate from Time Lord Academy…

BBC DOCTOR WHO

Tales of Trenzalore

THE ELEVENTH DOCTOR'S LAST STAND

ISBN 978 1 849 90844 3

As it had been foretold, the armies of the Universe gathered at Trenzalore. Only one thing stood between the planet and destruction – the Doctor. For nine hundred years, he defended the planet, and the tiny town of Christmas, against the forces that would destroy it.

Some of what happened during those terrible years is well documented. But most of it has remained shrouded in mystery and darkness. Until now.

This is a glimpse of just some of the terrors the people faced, the monstrous threats the Doctor defeated. These are the tales of the monsters who found themselves afraid - and of the one man who was not.

Tales of Trenzalore collects four of the Doctor's adventures from different periods during the Siege of Trenzalore and the ensuing battle:

'Let it Snow' by Justin Richards
'An Apple a Day' by George Mann
'Strangers in the Outland' by Paul Finch
'The Dreaming' by Mark Morris

BBC

DOCTOR WHO

HARVEST OF TIME
ALASTAIR REYNOLDS
ISBN 978 1 849 90419 3

A forgotten enemy. An old adversary. A terrible alliance.

From a ruined world at the end of time, the vicious Sild
make preparations to conquer the past and rewrite history.
But to do it they will need to enslave an intellect greater
than their own…

On Earth, UNIT is called in to examine a mysterious
incident on a North Sea drilling platform. They've hardly
begun, though, when something even stranger takes hold: the
Brigadier and others are starting to forget about
UNIT's highest-profile prisoner.

As the Sild invasion begins, the Doctor faces a terrible
dilemma. To save the universe, he must save his
arch-nemesis… the Master.